All the characters and events depict fictitious. C. B. C.

THE FIFTH TUMBLER

CLYDE B. CLASON

THE FIFTH
TUMBLER

Introducing Professor Theocritus
Lucius Westborough, a mild little man
who meddled in murder—with
surprising results.

CONTENTS

THE FIFTH TUMBLER

PART ONE: *Thursday Evening*

I

DOORS! ENIGMATIC DOORS opening from darkened corridors. Closed doors hiding lust and laughter, sorrow and death. Adjacent lives isolated by thin partitions as effectively as though separated by miles of bleak desert. Hundreds of people, unaware of each other's existence, clustered under a single big roof. Mysterious and inscrutable doors! Baffling corridors!

"Dear me!" mused Theocritus Lucius Westborough, the sole occupant of the large double bedroom designated as number 312. "A hotel is like a giant beehive!" It amused him to enlarge upon this simile. Worker bees: out of the hive by eight in the morning and gone until six. Queen bees: imposing black-clad dowagers. "Their husbands, ironically enough, have toiled to premature graves in order that these elderly women might spend the remainder of their lives, bored and miserable, in doing nothing. Poor souls, I am sorry for them. *Labor est etiam ipsa voluptas,*" quoted Westborough, who was addicted to bromides in foreign languages.

Workers? Queens? Oh yes, and of course drones. "I am one—thanks to government bonds and James' kindly forethought. I should be inclined to place that porcine Mr. Swink in the same category. Also, sadly against her will, I fear, that poor child Miss Gant."

Westborough picked up his fountain pen and resumed the writing of a foreword to a manuscript for which, after many months, he had found a publisher. The manuscript was entitled, *Trajan: His Life and Times,* and Westborough had devoted at least ten years to its preparation. He wrote:

"Although it is singularly unfortunate the works of Trajan's four biographers—Marius Maximus, Fabius Marcellinus, Aurelius Verus, and Statius Valens—have been lost, an imperishable record of the

1

great emperor remains in the Trajan column, which describes the campaign against the Dacians more eloquently than could any book account. This tall shaft, as high as a ten-story building and weathered to the color of bronze, is covered with a continuous spiral of carvings in which are represented more than twenty-five hundred human figures. To counteract the visual effect of distance, the artist, Apollodorus, designed the groups progressively larger as the spiral ascended the summit. Curiously enough, a statue of St. Peter now occupies the top of the monument where once stood in lonely grandeur the colossal figure of the great emperor."

Westborough's pen paused—he had said "great emperor" before, and, as he racked his mind for a synonym, his thoughts again strayed.

"Gant! That's an odd name. Dear me, I wonder if it can be traced to John of Gaunt and the Black Prince?"

In room 309 Chris Larson's alarm clock measured off seconds with raucous zeal. It was not one of your new electric alarms, adjustable to a soft or loud call to suit the sleeper's whim, but a battered wreck. Chris had bought it for $1.29 three years ago and had thrown it across the room at least twice since then. Nevertheless, it continued to run: loudly if not accurately, and, by dint of frequent manipulations of the hands, it would even give a reasonably true approximation to the correct hour. It now said, "twenty minutes to eleven," and, since Chris had set it at five, it was probably not off more than three minutes.

Chris yawned. He was a tall Scandinavian, tawny-haired and fair-skinned. He smothered a second yawn and adjusted the shade of the desk lamp. The light, streaming down upon his book, revealed queer-looking symbols like long slanting "S's." Chris read, "The rate of chemical reaction with respect to the time is proportional to the quantity of substance still unchanged in the mixture."

It was a problem regarding the decomposition of radium, and Larson chewed thoughtfully at the end of his pencil. At length he turned to a table of natural logarithms and ran the pencil along one of the many columns of figures.

"Her name is Yvonne," he thought, jotting a number upon a scratch pad. "Yvonne Gant. Yes, and her hair is bronze and her eyes are a light purple. Or would you call them violet?" His pencil commenced a sudden and furious tattoo against the surface of the desk. "Imagine that low scum Swink trying to get away with the trick he pulled. I should've taken a poke at him. Yeah—and lost my job." The pencil dropped unheeded to the floor. "Don't be a fool. I couldn't keep a girl like that in stockings. But her mouth has the cutest little crinkle . . . purple eyes . . . Yvonne Gant . . ."

In room 311 Yvonne Gant labored with commendable persistence to mend a run in a silk stocking. She thought, "It's my last decent pair, too. Oh well, maybe it'll hold. Maybe nothing! It's got to!"

Miss Gant, a tall girl with finely chiseled features and the reddish-bronze hair upon which Chris Larson had remarked, was wearing a peacock blue negligee which spoke eloquently of more prosperous times. She finished her darning and bit off the end of the thread. "There! If that doesn't stay, I'm out of luck."

She filled the porcelain basin in her bathroom with warm water and sloshed an oval cake of the hotel's soap until the surface of the water was covered with a copious layer of stiff suds. "Wonder if it hurts when they throw you out?" Miss Gant asked and smiled at the reflection in the Venetian mirror above the bowl.

"It's your own fault, you know. Nobody forced you to stay here." "It's not your fault," the reflection said consolingly. "Who was to know that the Merdock Company would go ker-phlooey? You had a fairly good job with them, didn't you? And you couldn't help it about Betty."

Miss Gant immersed the stockings in the washbasin and swished them vigorously among the soapsuds. "There are just two kinds of fat men," she generalized. "One kind is fat and jolly. You always like

3

to have them around. The other kind is fat and nasty, and Mr. Swink is like that. Little pig eyes! Ugh!"

She pushed down the white knob which opened the drain, and the suds gurgled down the pipe. Then she opened the tap and filled the bowl with fresh water. Immersing the stockings for the second time, Miss Gant thought:

"He's sweet, that boy! Knows how to handle people, too! I don't know what I'd have done without him the other night. He hasn't a cent, of course. Why is it the nice ones never have? But fat porkers like Swink always have plenty." Miss Gant surveyed the reflection with a Mona Lisa smile. "*He'd* pay my bill fast enough! No doubt about that. Ugh! Well, I've managed to get along without having to sleep with anyone yet, and if I do, it won't be with Mr. Elmo Swink." Miss Gant's laughter echoed clear and tinkling. " 'There are things worse than death,' said the Lady Yvonne as she let down her golden tresses and rinsed her silken hose."

Room 317 was a double room with twin beds, but tonight Fred Hammond had it all to himself. He was sandy-haired and ruddy complexioned, a large man just beginning to turn portly. His cigar— his fourth that evening —had suddenly developed a vile taste, for no reason at all that Hammond could fathom. He scowled. The tobacco leaves crumpled apart as he crushed the butt against the bottom of a glass ash tray.

"I'd like a drink," Hammond thought. In his grip was a pint of Old Apple left over from his trip on the road. "I could call room service for a bottle of White Rock." Then he vetoed this plan. "Hell, I don't like to drink alone."

Pacing restlessly across the room he paused to seat himself at the hotel writing desk and commenced to scribble upon a sheet of hotel stationery. Hammond's pencil was a thing of onyx and gold, shaped to a sharp point at the end where more plebeian pencils boasted only of an eraser. He dug viciously at the paper, and the lead cracked. Hammond turned the gold tip to bring a new lead into place and renewed his artistic efforts by drawing a circle, which, although a

4

long ways from the famous freehand circle of Giotto, was yet a reasonably good approximation to the curve.

"She's been gone a long time. I should have gone with her and not pulled that headache stall. I wish I had. We get so few evenings together."

He divided the circle into quarters and commenced the shading of opposite segments. "Poor Norah! This is a hell of a life for her. A woman ought to have a home of her own, but when I'm on the road all the time . . . We'd have to get one though if we ever have a kid. Wonder what it would be like to have a little shaver that was mine and Norah's. Norah wants a girl . . . that wouldn't be so bad ... a girl growing up to look like Norah. . . . I'd rather have a boy. I might be able to make a football player out of him."

He abandoned the circle as offering no further possibilities and tried his hand at a caricature of his sales manager, Thompson. "If that guy is a sales manager, I'm first cousin to the Prince of Wales! I'm sick of his sales contests. He sets a quota twice as high as it should be and expects us to take it and like it if he sugar coats it with enough hooey. We've been baseball players and prospectors and airplane pilots; we've ascended the stratosphere, and we've gone to the Antarctic with Admiral Byrd. Now he tells us we're going to dig for treasure in King Solomon's Mines. Banana juice! Does he think we're a bunch of ten-year-olds?"

Hammond completed the final touches to his sketch and drew a hand thumbing a nose at Thompson's profile. "You know what you can do to King Solomon's Mines, don't you?" he apostrophized the portrait. "Why the hell don't you tell us to go out and do a good old-fashioned job of selling? I'll bet you never even thought of that, you louse!"

Hammond crumpled up the caricature—the likeness had not been very creditable—and tossed it at the wastebasket. "Damn those old harpies! They sit in the lobby like a bunch of vultures, and I'd like a five-spot for every refutation they've busted." He opened the drawer of the writing desk and felt absent-mindedly within. "I shouldn't let their lousy gossip get under my skin. They were lying. Of course they were lying!" There was a Gideon Bible in the drawer, and Hammond thumbed through it aimlessly until he realized what it was and dropped it like a hot potato. "But I'd give all I've won in poker the last six months if I hadn't heard them."

He took a second sheet of hotel stationery and began another cartoon, muttering under his breath as he sketched.

"Damn that fat hog! There's what he looks like. Diamond stickpin and all. Promoter, is he? Kind of swine that runs after widows' insurance money, I'd say. And if Norah . . ."

In room 319 Benny Devon lit a cigarette. He smoked incessantly, and he usually lit one with the butt from the last. Devon was not his real name. He had taken it from a sign glimpsed on a Chicago streetcar.

"I had the pete all lathered and was ready to slip in the oil when that rube cop stuck his face through the window," Devon reminisced. "Jeez! I didn't mean to jimmy the bull, but could I help it? This town's lousy with dicks, and if some cop gets wise, I'll get a stretch that'll be no valentine."

Devon shrugged his narrow shoulders and tilted his chair to an angle of thirty degrees. He put his feet upon the bed, his shoes leaving a black stain on the clean spread. "That fat mug Swink!" he exclaimed. "The rock he wears is worth half a grand if it's worth a cent. But I don't dare chance it here. Besides, I'm a box man and not a flat worker. And a rock like that lying around waiting to be picked up! Jeez!"

Mrs. Sarah Blakely of room 310 was combing her hair. Mrs. Blakely's hair was faded and lifeless, but such as it was it was her own. She wove the strands into braids and fastened the ends with rubber bands.

"If you ask me, that Gant girl is no better than she should be!" thought Mrs. Blakely, her fingers digging viciously into the cold

6

cream jar. "There are two sides to everything, as I said to Esther this morning." She patted the grease onto her wrinkled face with vigorous slaps. "The Hammond woman is another chippy—or she'd like to be! Her husband ought to stay home and watch the hussy."

Mrs. Blakely raised her head and listened. She had eyes which saw like a hawk and ears which could hear the drop of a pin twenty feet away. But the noise she heard now did not call for any such delicate perception of the senses. It was the heavy, disorganized tread of an inebriated man in the corridor. "That must be Mr. Swink," thought Mrs. Blakely. "It sounds like him, but I didn't know he was a drinking man. If I open the door a trifle I can tell for sure."

She tiptoed to the door and peeked into the corridor. A fat man was fumbling with a keyhole. "He's drunk as a lord," Mrs. Blakely reflected. "And to think I let that man take me to lunch!" She watched his clumsy efforts to open the door, and then Mrs. Blakely's excellent ears brought her another sound. A sound which had no business in the west corridor of the third floor of the Hotel Equable. Mrs. Blakely heard the tinkle of broken glass.

"Bottle on his hip!" she reflected. Then she remembered that Prohibition was a thing of the past, and it was neither convenient nor fashionable to carry bottles in that manner. The fat man entered the room. He didn't close the door, however, and Mrs. Blakely thought that was funny. Then she heard a second sound, and there was no mistaking what that was.

Mrs. Blakely crossed the corridor and peeped through the half-opened door. And Mrs. Blakely screamed.

II

CHRIS LARSON shoved aside his book. It was ten minutes to eleven, and he went on duty at the hour. He rose to his feet, stretched his long muscular arms, and then walked over to the bathroom where he lathered his hands with careful thoroughness.

From the hall he heard a boisterous racket; heavy tramping. "Swink's drunk again," Chris speculated. More tramping and a noisy fumbling. "The dirty hog." Silence reigned for perhaps a minute, and then someone screamed.

It was a feminine scream, piercing and shrill, and it penetrated the corridor. A second scream, only a trifle subdued in tone, followed the first, and then a third as Chris raced into the corridor. The screamer was a stout woman in a gray flannel robe. She was standing at the entrance to Swink's room, number 315, which should have been 313 and wasn't.

Other people came into the hall. Mr. Hammond stuck his head out from 317, and there were Miss Gant of 311 (she was wearing some sort of fluffy blue thing) and Mr. Devon of 319. Also owlish little Mr. Westborough from 312.

"What's going on?" Chris questioned.

"Mr. Swink!" Mrs. Blakely gasped hysterically. "I think he's—dead!"

The door stood open about three inches, allowing Chris to peek within the room. Swink, like an enormous Billiken, was lying doubled up on the floor. Someone had cut out a section of the carpet and folded it back, leaving a strip of bare floor about three feet from the doorway. There was a faint odor in the room which Chris sniffed inquisitively. "Good God!" he choked and turned at once to the group clustered about the door. "Please go to your rooms and open the windows. There's a dangerous gas in here. It's—"

Mrs. Blakely shrieked. There was a frantic scurrying, followed by the slamming of multitudinous doors. Adjusting a handkerchief to cover his nose and mouth, Larson dashed for the window. It was locked. He fumbled for the catch and then threw the window wide open. When he could no longer smell the faint odor he recrossed the room and bent down beside the figure on the floor.

Swink's pale, cold eyes were fixed in a glazed stare. A trickle of froth showed on his thick lips, and the fingers of one hand were rigidly clenched against the palm.

Unbuttoning the coat and vest, Chris laid his hand over the other's heart. He could feel no beating, nor were there the faintest signs of respiration. "It got him all right," he thought. "It can work as fast as two minutes, I've heard." His eyes, scanning the room, came to rest upon an object near the door—something which had no business being in the room—the top fragment of a broken glass tube.

He started to pick the thing up, but remembered, just before his fingers reached it, the admonition, "Don't touch anything until the police come." There was, however, nothing which would prevent him from looking, and he inspected the fragment with a scientific interest. The cork was still jammed within the mouth; there was nothing out of the ordinary about that. But a piece of string had been wound about the rim of the tube and tied in a loop. "What the devil!" Chris ejaculated, getting down on his hands and knees. He found several other fragments, one a large portion of the lower half of the tube, and he found something else. This last object was a wire—it looked like a rather large hairpin. It had been straightened out, however, and then, at a point about two fifths of the distance between the two ends, bent again at right angles. The shorter side of the angle had been bent once more so that it terminated in a small hook.

Chris rose to his feet; it wasn't his business to play detective. That was up to the police—and Jerry Spanger. He had to notify them right away, but was it wise to use the phone in this room? There might be fingerprints. He closed the door behind him, and it locked automatically.

Within the security of his own room Larson picked up the telephone receiver and explained the circumstances to the operator, Miss Devlin. "And tell Jerry Spanger," he added.

Three men stood gravely in a semicircle, like the judges appointed to pass sentence upon the Egyptian dead. Half an hour had elapsed since Chris Larson had found the corpulent body of Elmo Swink, and that body was still lying upon the floor awaiting the arrival of the medical examiner. Larson's eyes now flitted from one to another of the trio.

First, Jerry Spanger, the Equable's house detective, who was rubbing a pudgy and perplexed hand across his closely cropped mustache. Jerry was about forty-five and inclined to put on weight. His face was round, jovial—almost cherubic. But, though he didn't look the part, Larson reflected, Spanger had the reputation of being a smart detective.

Second, Captain Terence O'Ryan, a colossal figure of a man in a blue uniform. Six feet four, if an inch, and with shoulders proportionately broad. Larson, no small man himself, eyed the giant appraisingly, deciding that he'd be a bad customer to mix with in a rough-and-tumble. O'Ryan was captain of the Water Tower station in whose district the Hotel Equable was located.

Lieutenant John Mack of the homicide section was the third member of the triumvirate. Mack was from police headquarters on South State Street. Of medium height and build, he was dressed with an attention to details which rendered him almost dapper. Yet his keen blue eyes were as sharp and piercing as those of a lynx. He surveyed with callous professional interest the motionless form on the floor.

"That's a queer way to bump off a guy!"

Mack turned his head in the giant's direction.

"You said, Terry, that Larson opened this window?"

Larson nodded before the other could reply.

"Yes. I smelt the characteristic odor of hydrocyanic acid and realized the air had to be cleared at once."

"Too late to help him, though?"

10

"Yes."

O'Ryan resumed his narrative. "I posted a couple of boys at each end of this corridor to keep anyone from going in or out. Then I sent Phelan and McCarter to talk to the room clerk and check up on the entrances. I figured our first step was to make darn sure that this is an inside job."

Mack nodded approvingly, and O'Ryan's face broke into a broad grin. It was plain to see, Chris Larson realized, that the big man had the utmost respect for the ability of his colleague from headquarters. Mack, although inferior in police rank to O'Ryan, was, more or less unconsciously, Chris believed, taking complete charge of the investigation. He stooped now to pick up the glass fragment of test tube which had earlier engaged Larson's attention. He held it carefully by the string.

"You said he died as soon as he got the door open?"

"He was dead when I found him," Larson replied, "and that was hardly more than two or three minutes afterwards."

"Humph!" Mack ejaculated. "Then either the whole room had been previously saturated with the gas, or this thing smashed when he opened the door."

"That's what happened," O'Ryan opined. "See how the carpet's been cut and folded outa the way. The only reason for doing that was to make sure the glass would smash when it hit the floor. It's plain enough to me."

"Then the tube had to be fastened to the door in some way," Mack reflected. He picked up the wire from the floor and asked, "What do you make of this hook thing?"

"It's nothing but an ordinary hairpin bent out of shape," Spanger pronounced.

"I don't see much sense to it," came from O'Ryan. "The hook could fit into that loop of string, but how would you get the thing fastened to the door?"

"This way," Mack answered. He closed the door and placed the long end of the wire between the top edge of the door and the door frame so that the short end, the one with the hook, hung vertically downwards. "Here's how he did it—see? When Swink opened the door, the wire was released, and the tube had to tumble to the floor. Swink stooped to see what it was and got a whiff of the gas."

Jerry Spanger's pudgy hand tugged at his mustache in thoughtful deliberation. "The only thing I'd like to know is how he got out again."

Mack returned no immediate answer. His eyes roved restlessly here and there about the bedroom. There wasn't a great deal to see. It was just a conventional hotel bedroom furnished comfortably but simply with a metal bedstead, a bureau, a desk, a large lounge chair, and two or three straight ones. But none of these were the objects of Mack's scrutiny. His eyes flitted from one to another of the three doors within the room. Finally he opened one of these to reveal a moderately large closet. Getting down upon his knees, Mack made a thorough inspection of the closet floor.

"He might've hid in here—although there aren't any signs of it."

"I don't think so," Larson objected. "For one thing it would be dangerous, and for another he didn't have a chance to get out without being seen. Mrs. Blakely watched Swink going into his room and screamed as soon as she heard him fall."

Mack nodded in confirmation. "I didn't think he did." He returned to the side of the dead man. "Have you looked in his pockets, Terry?" O'Ryan shook his head. Mack pulled out a wallet and hurriedly examined its contents. "Nearly five hundred bucks on him." He glanced toward the top of the dresser. "The rock in that stick pin is worth another five hundred or I miss my guess. And it's right in plain sight where anybody could've picked it up."

He rose to his feet and walked toward one of the two inner doors he had not previously inspected. "Where do these doors lead to?"

12

"Rooms on either side," Spanger answered. "Every room on the corridor is connected that way; for that matter, nearly every room in the hotel. It makes for flexibility. You can turn any two adjacent rooms into a suite at a minute's notice."

Mack's thumb and forefinger closed about the narrow ring between the latch and the doorknob, and he turned the handle without touching the knob. He tugged and pronounced the door locked, then repeated the experiment on the door at the opposite side of the room.

"Both of 'em are locked."

Spanger nodded confirmatively. "They should be. They're never opened without orders from the front office."

"The office keeps the key?"

"Yes."

Mack asked another question. "Do these doors have special keys of their own or will one of your ordinary passkeys work on 'em?"

"Passkey will unlock any door in the hotel," Spanger pronounced with finality. "That is, the ones we keep at the office will. The maids' floor keys will only work on one floor."

Mack jerked a large and square thumb toward one door. "Who has that room!"

"A Miss Gant," Larson answered. "She used to share a double room with another girl, but her roommate left the hotel a few days ago, and she moved into this single."

"Anybody in the room on the other side?"

"It's a double room occupied by a Mr. and Mrs. Hammond. He's away most of the time. Salesman, I believe."

"You said that a number of people rooming off this corridor were in the hall after Mrs. Blakely screamed. Either Miss Gant or the Hammonds among them?"

13

"I remember Miss Gant," Chris answered promptly. He ransacked his memory. "Yes, and Mr. Hammond. I don't believe I saw Mrs. Hammond."

"Want 'em in, Johnny?" O'Ryan asked. Mack shook his head.

"Not yet. Another point I want to clear up before Doc Hildreth gets here. Larson, how'd you know Swink had been gassed by hydrocyanic acid?"

"By the smell."

"Hydrocyanic acid is the same as prussic acid, isn't it?"

"Yes."

"I always thought that was a liquid."

"It is—a very volatile liquid, boiling at 78 degrees," Chris Larson explained.

"Well, that's close to room temperature. I suppose he could inhale enough vapor to kill him. It ought to be easy to check up where the stuff was bought. There's a fifty-dollar fine for any druggist who doesn't keep a record of his sales of arsenic, strychnine, corrosive sublimate, or prussic acid, or lets them out of the store without a prescription."

Larson shook his head slowly. "I don't believe he bought this at a drugstore."

"Why not?"

"Prussic acid is used for medicinal purposes only in solution—about two percent, I believe. Inhaling the solution might make a man feel dizzy and probably give him a headache, but it shouldn't kill him."

"Something did."

"Inhaling anhydrous prussic acid would do the job all right."

"An—what?"

"Anhydrous. Prussic acid without water."

"Where do you buy that?"

"You don't—you make it."

Mack looked incredulous.

"That's a job for a chemist, isn't it?"

"Not necessarily. All one has to do is put some acid in the test tube, add potassium or sodium cyanide, and cork up the tube. There's a chemical reaction which gives you prussic acid vapor and a sodium or potassium salt."

"That's a new one on me!" O'Ryan exclaimed.

"In the old days they used that method to kill the insects on fruit trees," Larson elaborated. "They covered the tree with a sort of tent, and then they took a two-gallon stone jug, put in some water, some concentrated sulphuric, and a charge of sodium cyanide. Then they uncorked the jug inside the tent and ran for it. Now, I believe, they usually spray the liquid hydrocyanic acid over the tree with a hand pump."

"Do you have to use sulphuric acid?" Mack inquired.

Larson shook his head. "No, any acid—even a weak one —will act on the cyanide."

Mack was writing busily in a black-covered notebook.

"Potassium or sodium cyanide, you say? Which do you think was used here?"

"Either would produce the reaction. Most potassium and sodium compounds are very similar—both in physical properties and their chemical action."

Mack scrutinized his informant quizzically.

"You seem to know a lot about it, Larson."

"I'm taking a chemical engineering course."

"I guessed that. Even so, I'm willing to bet you know more about cyanides than you'll find in your college textbook."

"I boned up on them on the side," Larson flared. "Thought I had a job with the United Cyanide Company, but it fell through. If you're trying to insinuate—"

"Now who said I was?" Mack interrupted quietly. "I've got a lot of people to see and a whole lot of questions to ask before I start forming opinions." He continued didactically as though to fix in his memory certain mental notes. "As far as opportunity is concerned, anybody in the hotel could've done it. That means any employee or any guest, do you understand? Not to mention the possibility of someone from outside. As far as motive is concerned, we'll know more when we get a few stories from people acquainted with Swink. And as far as method—" "He shook his head in a puzzled manner. "There're several important points to clear up. I want to know—" He broke off abruptly as two blue-coated patrolmen entered the room.

"Phelan and McCarter!" O'Ryan exclaimed. "What'd you find out, boys?"

Patrolman Phelan was the first to answer. "I talked to the room clerk as you told me, chief. From the desk he has a clear view of both entrances to the lobby as well as the elevators." He handed a paper to O'Ryan, who read it carefully. "There's a list, as nearly as he can remember, of everybody asking for their keys since he went on duty at three-thirty. He's positive no strangers went up alone, and the elevator men tell the same story."

"Well, McCarter?" O'Ryan asked.

"I went to the back part of the hotel and started asking questions," the patrolman replied with the air of one who has performed a duty both thoroughly and conscientiously. "Seems there's a timekeeper—thin-lipped guy with glasses—who has to stand by the employees' entrance and check everyone going out— see? This is a big place, and the management's taking no chances on

16

a guy sneaking out and going home when he's supposed to be working. Well, this guy is sure that no one left the hotel who didn't work here—and that no one came in who wasn't supposed to."

"Did you think about the fire escapes?" O'Ryan catechized.

McCarter's voice soared triumphantly. "You bet I did, chief. There are two fire escapes leading to the alley. Both of them stop at the second floor, but the stairs swing down when a guy gets on 'em, and when he gets off, a weight pulls 'em back up again."

"Practically every fire escape in town is built that way," O'Ryan grumbled. "Did you think to look at the doors?"

"Sure we did. Phelan and I went over every fire-escape door in the hotel—some job!"

"Well?" O'Ryan interrogated. "Find that somebody could beat it that way?"

McCarter shook his head. "Every damn one of 'em was bolted from the inside, chief."

III

"IT'S AN INSIDE JOB." O'Ryan grinned like a pleased Cheshire cat.

"Fat lot of help that is!" Mack snorted deprecatingly. "Yeah—an inside job with only four to five hundred rooms in this hotel and maybe a hundred and fifty people working here. We'll be up all night, Terry."

"Well, that's what we're paid for, ain't it?" O'Ryan turned to the house detective. "When you were on the force, Jerry, you weren't a bad cop. What's your slant on this?"

Spanger waved a pudgy hand.

"I didn't like Swink myself—fat, slimy sort of fellow. Maybe two or three other people felt the same way about him. But as for what happened tonight—well, I can't tell you a damn thing. I went to my

17

room early and got off my shoes. Feet were burning something fierce."

"You used that feet stall a hundred times a week when you were on the jewelry detail," Mack cut in. "Tell me what you had against Swink, anyhow."

Spanger's blue eyes opened as wide as those of a baby. "Just a hunch, but I don't have to tell you what hunches mean in this racket. I thought the fellow'd bear watching, and I kept an eye on him whenever I got the chance. But I didn't learn anything."

"Have any enemies in the hotel?"

"None as far as I know. Nor any friends either. In fact I've only seen him with one man. Guy by the name of Chilton."

"Chilton?"

"Yeh. He's in 305 down the hall. Signed the register as James Chilton of New York when he blew in last Monday. He told Collins, the room clerk, that he was a broker."

"Well, if he's broker than I am I'd like to meet him!" O'Ryan exclaimed. No one smiled at this witticism, and the giant instantly sobered. "Shall we have him in, Johnny?"

Mack reached in his vest pocket for a cigar and spat the end into the wastebasket. "First I want to get Larson's story straightened out. You're the night clerk here, aren't you, Larson?"

"Yes. I go on duty at eleven."

"Been in your room all evening?"

"Yes."

"Sleeping?"

Chris smiled. "Until nine. I set the alarm clock for that time, and then I get up and study for a couple of hours."

"Study?" For the minute Mack's face looked uncomprehending. "Yeh, I remember you told me about it. Chemistry tonight, was it?"

18

"No, I was working a problem in calculus."

"Calculus? Some sort of mathematics, huh?"

"You've said it!" Larson exclaimed with a rueful face. "Had to do with a logarithmic derivative, and when you integrate you get an exponential function."

"I get a headache," Mack said with conviction. "Anyway, you were pretty well wrapped up in the logarithmic what-you-may-call-it, weren't you?"

"I guess so."

"So you couldn't hear a noise in the hall?"

"What sort of noise?"

"Like somebody trying to get into a room that didn't belong to him."

"If I had, I'd have investigated," Larson declared. Mack regarded the night clerk with a thoughtful expression.

"Work pretty hard, Larson?"

Chris Larson thought of his daily routine—and smiled. Off duty at seven in the morning. A hastily snatched two hours' sleep and then a grand rush to the "L" to make a ten o'clock class in Organic. More classes. Lab. Classes. Lab. Through at four and back to the hotel. Grab a bite to eat and sleep till nine. That alarm clock! Damn the thing anyway! Always interrupting what promised to be the soundest and most refreshing sleep you've ever known. Then study—two hours of it. It isn't enough. You know that. Not half enough. You're falling behind in your classes. But your crammed schedule just doesn't allow room for another minute—outside of Sundays and the few minutes you can put in on the "L." Now you're on duty again. Night clerk. Supreme boss during the wee small hours—and very little to boss. Complaints. Somebody's radio is bothering somebody else. Mrs. Blakely thinks there's a mouse in her room. You have to get the night houseman to turn everything inside out and assure her there isn't the slightest vestige of a rodent. Make out the room value sheet. If you're lucky, it checks with the cashier's record. But sometimes the cashier has forgotten to pull an account after it's been paid. Then you look in the "departure book." If the name shows there you have a "sleeper"—room shows occupied in the room rack but it's really vacant. Sleepers are bad medicine—and a damn nuisance. Slightly drunk middle-aged fellow comes in with flashy girl and wants a room for the night. You're sorry, but the hotel is full. "What're you trying to tell me, fellow? This here's my wife." You are still sorry, but all the rooms are occupied. He goes out muttering vengeance, and the girl shrills profanity after you. You turn back to the room value sheet. The cashier's record is checked at last, and now you can get the house count and the house value. Somebody comes in drunk and you have to see he gets to his room without falling down the elevator shaft. Now you get to work on the bills—stacks and stacks of them. You look out and sky is getting lighter. Presently the sun will stain the clouds a brilliant crimson—but you never see it. It's seven o'clock, and you're through at last. Your eyes are sodden and heavy. There's lead in your veins instead of blood. You never get enough sleep, never get . . . enough sleep . . . sleep.

Chris Larson yawned and turned to the detective.

"Yes," he said. "I probably do."

Whatever Mack had in mind he did not pursue farther. Instead: "Who's the manager?"

"Mr. Swann—Victor Swann."

"Where's he?"

"Out," Chris answered laconically.

"Yep," Spanger confirmed. "Took his wife and went out on a big party tonight. Collins is keeping the telephone wires hot trying to find out where. Swann'll be tickled to death to hear about this—I don't think. It sure won't do the hotel no good."

20

Mack seemed not to be listening to this interjection. "If you go on at eleven, Larson, you ought to be at the desk now."

"Larry Collins is staying on. Larry figured you might want to talk to him."

"Smart fellow," Mack grunted approvingly. "If everyone used his head that well, our job would be a whole lot easier. Well, Larson, you'd probably better stick around here a while longer, then. I may have to ask a question or two—about chemistry."

"Glad to do anything I can to help out," Chris smiled.

"What's next on the program?" O'Ryan put in. "Want Chilton?"

"Yeh, get him. If he was with Swink this evening we ought to get a good check on the time element."

O'Ryan halted before touching the doorknob.

"Having this checked for prints, aren't you?"

"Sure—everything in the room'll be checked. Jimmy Selzer of the Identification Bureau is downstairs now—waiting till Doc Hildreth gets through making his report. We won't find any prints, though."

"No?"

"Naw," Mack grunted disgustedly. "A babe in the cradle would have better sense than to touch that knob with bare hands." Larson chuckled. "Well, fellow, what's so funny?" Mack demanded truculently.

"You'll find a full set of my prints on it. I closed the door to keep the gas out of the corridor."

"Oh, sure!" Mack gibed. "Fixing up an alibi for yourself already, huh?"

The fair complexion of the big Scandinavian turned an indignant pink, and he breathed heavily.

"If you mean—"

"I don't mean. I never mean anything at this stage of the game. I thought I told you that before, Larson."

The night clerk's tensed muscles relaxed. "Sorry. Kind of hard to realize that I'm a legitimate suspect."

"Don't worry about it, Chris," Spanger admonished. "Johnny Mack'll give you a square deal every time."

"I'll have Chilton brought in," O'Ryan declared. He threw the door open to reveal an excited controversy. The patrolman stationed on duty in the corridor was remonstrating audibly.

"Hey, you, I said you couldn't go in there. When they want you they'll send for you."

"But I have information of vital importance to convey," the other began, then stopped hastily as he caught sight of O'Ryan.

"What's the fuss about, Clancy?" the latter asked. The bluecoat glowered belligerently at the little man in the corridor.

"This guy started to walk in on you, chief. I stopped him just as he put his hand on the doorknob."

"Sweet mess of prints there'll be for Jimmy," Mack grumbled.

From his full height of six feet four inches O'Ryan looked down at the intruder, who couldn't have been more than five feet six and was narrow shouldered, flat chested, and scrawny necked in addition. His thin hands were delicate and small fingered, and his face was triangular: broad and wide at the forehead, narrowing toward a small, pointed chin. His sparse hair was silvery and his eyes peeked owlishly from behind a pair of gold-rimmed bifocals. Chris recognized him at once.

"What's your name?" O'Ryan demanded gruffly.

"Westborough."

"What you want here?"

"My room is across the corridor. I recalled overhearing a fragment of conversation from this room which may or may not be important to you."

O'Ryan paused for a few seconds to scrutinize the other intently. "Go on in," he said at length.

Westborough stepped over the threshold and surveyed the little group inside the room. He looked curiously at the form on the floor, then nodded at Chris Larson.

"Good-evening, Mr. Larson. I don't believe I am acquainted with you other gentlemen."

"We'll skip the introductions," Mack said shortly. "If you've got anything to say, make it snappy." He brought out a notebook. "What's your full name?"

"Theocritus Lucius Westborough."

"Good Lord!" O'Ryan commented from the doorway. "How your folks must have hated you."

The little man smiled cheerfully.

"It does seem a bit too much, doesn't it? To save you the trouble of asking any more questions, I'll tell you that my room is number 312 across the corridor and that I have no particular occupation."

"What's this conversation you heard?" Mack cut in.

"It can hardly be called a conversation since it was entirely one-sided. More in the nature of a monologue—at least the part I chanced to overhear."

"Who was talking?"

"Mr. Swink."

"Where?"

"In this room two or three evenings ago. As I opened the door of my own room and started toward the elevator on my way to dinner

23

I heard him saying, 'I know enough to put you behind bars. Now I want ten grand and I'll give you just one week to dig it up.' "

"Is that all you heard?"

"Yes, I caught those few words on my way down the corridor, but, as the matter did not concern me, I did not stop to listen to any more."

"You don't know who he was talking to?"

"I really haven't the faintest idea. He may even have been talking to himself."

"Was his door open?"

"No, closed. Ordinarily I shouldn't have heard anything, but he was undoubtedly excited, and his voice carried."

"When did you hear this conversation?"

"Let me see. This is Thursday. It must have been either Monday or Tuesday. Monday I believe."

"At what time?"

"Just before I had dinner."

"Can't you give us a better idea of the time than that? It might be important."

Westborough flushed with embarrassment.

"Dear me, I am sorry, but I am afraid I am unable to do so. You see I am not a person of extremely regular habits, and I am liable to go to dinner almost any time from five-thirty to eight o'clock."

"Did you eat in the dining room downstairs?"

"Yes."

"Well, we may be able to find the time later on from a waiter or somebody." Mack peered quizzically at the undersized man. "What do you know about tonight's business?"

"I? Nothing at all—Lieutenant Mack, isn't it? I have been in my room since dinner time—since seven-thirty. I really did look at my watch tonight. Although I don't imagine that will be very helpful, will it?"

"Did you hear any noise going on? Anything at all suspicious?"

"I heard Mr. Swink coming down the corridor. He was stumbling heavily as though he had been drinking too much, and he made quite a little noise inserting his key into the keyhole."

"But you heard nothing before that?"

"Nothing at all. I was completely absorbed in my thoughts."

"Thinking about anybody in the hotel?"

"Oh dear, no! I was thinking about Trajan."

"Who the hell's Trajan?"

"One of the five emperors who ruled Rome from 96 to 180 A.D. I've written a book—*Trajan: His Life and Times*—shortly to be printed."

"Out of my line, I'm afraid," Mack declared.

A short globular man carrying a much-worn black bag burst briskly into the room. He glanced downward to the floor. "What the devil happened to this fellow?"

"That's for you to find out, Doc," Mack grinned amiably. He turned to Westborough. "You can go now."

The little man was watching the doctor with an obvious interest. "Lieutenant Mack," he said, "I wonder if you remember my brother, James Westborough."

"Jim Westborough!" Mack exclaimed. "My God, yes! He saved my bacon when I was framed in as dirty a deal as was ever cooked up. I'll say I remember Jim Westborough! And he's your brother?"

"Was," the other corrected gravely.

Mack said slowly, "I heard about that. Angina pectoris, wasn't it?"

"Yes."

"There'll be a lot of people miss him—but I haven't time to talk about it now. Drop in at headquarters some time, will you? I'd like to have a good chat with Jim Westborough's brother."

"I shall be glad to. However, I should like first to ask a favor of you tonight. This is the first murder case in which I have been even remotely involved. I find it most interesting. If I won't be too much in the way . . ."

"How about it, Terry?" Mack inquired of his associate.

"If Westborough wants to stick around, let him stick. I knew Jim Westborough myself."

Dr. Basil Hildreth straightened up and faced the group.

"This is the damnedest way to kill a guy I ever met in my life. Funny part of it is that the damn scheme worked. It should have been a complete flop."

"What do you mean by that, Doc?" Mack asked.

"The symptoms all point to prussic acid poisoning: signs of convulsions, fingers clenched, pupils dilated. But there's no perceptible odor about the lips. There is on the contrary an odor about the nostrils. If he didn't swallow it, he must have breathed it."

"Well, what of it?"

"The prussic acid you buy is the two percent aqueous solution of the United States Pharmacopoeia—*Acidum Hydrocyanicum Dilutum*. I never heard of anyone dying from inhaling the fumes. I don't say it can't be done, mind you, but I never heard of it."

The doctor bent to pick up one of the fragments of the test tube, and Mack winked at O'Ryan.

"This is a different kind of prussic acid, Doc. This is the An-something or other kind."

"Anhydrous?"

O'Ryan returned Mack's wink from behind the doctor's back.

"Don't expect Doc to know what that means. He's never been to college."

"Anhydrous prussic acid would do it all right," the doctor mumbled, plainly chagrined. He inspected the top of the test tube with an air of detached indifference. "I suppose someone put potassium cyanide with an acid in this thing?"

"That's the way we've doped it out."

"Yes, the odor of bitter almonds still clings. There is no doubt but what prussic acid was contained in this tube.

"The fellow who engineered this job," the doctor continued, "took considerable of a chance unless he knew he could count upon our fat friend bending down to see what fell. The lethal concentration for prussic acid vapor is rather high—it was probably one of the least efficient gases used in the World War. There's a record of a fellow who breathed air containing one part in two thousand for a full one and a half minutes. Now carbon monoxide—"

"Carbon monoxide," Mack declared emphatically, "has got about as much to do with this as my aunt Harriet up at Niles, Michigan."

"This is an interesting case in several ways," Dr. Hildreth mused as though to himself. "Once the vapor got into his lungs it would traverse the membranes by osmosis."

"All right, Doc. But how does a fellow manage to get hold of this cyanide?"

"Sodium or potassium?"

Mack grinned. "Either, as far as I'm concerned."

"Both of 'em have industrial uses, I believe," the doctor replied, "but industrial chemistry's out of my line."

"What do you know about it, Larson? You seem to be pretty well up on the subject."

"The biggest use of sodium cyanide is in gold smelting. However, I don't know of any gold smelters in Chicago, so that won't help you much. Sodium cyanide is also used in case-hardening steel. The mild steel is immersed in a fused cyanide solution"

"Well, that's something," Mack interrupted. "There are a few steel works. Anything else?"

"Potassium cyanide is used in silver and gold plating."

"Silver plating?" O'Ryan echoed. "There's a building right in tins district that's lousy with silver platers."

Mack perked his head like a dog scenting the chase. "That's a lead we can follow up." His cigar bobbed thoughtfully at the side of his mouth. "Cyanide's also used in photography, isn't it?"

"Yes, a number of photographers use it as an intensifier solution. So do photo-engravers. You see, potassium cyanide is a very active solvent for all the silver halides . . ."

"You're getting too technical for me," Mack interrupted. "I gather, though, that we can add both photographers and engravers to the list of places where the cyanide might have come from?"

"Yes."

"This guy's been dead about an hour, I'd say," Dr. Hildreth pronounced.

Larson consulted his watch. The hands showed a quarter to twelve.

"That checks with the time he opened the door," Mack declared. He winked again at O'Ryan. "I suppose, Doc, you've got a dozen reasons why it was homicide and not suicide?"

"I can't tell you from the medical evidence," Dr. Hildreth snapped. "Neither can anybody else. All I can say is that if he did kill himself, he went to a hell of a lot of trouble!"

"Reminds me of how they used to pull out my first teeth by tying 'em to a door," O'Ryan commented jocularly. "Maybe he figured that stunt would make it easier to get into the next world."

"Want the stiff at the morgue, Doc?" Mack inquired.

"Sure, shoot him down there, and I'll do a post." He snapped shut the catch of his bag. "There's not a thing more I can tell you now, not a thing."

"O. K., Doc, and thanks. So long."

"So long," the doctor grunted on his way out of the door.

Mack turned to O'Ryan.

"Now that Doc Hildreth's through, we can get down to work. Let's turn this room over to Jimmy Selzer."

He went to the door and bellowed down the corridor; in a few seconds, a spectacled youth carrying a camera and its tripod base came into the room.

"Lot of work for you, Jimmy," Mack directed. "I want some pix showing just where this guy fell and a close-up showing how he's lying. Also I want you to go over every likely spot in the room with your brush and mercury powder. You should find Larson's and Westborough's prints on the doorknob, so better take their impressions now. Also get Swink's before we have him carted off to the morgue."

"O. K., Johnny," Jimmy Selzer called cheerfully.

"We've got to get out of here while Jimmy does his stuff," Mack told Larson. "Any vacant rooms in this corridor?"

"Why don't you gentlemen make use of my room?" Westborough suggested.

"Good idea," Mack approved.

He and O'Ryan walked across the corridor followed by the house detective. Larson and Westborough were halted on the threshold by Jimmy Selzer.

"If you two are Larson and Westborough," he said, "I have to take your fingerprints."

In a surprisingly short time both Larson and Westborough had been fingerprinted. As they walked into the latter's room across the corridor, the patrolman stationed at the end of the corridor called.

"Man, two women, and a kid say they want to get to their rooms. Names are Graham and Hammond. Ask Captain O'Ryan if it's all right, will you?"

Chris found O'Ryan and Mack conversing with Patrolman Phelan. He told O'Ryan what the policeman in the corridor had said.

"Do they have rooms here?" O'Ryan asked.

"Yes," Chris replied. "The Grahams are next door to Mr. Westborough and the Hammonds are across the hall."

"Next door to Swink, huh?"

"Yes."

"Tell Clancy it's O. K. No, I'll take a look at them myself. I want to get Chilton up here anyway."

O'Ryan strode out of the door. "Sweet job this is going to be," Mack complained to Spanger. "We'll probably have to see everybody in the hotel. Wish we'd get one of the swell breaks you read about— some way we could localize the killer to this corridor, for instance."

Spanger crashed a fist against the palm of his other hand.

"By God, Johnny, I may be able to help you at that. Just remembered there's a kindergarten teacher living down the south corridor by the name of Effie Colmar. Homely kind of dame that will never see thirty-five again."

"Well, what of it?"

"This virgin, it seems, has a brother by the name of Marcus. I guess she told me his name was Marcus. He was going to take her out to dinner tonight, and she wanted a good chin with him."

"I don't see that has—"

"Wait a minute, Johnny, and you will. I gathered that Mark lives out of town and Sister doesn't see him any too often. She wanted to talk to him in her own room instead of the lounge, so she comes to your uncle Jerry for permission. It was time wasted, because I never would have suspected anyone with a mug like hers anyhow."

"Come down to earth, Jerry. What's it all about?"

"Well, I told her sure, she could have her brother in her room, but I suggested, to make everything aboveboard, she—" Spanger paused portentously, and Mack snapped:

"She should leave the door open, I suppose!"

Spanger looked crestfallen at the anticipation of his dramatic climax. "Yep, and that's just what she did. And she or Mark must have been able to see everyone who passed along the corridor on their way to the rooms in this corridor."

"There's another corridor on the north, isn't there?" Mack asked.

"Yes, but it's not used nearly as much. The elevator shaft is off the south corridor, and it's the natural passageway to this part of the hotel."

"Can't help that. As long as anybody could have sneaked through the north corridor, we'll still have to quiz everyone in the hotel."

Chris Larson had a sudden inspiration. "The linen room—" he began, when he was interrupted by the return of O'Ryan with James Chilton in custody.

IV

CHILTON LOOKED the successful broker he purported to be—if anything a shade too perfectly. He was tall and dignified, his hair splashed with gray about the temples. His tailored English tweed couldn't have cost less than a hundred, and his heavy rep necktie had probably set him back a five spot, Chris speculated.

Mack rose from his chair at Westborough's desk. "Sit down here, Chilton." The chair he indicated directly faced the desk lamp, and Chilton frowned.

"See here, I don't like third-degree methods. I'm not legally required to answer any questions."

"He's right about that," Spanger put in. "You're going to have to be careful about the way you talk to our guests, Johnny."

"Want me to wrap 'em up in cotton wool?" Mack sneered. "All of you are going to find it wiser to cooperate. Where's your home town, Chilton?"

Chilton crossed his legs with a slow and languid assurance. "New York. I don't mind telling you that."

"Oh, don't you? Well, what do you do in New York?"

Chilton stretched a hand toward the desk lamp and tilted its shade. "I'm a broker. And I don't believe that a light should glare. Do you?"

O'Ryan furiously rearranged the shade. "Yes," he roared. "You let that lamp alone."

Chilton shrugged his shoulders. They were rather a good pair of shoulders too, Chris Larson thought.

"My error."

"What's your firm?" Mack demanded.

"Crabb and Cunningham."

He gave the address, which Mack noted in his little black book. Then:

"What're you doing in Chicago, Chilton?"

"Business," Chilton replied sullenly. Mack's next question was tinged with suspicion.

"What sort of business?"

"That concerns me and my firm."

"Maybe so." Mack relaxed in the manner of a fisherman allowing his victim more line. He went on in a silky tone. "How long have you been staying here?"

"I registered Monday."

"Morning or afternoon?"

"Morning."

Mack counted on his fingers. "Four full days you've been here." He shot out with sudden force. "How many calls have you made in that time?"

Chilton uncrossed his legs and fumbled for a cigarette. "None."

"None," Mack repeated sarcastically. "Four days and not one call? Why not?"

"People are out of town," Chilton mumbled evasively.

"And you didn't find that out before you left New York?" Chilton was silent. "For a so-called big business man you don't seem very efficient."

Chilton smouldered at the taunt. "It's none of your business, but this is a combination business and pleasure trip. I have plenty of time to wait for my customers."

"Why didn't you bring your wife along?" Mack inquired.

"He says he's on a pleasure trip," O'Ryan contributed jovially.

Chilton flushed. "Again it's none of your business, but I don't happen to be married."

"April's a funny month and Chicago's a funny town for a vacation. That is, for a fellow from New York."

"I also came on business," Chilton reminded.

"An answer both ways. Convenient, isn't it?"

Chilton made no reply but shifted nervously in his seat. Lieutenant Mack seemed to be getting under his guard, Larson reflected. The night clerk couldn't help but admire the deftness with which the detective was conducting this interview.

"Why don't you tell the truth, Chilton?" Mack suggested. The broker rose indignantly to his feet.

"See here! I'm not going to be called a liar"

The pressure of O'Ryan's gigantic hand on his shoulder forced him back to his chair.

"You're going to sit right there! See?"

Mack shifted his line of attack. "You knew Elmo Swink?" Chilton nodded. "Very well?" Mack asked.

"It depends on what you mean by very well."

"Well, what do you mean?"

"I never saw him before I registered here."

"How'd you get acquainted with him, then?"

"How do such things usually start?" Chilton tilted his chair backward and recrossed his ankles. "I sat next to him in the bar a couple of evenings ago. Strangers usually start talking after they've poured down two or three Scotch-and-sodas."

"Tried to sell you something, didn't he?"

Chilton glanced at the detective's face with grudging admiration. "That's not a bad guess."

"No guess at all," Mack disclaimed. "You've been seen with him a lot around the hotel during the last few days. Either you were trying to sell him something, or he was trying to sell you something."

"He was."

"Well, what was it?"

"A mine in Colorado—the Link of Gold."

"Did you bite?"

"I'm no sucker," Chilton declared vehemently. "There's been considerable of a boom in Western mining lately, and his proposition seemed like a good buy, but—the motto of my firm is, 'Before you invest, investigate.' "

"The Link of Gold," Mack repeated, writing down the name in the ubiquitous notebook. "Did Swink tell you where it was located?"

"Near Georgetown."

"Swink strike you as being on the level?" Mack questioned, restoring the notebook to his pocket.

"He did—and I've been up against a lot of con men too. I'm able to tell them pretty well by now."

"But you didn't commit yourself?"

"Don't be absurd. I wouldn't put in a cent without a detailed report from my own agent."

"Which you didn't get?"

"Not yet."

"You had dinner with Swink last Monday night, didn't you?" Mack inquired with assumed casualness.

"Not last Monday," Chilton replied quickly, "tonight."

"My mistake. You didn't see him Monday, then?"

"I didn't know him Monday. I didn't meet him until Tuesday."

"And you weren't with him last night?"

"No, I didn't see him last night."

"But you did have dinner with him tonight?"

"Yes."

"His suggestion or yours?"

"His. He called me on the telephone just before dinner and asked me to be his guest."

"What time?"

"I suppose we went down together a few minutes after seven. I remember we had finished our meal at eight."

"What did you do then?"

"Sat around the lobby for a while and smoked our cigars."

"Did either of you leave the lobby at any time before quarter to eleven?"

"We both did."

"Together?"

"Yes."

"Where'd you go?"

"Up to Swink's room. He had some production charts he wanted me to look over."

"What time was this?"

"About eight-thirty."

"How long'd you stay in Swink's room?"

"Maybe twenty-five minutes."

"Then you left Swink's room about five minutes to nine?"

"Yes."

"Who went out first—you or he?"

"I did, naturally."

"Did you see him lock his door?"

"It's a spring lock and doesn't require locking."

"But you heard the door close behind you?"

"Yes."

"Everything all right in Swink's room when you went in?"

"As far as I could tell."

"Did you see a diamond stick pin lying on his dresser?"

"I think there was one—yes."

Mack had again produced his notebook and was jotting down an abbreviated summary of the laconic conversation.

"Where'd you and Swink go after you left his room?"

"To the bar."

"And you stayed there with him the rest of the evening?"

"Yes. We didn't leave until nearly eleven."

"Then what did you do?"

"Went to our rooms."

"You left him in the west corridor?"

"Yes, my room's down at the other end."

"See anyone around when you said good-night?"

"Nobody."

"You didn't wait in the corridor until Swink had opened his door?"

"No, I went straight to my room and took off my coat. Right after that I heard someone scream and rushed out. There were a lot of people in the hall."

"Yes, I know." Mack dismissed the subject as of no importance. "Did you leave Swink at any time while you were in the bar?"

"Yes—a little after ten."

"Why?"

"I suppose I'd better tell you the truth," Chilton began hesitantly. "One of the rear suspender buttons on my trousers popped off. So I slipped down into the washroom in the basement and had the porter sew it on."

"How long were you gone?"

"About fifteen minutes."

"You didn't go back to your own room or up to the third floor?"

"No."

"Sure of that?"

"Yes."

Mack terminated the interview.

"All right, Chilton. That's all we want to know tonight. I'd advise you to stay in the hotel for the next few days, though. Don't try to check out without seeing me first."

"You mean I'm under suspicion?" Chilton demanded angrily.

"Everyone's under suspicion until we get this thing cleared up," Mack said quietly, "you no more than anyone else."

Chilton opened his mouth as though he would like to say something, closed it again, and strode out of the room without glancing behind him. Mack turned to O'Ryan.

"How does that story strike you, Terry?"

O'Ryan pulled a paper from his pocket and scanned it carefully.

"Phelan wants me to get him a transfer to the detective division, and I think I'm going to do it. I sent him down to have a talk with the room clerk and see what he could find out. Here's what he says." He began to read from the notes.

"About eight-thirty, Swink, accompanied by Chilton, asked for the key of his room and went to the elevator. The elevator pilot stopped at the third floor and both men got off. He picked them up again half an hour later and both men were observed by the room clerk to go in the direction of the bar. The bartender remembers that Chilton excused himself from Swink and was gone a quarter of an hour or so. He isn't quite sure of the time but thinks it was sometime after ten. Both men left the bar again shortly before eleven. Elevator men do not remember taking Chilton up alone at any time."

"That checks with what Chilton told us."

"Almost too well. Of course, there's one thing."

"What's that?"

"There are stairs leading up to the third floor. Chilton wouldn't have to take the elevator."

"But nobody saw him walking up."

"Phelan didn't find anyone who did." O'Ryan heaved a colossal sigh. "What do *you* think of his story, Johnny?"

Mack said slowly:
"The last part sounded better than the first."

"You think there's something fishy about him?"

"Figure it out for yourself. He's been here since Monday—he came on business and he admits he hasn't done any. I'm going to wire New York to get in touch with Crabb and Cunningham."

O'Ryan looked at his watch.

"Any idea of how many people we've got to talk to, Johnny?" he said somewhat crossly. "If you take as long with everyone as you did with Chilton, we'll be on the job till next Christmas."

"Maybe not," Mack said cheerfully, "Jerry Spanger knows a kindergarten teacher who may save us a peck of trouble."

He explained about Effie Colmar and the proprieties, and O'Ryan grinned broadly.

"Thank God for one woman who's afraid of what the old hens will say." His face grew sober again almost instantly. "There's another corridor, however."

"Pardon me," Chris Larson interrupted, "but I thought of something just before you brought Chilton in. The linen room is on the north corridor, and our night housekeeper, Miss Kriskrowski, spends two or three hours there every evening making a check of supplies. She usually leaves the door open too," he added.

O'Ryan's ham-like hand descended across Mack's shoulder in a slap that could have been heard at the opposite end of the corridor.

"That's the ticket! Now we're beginning to get somewhere. Jerry, bring in your kindergarten teacher and then we'll talk to Miss Criss-cross."

"Kriskrowski," Larson corrected.

"Well, whatever her name is."

Effie Colmar was, as Jerry Spanger had described her, a spinster of about thirty-five, a trifle near-sighted and wearing nose glasses, which gave her thin face a slightly pinched look. Her straw-colored hair was gathered up at the back in a plain but efficient knot. Spanger had given her just five minutes to "make yourself decent," and the results of the hasty toilet were apparent.

"Miss Colmar," Mack began without preamble, "your brother spent this evening with you, didn't he?"

"Yes. Marcus doesn't get up from Springfield very often, and it was so nice to see him. He's a dear boy— always so thoughtful."

Mack cut this laudation short.

"You spoke to Mr. Spanger about entertaining him in your room, and Mr. Spanger told you that it would be all right if you left the door open, didn't he?"

"Why—yes. I won't get into trouble with the management over it, will I?"

"I don't know why you should. You did leave the door open, didn't you?"

"Indeed we did. Every minute of the time."

"What time did your brother leave you, Miss Colmar?"

"It wasn't quite eleven."

"And what time did you and he go up to your room?"

"Let me see—we had just had dinner—such a lovely dinner too. Yes, it must have been about seven."

"With the door open all that time you should have been able to see everyone who passed down the corridor."

"Oh, we did." She giggled nervously. "I'm afraid I'm inclined to take just a wee bit too much interest in the doings of my neighbors. I pointed out everyone who passed to Marcus and we would speculate on who they were and what they were doing. Of course, I'm not really acquainted with any of them, but it's fun to pretend."

"Good girl!" Mack commented. "Now if you can tell me who they were, you'll be a big help. This is a murder case we're investigating."

"Right in this hotel!" Her colorless eyes looked startled. "Why, that's too thrilling! I'm glad to do anything I can. Of course, though, I don't know any of their names—I mean I'm not sure."

"Describe them, then."

41

"I'll try." Her forehead puckered. "Well, for one I noticed this gentleman." Her glance designated Westborough. "Marcus and I thought he must be a college professor—he looked so absent-minded and scholarly."

"What time did you see him?"

"Oh, dear, do I have to tell the time too? I'm afraid I didn't notice that very much."

"Was he going toward the elevator or away from it?" Mack wanted to know.

She looked at him archly. "Won't it simplify matters if I just say in or out? 'In' when they were going away from the elevator and 'out' when they were going toward it?"

"O. K., Sister," Mack assented wearily.

"This gentleman—in—seven to eight o'clock. Is that the way you want me to put it?"

"You're doing fine!"

"Then there was a party—two women, young, stylishly dressed, one a blonde and the other an Irish brunette with blue eyes. At least they should have been blue—I didn't actually notice. Also a tall, rather thin man, and a little boy—out—at about eight-thirty. I'm sure of that time because Marcus had just looked at his watch."

"That would be the Graham family," Spanger interpolated, "and the brunette sounds like Mrs. Hammond."

"Oh, I forgot," Miss Colmar began in a rapid gush of words. "In—just before the other party went out—two men. One tall, handsome, with gray temples. He looked just like a movie actor. The other was a fat, dumpy man, not very attractive. Out—same two somewhere near nine o'clock."

"Anyone else?"

"Yes, in—nine-thirty—imposing-looking dowager. I know her—it's Mrs. Blakely. I can't say I exactly like her, although she's been lovely to me. In—probably ten o'clock—a little shriveled-up man with a face like a fox."

"That sounds like Mr. Devon," Chris Larson smiled.

"I forgot again. In—maybe fifteen minutes before Mr. Devon—tall, lovely girl with striking bronze hair."

"And that's Miss Gant," Larson interrupted again.

Miss Colmar's brow wrinkled.

"Now that must be all. No, it isn't quite. I went to the elevator with Marcus and said good-night to him there. While we were waiting, an 'up' car stopped and two men got off. Same two we'd seen before. The tall handsome man and the fat dumpy one." She simpered. "I fear they had both been looking upon the 'wine while it is red in the cup' or do people drink nothing but highballs now? Anyway, my tall handsome man was helping my unpleasant fat one along the corridor. In—maybe ten minutes to eleven."

She stopped, finally out of breath, and Mack put in a word or two.

"You're sure you saw nobody else, Miss Colmar?"

"Not another soul, take oath and hope to die!" She raised her right hand kittenishly. "After Marcus left me I had a hot shower and then went to bed. That's all I knew until Mr. Spanger woke me up."

"You didn't hear a scream just after you left your brother?"

"Was there a scream? No, I didn't hear it, but then I was in the bathroom with the water running." She paused again, and Mack asked:

"You didn't at any time see your tall handsome man who looked like a movie actor go up or down the corridor without his short dumpy friend, did you?"

"No, I'm sure he didn't."

43

"You sure you would have noticed him?"

"We were facing the door all the time. I didn't want to be taken by surprise by the manager, even though I had asked Mr. Spanger's permission."

She giggled again, and Mack made haste to say, "We don't want to keep you up any longer, Miss Colmar. You've helped us a lot."

"Have I really helped you? It's just too thrilling to be a part of a real live murder case."

Jerry Spanger escorted her to the door and Mack gave a disgusted shrug.

"There may be sillier dames, but I've never met one." O'Ryan was consulting the list he had received from Patrolman Phelan. "How does her dope check with yours, Terry?"

"Tallies pretty close. Graham handed in his key at the desk around eight-thirty and went out with his wife and Mrs. Hammond. Westborough asked for his key about seven-thirty. Mrs. Blakely, between nine and ten; Devon, between ten and ten-thirty. No dope on Miss Gant." He restored the list to his pocket. "Your girlfriend didn't see Chilton come back alone either."

"No." Mack was thoughtful. "If you want any help in getting Phelan transferred to the detective division, I'm your man, Terry. And now let's hear from Kriskrowski."

O'Ryan looked at him in admiration. "I couldn't remember that name, Johnny. Not unless I'd seen it in black and white."

Miss Kriskrowski was a large woman with flashing black eyes and straight black hair strained back from the forehead. Her Slavic ancestry was apparent in every feature. Her voice was hard, efficient, and metallic. She gave as little information in response to a question as was conveniently possible, and it was at first difficult to draw her out.

However, at the end of ten minutes Mack and O'Ryan had elicited the following facts.

—That she had been working in the linen room from eight forty-five until after eleven.

—That the door had been open during the entire time.

—That she would have noticed anybody who had passed down the north corridor.

—That nobody had passed down the north corridor—either "in" or "out"—with the exception of a chambermaid.

—That the chambermaid was in the west corridor about nine o'clock as she was every evening.

—That she could and would give the chambermaid's name (Mack's notebook was again requisitioned into service), but that it would be of no use trying to talk to her this evening because she went off duty at eleven o'clock.

—That hotel guests were the most unbelievable ingrates on earth, that a great many towels were always missing, and that nobody could credit the monstrous things they did to sheets.

—That in spite of the extreme care lavished upon their rooms, they could still find it in their hearts to complain.

Miss Kriskrowski was dismissed, and O'Ryan was jubilant. With the advice and assistance of Larson and Spanger, he constructed an improvised floor plan of the third floor. Westborough was an attentive spectator to this phase of the investigation, even going so far as to make a copy of the diagram. "For my own reference," the little man explained apologetically.

The sketch completed, O'Ryan's big blunt forefinger hovered directly between two wavering parallel lines marked, "west corridor."

"The only people we need bother about, Johnny, are right here. There are some vacant rooms, Larson says, and that makes things easier. I'm going to have Phelan and McCarter go through every room in this corridor. They might find some of the cyanide or maybe find the box the stuff was carried in."

"You can't start poking into people's rooms without a warrant," Spanger protested.

O'Ryan gave him a friendly push into a chair. It was meant for a friendly push, Larson believed, but Spanger sat down—hard. "Be your age, Jerry," the police captain advised.

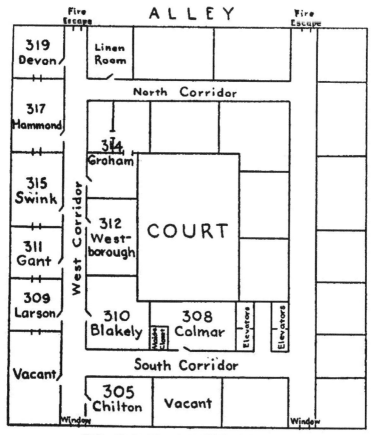

Plan drawn from a sketch in the notebook of
Theocritus Lucius Westborough

46

"Swann won't like it," Spanger remonstrated, fussily anxious to shield the hotel's guests from annoyance. Mack left them arguing to go across the corridor and bawl for Jimmy Selzer. The spectacled youth appeared at once.

"Any prints?" Mack inquired.

Selzer shook his head. "Only on the doorknob. I've used the gray dust over nearly all the likely places, too. The housekeeping staff here do a slick job of keeping things clean."

"Whose prints were on the doorknob?"

"Swink's, Larson's, and Westborough's—all messed up together. It was a tough job to make 'em out."

"Find any prints you couldn't identify?"

"Nope—just found those three."

"Stiff gone to the morgue?"

"Yep. Didn't you tell 'em to give it a ride?"

"Terry O'Ryan did." Mack concluded the conversation. "When you're through we'll move back in here. But be sure to get pix of the prints on the doorknob."

"Already got 'em," the efficient Selzer answered.

Mack returned to Westborough's bedroom. O'Ryan had won the argument with the house detective and assured the homicide section lieutenant that Phelan and McCarter were now at work.

"Searching their persons, too?" Mack inquired.

"Sure! Job's no good unless it's done thoroughly."

"Swann isn't going to like this at all," the discomfited Spanger grumbled.

O'Ryan chuckled. "We should take orders from him."

"Just the same, you ought to have a warrant," Spanger stubbornly maintained.

47

"What about searching the women?" Mack queried. "You got to get a matron up here, Terry."

O'Ryan made a wry face and reached for the telephone. "Now how the devil did that detail slip my mind?"

Mack seated himself at the writing desk, took a sheet of notepaper from the drawer, and wrote eight names in a large, bold chirography. Very slowly he made check marks opposite the first three names on his list. Then he folded the paper and placed it in his pocket.

"No guy can do a job like this without leaving back tracks," he declared, rising to his feet. "People remember and people talk." He reached for a packet of matches and relit his cigar. "If we have luck with just one lead, we've got our man. And we have three leads."

"The cyanide's one," O'Ryan averred.

"Yep," Mack agreed, "that's number one. He had to get it somewhere. There seem to be a lot of likely places—steel works, silver-plating plants, engravers, photographers, photographer's supply houses—but it's just a matter of routine to run 'em down one by one."

"Then there's the acid," O'Ryan suggested.

"That's harder. Larson says almost any acid might have been used. He thinks sulphuric, but he won't swear to it. And even if it was sulphuric, that doesn't help much because that stuff is used damn near everywhere. However, it's a lead."

"What's your third?"

"The test tube," Mack proclaimed. "You buy those things at chemical supply houses, and there aren't so many of those, are there, Larson?"

"Probably more than you think."

"Anyway," Mack went on, "it shouldn't be an impossible job to run it down. We might get pix of everyone in this corridor, and go call on supply houses with 'em. Then if we got an identification—"

"I've got a hunch, Johnny," O'Ryan interrupted. What his hunch was nobody ever learned, for at that moment Patrolman Phelan burst excitedly into the room.

"Chief, I've found out where your test tube came from!"

V

"THE HELL YOU SAY!" O'Ryan shouted. "Where?"

"Remember the family that got in around midnight? Had a kid about eleven years old."

"Sure I place 'em. Mr. and Mrs. Ronald E. Graham. Another woman, Mrs. Hammond, was with them."

Phelan nodded.

"That's the party. The Graham kid—he's called Cedric, the poor little devil—is bugs on chemistry, and his folks bought him a set. It's a big cardboard box with a lot of tubes and jars and bottles in it."

O'Ryan grinned understandingly.

"I know what you mean. My own youngster wants me to get him one."

"Well, it seems the kid got into some sort of trouble with the set," Phelan went on. "Made the damnedest stinking stuff you ever heard of, and his folks took it away from him and locked it up in a closet, way on the top shelf. Me and McCarter were going through the room and we found it—one of the glass tubes that you use for mixing up the chemicals is gone!"

"Kid might have broken it," O'Ryan speculated.

"He says he didn't. Swears the set was O.K. when his folks took it away from him."

O'Ryan sprang toward the door.

"Come on, Johnny. We're going to look into this."

Chris had seen Mr. Graham several times before and had liked the man from the first. He was nearly as tall as the big O'Ryan, but was far from being as broad. He had a lean bronzed face, light hair and a light mustache, and a lantern jaw. By that curious law which seems to insure the attraction of opposites, Mrs. Graham wasn't much over five feet: a little blonde with wide blue eyes. She didn't look a day over twenty-two, but her son, Cedric, at least eleven, gave the lie to her appearance. Cedric, who resembled neither parent, was a thin, somewhat nervous youngster with an air of bored detachment, obviously assumed as a mask in the presence of adults.

"Come in," Graham invited cordially. "Captain O'Ryan, isn't it? I've seen your name often in the papers, but I never imagined I'd have the honor of meeting you face to face."

"I could name a lot of folks who don't call it no honor," O'Ryan chuckled.

"Won't you sit down?" Mrs. Graham invited, bustling about hospitably. "Cedric, run into the bedroom and bring another chair. That's the worst part of living in a hotel," she apologized. "I do hope we will be able to find a real home again soon."

"Never mind, ma'am," O'Ryan expostulated. "Where's that chemistry set of your son's?"

"On the table."

O'Ryan lifted the gaudy lithographed lid of a cardboard box labeled "Magic Marvels of Chemistry." Strips of elastic held in place various bottles, phials, and short wooden cylinders. A wooden rack in the center held several test tubes, some empty, others containing various chemicals. There was a conspicuous vacant space in the middle of the rack.

Mack selected one of the test tubes and held it between his thumb and forefinger. "Same kind all right," he pronounced. As his eyes ranged over the names printed on the bottles, he whistled sharply.

O'Ryan peered over his shoulder. "What do you see, Johnny?" Mack pointed to a label on one of the bottles.

Larson leaned forward to read, "Sulphuric Acid—Very Dangerous." He compared the other bottles and their labels, then said slowly, "There's something wrong about this. I didn't think a manufacturer would put anything like sulphuric in the hands of kids. And I was right. This bottle doesn't belong with the set. It's a different kind, for one thing, and the label is hand lettered and not printed."

"Neat job of lettering, though," Mack commented. He turned to Graham. "Seems to me you have some explaining to do."

"Papa bought it," Cedric chimed in. "I asked him to and he did. Didn't you, Papa?"

"Is that right, Graham?"

"Yes, Cedric wanted to make some experiments that called for this stuff. I didn't want to let him have it, but he teased so that we finally compromised. I bought the bottle and put him on his honor never to open it unless I was there to supervise the operation."

"I never did either," Cedric piped in a shrill soprano.

"I begged him not to get it," Mrs. Graham lamented. "It's dangerous, isn't it, Mr. Larson?"

"Yes," Chris said, "particularly so in the concentrated form. It has a very powerful attraction for water, which causes it to char organic tissues. A single drop could result in a severe burn."

Mrs. Graham addressed her husband firmly.

"You'll have to throw that stuff out right away, Ronald. I'm not going to have it around here another minute."

"A fair amount's been used," Mack observed. "What did you want stuff like this for, sonny?"

"It dissolves iron and frees hydrogen," the boy explained in an eager torrent of words. "I wanted to make hydrogen, and Papa helped me."

"Your son has what it takes to be a chemist all right," Larson smiled at Mrs. Graham.

"Will it do that, Larson?" Mack inquired.

"Cedric's perfectly correct about that experiment."

Graham chuckled. "Cedric and I had ourselves a big time one Saturday afternoon while his mother was at a bridge party. We put some iron filings in the bottom of a test tube and added just enough of the stuff to cover 'em. Pretty soon the filings began to melt away and the gas started bubbling through the acid. Then we touched a match to it and got a pale blue flame."

"How long ago was all this?" Mack asked.

"About a month ago," Mrs. Graham put in. "I remember because it was the day of Ethel's party, and that was on the sixteenth."

"Where'd you buy the acid?" asked Mack abruptly. Graham told him, and Mack made another entry in the inevitable notebook. Then he asked Larson. "How long has Swink been in this hotel?"

"About two weeks."

"That's right," Jerry Spanger confirmed. "I took particular note of the day he moved in because he looked like some sort of bunco-steerer to me."

"How well did you people know Swink?" Mack inquired of the Grahams.

"Know him?" Graham echoed. "We've scarcely seen the fellow."

"Was he that fat man across the hall?" Mrs. Graham asked. "He nodded good-morning to me once."

"Do you wear hairpins, Mrs. Graham?" Mack interrogated.

Luella Graham started. "Why, of course."

"I'd like to have one of 'em."

With a perplexed expression on her face, Mrs. Graham stretched a soft, plump hand to her hair. Larson noted her nails were stained a vivid crimson.

"I can't imagine why on earth you want it, but it's yours."

Mack scrutinized the hairpin with absorbed attention.

"Graham, a guy was murdered across the hall this evening," he began curtly. "Someone made some poison gas in a test tube and hung it over his door. The test tube was just like these in your son's set and there's one of those missing. Sulphuric acid might have been used to make the gas. You've got some here. A wire hairpin was used to hook the test tube over the door—and your wife wears the same kind. I want the truth from you, Graham," he demanded sternly. "Where were you tonight?"

"I don't like your tone," Graham barked, his jaw setting in a grim line. "I think still less of your methods, and I refuse to be bullied by either."

"You'll answer my question," Mack blustered, "or I'll—"

Westborough, who had been an eagerly interested spectator ever since he had been granted permission to watch the investigation, had up to this minute contributed nothing to the discussion. Now he interrupted to break the tension.

"I don't think your case can be solved so easily, Lieutenant Mack. You see everyone rooming off this corridor had been unpleasantly reminded that Cedric owned a chemical set."

"I'll say they were!" Jerry Spanger chortled. "We had one sweet time."

"What happened?" asked Mack, his eyes remaining upon Graham.

"Well, the kid came home from school, his mother was out, and he got down his chemical set to play with. Pretty soon he had stirred up the stinkingest mess you've ever smelt—like ten thousand eggs that had been rotting since the year one. Then he ran up and down the corridor, popping in wherever anyone happened to be home to let them smell it." Spanger chuckled. "Seems like that damn rotten egg stink hung on for hours. You never smelt anything so terrible."

"It was hydrogen sulphide," Cedric told him. "It did smell, I guess."

"Gracious, I was afraid we were all going to be asked to leave the hotel," Mrs. Graham broke in. "I locked Cedric's chemical set in the closet, and he hasn't been allowed to play with it since."

"I don't care," Cedric announced sulkily. "Rotten old set isn't good for anything but a lot of baby tricks. When I grow up, I'm going to get me a real laboratory, and I'll make anything I want to then, you bet."

"How do you make hydrogen sulphide?" Mack inquired.

"Any sulphide will give it when acted upon by a dilute acid," Larson replied. "Just add some hydrochloric acid to ferrous sulphide, for instance, and you'll get your rotten egg smell."

"I didn't have any hydrochloric acid," Cedric informed. "I dissolved sodium thiosulphate in water and added ferric sulphide. It worked, too."

"It sure did," Spanger confirmed.

"And everybody on the floor knew about this?" Mack questioned.

"I didn't hear 'em talk about much else for the next two days. A fellow would have to be blind, deaf, dumb, and then have his smeller amputated not to know what the kid had been up to."

Mack's manner toward Graham underwent a visible alteration. "I don't mind telling you that if everyone on the floor knew your son had the chemical set, it does make the case look a bit different."

Graham said, "You asked me what we did tonight. Mrs. Graham and I took Cedric to a movie—afterwards we all stopped for a bite to eat. Mrs. Hammond was with us."

"Where was her husband?" O'Ryan asked.

"He had a headache or something."

"He's away most of the time," Mrs. Graham put in, "and Mr. Graham and I have sort of made it a habit to ask Norah to go with us whenever we go to a show. I'd forgotten that Fred'd be home tonight, or we wouldn't have asked her. Of course, she didn't have to go with us, but Fred acted kind of funny—practically insisted that she should go without him."

"What time'd you leave?"

"Rather early," Graham replied. "I didn't look at the time."

"I did," Mrs. Graham confessed. "It was just eight-thirty by the clock in the lobby."

"What'd you do with the key to your room?" Mack wanted to know. "Take it with you?"

"No, Mr. Graham turned it in at the desk. We always do that when we go out."

"There are three of you," Mack reminded. "Don't you have more than one key?"

Graham shook his head. "I suppose we could get another, but we don't really need it."

"That means your one and only room key was down at the desk from eight thirty until—what time'd you get back?"

"About a quarter to twelve."

"That's a long time to spend at a movie."

"It was a long show. We went down to the Loop—United Artists, if you want to know where. Then we had something to eat, and—"

"Good show?"

"Mr. Graham certainly thought it was," Mrs. Graham informed. "He couldn't talk of anything else all the way home. It was a gangster picture. I don't think so much of them."

"There was lots of shooting," Cedric volunteered. "The gangsters had the two G men all tied up and were going to turn a machine gun on them, but the third G man came in from the window and—"

"Mrs. Hammond like it?" Mack interrupted.

"Norah was rather quiet all evening," Mrs. Graham replied thoughtfully. "She seemed worried about something—Fred, I suppose."

"Humph!" Mack's exclamation might have stood for nearly anything. "You told me, Mrs. Graham, that you locked this set in the closet when you took it away from your boy."

"Yes."

"Was the closet door locked while you were gone?"

"No, we unlocked it to get our hats and coats and didn't lock it again."

"It's unlocked most of the time," Cedric contributed. "Mama never can remember to lock it."

Mrs. Graham darted an angry glance at her offspring. "Cedric, if you've been taking advantage of me"

"Cedric wouldn't do that," Mack cut in. "Are you pretty good at remembering things, Cedric?"

"Pretty good."

Mack held up the sulphuric acid bottle. "Has any of this gone since you and your father experimented with it?"

Cedric wrinkled his small forehead in intense concentration. "Gosh, I can't remember! I don't believe Papa and I left any more than that in the bottle."

56

"Cedric, did you tell anyone else in the hotel about this bottle of acid?" Westborough inquired excitedly.

"I don't think so," the boy replied after some deliberation. "Did you?" Westborough asked of Graham.

"I don't remember talking about it."

"And you, Mrs. Graham?"

"Let me think. Yes, I might've mentioned it to Mrs. Hammond."

"What're you driving at, Mr. Westborough?" Mack asked.

"Don't you see?" Westborough exclaimed with a nervous agitation. "The murderer undoubtedly knew that he could secure this tube from the boy's chemical set. But there is a strong probability that he didn't know about the sulphuric acid, since it is not usually included with sets of this character. Therefore—"

"I get it," Mack snapped. "He had to have some acid of his own before he came in here."

"Well, if that's the case, it's in some room off this corridor," O'Ryan was prompt to declare. "We know that he didn't leave the corridor afterwards."

"I think," Westborough pronounced gravely, "that you have hit the nail squarely on the head."

VI

BACK ONCE MORE in the room which Elmo Swink had occupied, Mack declaimed, "I want more facts before I start putting two and two together. Let's talk to Mrs. Blakely. She was the first to find the body, and we haven't got her story yet."

"You'll get plenty of facts from her," Spanger snickered. "That hen's the biggest gossip in the hotel—and that's saying something."

"Well, have her in," Mack directed. O'Ryan bellowed instructions to his henchmen. "The more she gossips, the more dope we'll get. An old girl like that has a lot of uses when it comes to finding out things about her neighbors."

That inert figure had been removed from the floor at last, Chris Larson noted. Someone, undoubtedly the diligent Jimmy Selzer, had gathered up the shattered fragments of the test tube and laid them upon the writing desk. Larson examined them with fresh interest. Unquestionably, he decided, the unbroken tube would have been of the size and shape of those found in the rack of Cedric Graham's chemical set. He inspected the sludge clinging to the bottom portion of the tube. Transparent crystals had formed at the edges.

"Are you going to have this analyzed?"

"I suppose so. Why?"

"If you find out what salt this is, you'll know whether sodium or potassium cyanide was used and also what acid."

Mack's mind was plainly intent along another trend of thought. "You know, Larson, people are a lot like your chemicals. You mix 'em up together in a test tube—that's this hotel—there's what you call a reaction, and somebody gets killed. Now I've been thinking—what do you call the things that make the fireworks start but don't take any part in it themselves?"

"Catalysts?" Chris volunteered.

"That sounds like it. Well, I've a hunch our old dame may turn out to be one of those. We'll get her to talking, and things will start happening. Although I can't see how she could have had a damn thing to do with putting the tube over Swink's door herself."

"Hire a hall," O'Ryan advised.

"Jerry says she's a gossip," Mack went on, ignoring the gibe. "An old dame like that with nothing to do but watch her neighbors! Why, I'll bet she can tell us everything about everybody in this corridor—even what the 'E' stands for in Graham's middle name."

"I'll take that bet," O'Ryan offered quickly. "Want to make it half a buck?"

Westborough was looking absent-mindedly out of the window.

"Dear me, it has started to rain again!"

Dressed in a clinging black gown which enhanced the opulence of her ample bosom, Sarah Blakely swept in the room like a magnificent ocean liner. Her little gray eyes, surveying the world through a large pair of horn-rimmed spectacles, were inquisitive and prying. Her nose was built along the architecture of an eagle's beak, and her lips were thin and uncompromising. Little folds of skin hung from her thick and flabby neck.

Her voice was harsh and belligerent.

"I've sat up for hours past my bedtime waiting for you to call me. I'm a law-abiding woman, and I want to tell the police everything I know."

"That's the right spirit!" Mack exclaimed with pretended heartiness. "Mrs. Blakely, I understand that you were the first to discover what had happened to Mr. Swink."

Sarah Blakely swelled visibly at this tribute to her importance. "I certainly did, Officer—I don't know your name."

"I'm Lieutenant Mack." He completed belated introductions. "This is Captain O'Ryan. I suppose you know Mr. Spanger and Mr. Larson and Mr. Westborough?"

"Yes, good-evening," Sarah Blakely acknowledged shortly, obviously feeling that these gentry were not worth her time. She seated herself in a chair, arranging her skirt with careful deliberation, while her small gray eyes dissected each separate feature of the room.

"Thank goodness, you've got rid of him! A lot of people tell me I'm psychic. I don't know whether that's true or not, although I think probably I am, but I do know I'd never be able to sleep again if I had to sit in the same room with a corpse." Her stout body shivered. "I never shirked a duty yet, and I don't intend to now. What do you want to know first, Captain Mack? Or are you Lieutenant O'Ryan?"

"Lieutenant Mack," the detective corrected. "Begin at the beginning, Mrs. Blakely, and tell us about this evening any way you want to."

"I went to my own room early," Mrs. Blakely declared positively. "I had a headache, have them often lately, must be these glasses. I told the oculist they ought to be changed the last time he examined my eyes, but he said it wasn't necessary. If you ask me, he's one of these conceited and opinionated little men who simply won't take advice. I ought to know how my own eyes feel, shouldn't I?"

"What time was it when you went to your room?" Mack interrupted.

"Well, it was some time after nine o'clock, but I don't think it was as late as ten. It must have been after nine o'clock, though, because I was talking to Esther Hatteras, who lives on the fifth floor—you know Mrs. Hatteras, don't you, Mr. Westborough? I said to her, 'Gracious, it's nine o'clock already—I don't know where time flies to. Seems like a body just can't start to do anything nowadays but what it's time to do something else.' And she said that was true. My poor George always used to say—"

"Can't you make a closer guess than between nine and ten?" Mack inquired, attempting to switch the conversation away from "poor George." But it was a futile attempt.

"George, that's my late husband, you know, he died three years ago, the poor fellow! Well, George had a saying, 'Time was made for slaves.' He ought to know, I guess, for if ever a man slaved at his work, George did. I used to tell him, 'You'll kill yourself if you keep it up,' and he told me, 'Sarah, when I go, I'd rather die in harness.' He might be alive now if he'd taken my advice. But George always was a stubborn man. I had a regular battle every year trying to get him to put on his winter underwear."

"I bet you did," Mack said conciliatingly, "but, Mrs. Blakely, we were talking about the time you went to your room."

"I declare it must have been after nine-thirty," the lady cogitated, "because Esther and I were in the lobby, and who should step out of the elevator but Mrs. Whippet. She has a Scotch terrier—one of those black, shaggy dogs with pointed ears—she takes out every night. It's always at nine-thirty—I've remarked on it several times."

Mack shuffled impatiently—probably annoyed at his imprudence in having given Mrs. Blakely a free hand, Larson decided.

"Then you didn't go to your room until after nine-thirty?"

"It couldn't have been much after nine-thirty, because I got on the same elevator that Mrs. Whippet came down in. I remember now because just before I had said to Esther"

"When did you hear Mr. Swink walking down the hall?" Mack made haste to put in.

"Now let me see. I don't know what time that was. After I got to my own room, I went to bed right away, or nearly right away."

"How did you know it was Swink you heard walking down the corridor?" Mack questioned.

"He walks with a heavier tread than anyone else. He should have dieted, I think. I put George on an eighteen-day diet at one time. He grumbled a lot about it, but I insisted that he stick to it, and he lost twenty pounds in two weeks. Well, as I was saying, Mr. Swink walks heavier than anyone else, and he stumbled around so I could tell he had had too much to drink. I must say I was disappointed in him, because I never thought he was a drinking man. Poor George liked an occasional glass of wine, but we never had anything stronger around the house, wouldn't have for anything—well, anyway, after I heard Mr. Swink I thought it wouldn't hurt to put my dressing gown on and take a look out in the hall. He might be in trouble, and a friendly hand never comes amiss, if I do say it. 'Do unto others as

61

you would have them do unto you' is a motto that I've always tried to live up to. 'Sarah, you're the most perfect practicing Christian I've ever known,' George used to say to me."

"Did you see Swink in the hall?" Mack asked.

"He was fumbling at the keyhole, and I must say that he was having a time of it. I stood in my doorway and watched him. Finally he got the door unlocked, and then, as he started to open it, I heard something fall. It sounded like glass breaking, and I thought, 'Mercy me! Is Mr. Swink carrying a bottle to bed with him?' He didn't try to close the door again, and I thought that was funny. Then I heard a thump, and I thought, 'Oh my goodness, Mr. Swink has had a stroke, I better go and see what I can do for him.' So I went across the hall and looked in through the door. Mr. Swink hadn't got around to turning on his light, but the light in the corridor was on, and I could see plainly into his room. He was lying there all doubled up, and you never saw such a sight in your life. Someone had deliberately ripped up his carpet and folded it back away from the door—an act of pure vandalism I'd call it. There were pieces of broken glass on the floor, and right then and there I knew something was wrong. My friends all say I'm psychic; anyway, I knew just as plainly as I know that you're sitting across from me now, Captain Mack, that Mr. Swink was dead. There was a funny smell, too. Then I knew somebody had murdered Mr. Swink, and I screamed. Mr. Hammond came running out of his room, and the Gant girl out of hers, and Mr. Westborough, and Mr. Larson. Yes, and Mr. Devon, too. Mr. Larson went in right away and opened the window. Then he said we'd better all go back to our rooms."

"How'd you know Swink had been murdered?" Mack demanded brusquely.

"I just sensed it, that's all! I can't tell you how I knew it, but it was as plain as the nose on your face—no offense intended, Captain Mack."

Mack fingered a rather prominent protuberance while O'Ryan roared.

"She's right about that beak of yours, Johnny."

The homicide squad lieutenant hastily changed the subject. "Did you know the dead man personally, Mrs. Blakely?"

"Well, I can't say I knew him very well, and, on the other hand, I certainly can't say that I didn't know him. He was very nice to me the other day. I had seen Mr. Swink coming in and out of his room several times, and I knew who he was when he came up to me in the lobby and said to me, 'Good-afternoon, madam, lovely weather, we're having, isn't it?' I said, 'I can't say that it is, because it's rained every day this month and will probably rain tomorrow as well.' And he smiled and said, 'That's what I mean.' Then we laughed, and he said, 'I really must introduce myself, since I am a new neighbor of yours. My name is Swink.' I told him who I was, and he said, 'Not Mrs. George Blakely?' and I said, 'Yes, George was my husband,' and he answered, 'Why, I used to know George well. One of the best fellows on earth. Only imagine meeting his wife under such circumstances.' And I said, 'Yes, the world is a small place, isn't it?' And he laughed and said, 'My dear Mrs. Blakely, you really must do me the honor of allowing me to take you to luncheon.' So we had lunch in the dining room, and I must say that Mr. Swink knew how to do things. Even better than George, who was rather awkward in public sometimes, as I used to tell him. Only I was quite surprised tonight to hear Mr. Swink coming in under the influence of alcohol. Because he told me at lunch that he had no use for it in any form. Oh well, we never really know the truth about anyone, I guess."

"Did he talk about a gold mine?" Mack probed. His informant waved her hands forward in surprise.

"Now how on earth did you know that? It's out in Colorado at a place called Georgetown. Isn't that a coincidence? As I said to Mr. Swink, 'Wouldn't it be a wonderful monument to George to invest his money in a town that bears his name?' Of course the money wouldn't be invested in the town; it would be in the mine, and that's called something else. Bobolink of Gold, I think, or is it just plain Link? Well, anyway, the principle would be the same whether it's the mine or the town, as I said to Mr. Swink."

"Did you sign on the dotted line?" Mack wanted to know.

"No, I didn't. As I said to Mr. Swink, 'My poor dear George was always of the opinion that I had to be looked after when he died, although I must say that when it came to matters of common sense I always got along better than he did, if I do say it. So George left his money tied up in trust, and I get an allowance and nothing else. Of course, if I want to change the investments I can, but I have to get the consent of George's lawyer, and he is inclined to be very unreasonable. Why, one time when I went to him he listened to me as solemnly as a judge until I got clear through, and then he said, laughing, 'My dear Mrs. Blakely. My respect for your husband's good judgment grows enormously every time you visit me.' Well, that's what I told Mr. Swink, and he didn't seem to like it very well. Said he didn't want to say a word against my lawyer but that a lot of them were conservative old fogies, and the depression proved that they weren't even able to hang on to money after they got it. Well, after lunch he told me how much he'd enjoyed meeting George's wife, and I told him it was certainly mutual. But I must say that I didn't see much of him after that."

"Do you know if Mr. Swink had any enemies in this hotel?" Mack cross-questioned.

"I can't say that he had exactly. Of course, Mr. Hammond probably didn't like him, and the Gant girl pretended she didn't either after she got caught with him in her own room."

"*What?*"

"That's a lie!" Chris Larson flamed.

"Larson, you are addressing a guest of this hotel," Spanger said quietly. The night clerk, his face a vivid, angry pink, stood motionless for a dramatic second. Finally:

64

"I beg your pardon, Mrs. Blakely," he apologized.

"I must say, young man, that if you go around calling many more people liars, you won't have your position long. I always understood that politeness was one of the first requirements for a hotel employee. I'm not going to complain to Mr. Swann this time—"

"I appreciate that, Mrs. Blakely." (Fat old sow, I'd like to choke her. This old harridan can throw her filth at Yvonne Gant to her heart's content, and I can't stop her. Yes, there is such a thing as slander, I suppose. If she goes too far, I'll warn her, job or no job.)

"Now we seem to be getting somewhere," Mack drawled. "Why didn't Hammond like Swink?"

Larson recalled Mack's prediction that Mrs. Blakely would serve as the catalyst in this human ferment and paid tribute to the detective's powers of divination. He watched the worthy lady vent a loud sniff and righteously fold her hands across her black gown. "Like a pious vulture," he thought. "Or perhaps a praying mantis. That insect," he reflected, "is in the habit of devouring her marital partner."

Mack repeated, "Why didn't Hammond like Swink?" and Sarah Blakely sniffed again.

"I don't know that he didn't. Mr. Hammond may be as blind as a bat for all I know. But I always say that if a man can't see what's going on right under his nose, he deserves to be taken in by a woman."

"What was going on?" Mack continued to probe.

"If ever a woman flirted right out in the open with a man that woman was Norah Hammond! And if ever a man was flirted with, that man was Mr. Swink! The way she smiled at him she might just as well have come right out in the open and said, 'I'd certainly like to get better acquainted with you, mister. My husband's away most of the time, and I get so lonely.' "

Mrs. Blakely's sarcastic attempt to mimic the inflections of the younger woman's voice was ludicrous, Larson thought, and a trifle disgusting. He put in quickly, "Mrs. Hammond smiles at nearly everybody she meets. She is Irish and a very friendly person."

"Irish, is she?" O'Ryan grunted approvingly. "That's to her credit."

"Humph!" Mrs. Blakely bridled. "I don't like her style myself. Maybe she does smile at everyone—a woman like that has no discrimination—but the way she smiled at Mr. Swink was entirely different from the way she smiles at everyone else, as I said to Esther Hatteras this afternoon. No sooner had I got through saying it than I looked up and who should I see but Mr. Hammond. Well, you could have knocked me down with a feather! Talk of your coincidences!"

"Did Hammond hear you gossiping?" Mack wanted to know.

"An exchange of confidences is not gossip," Mrs. Blakely replied testily. "I don't know whether Mr. Hammond heard us or not. If he did, he didn't say anything. But then he naturally wouldn't. No man likes to learn that his wife is making a fool of him behind his back. 'Mr. Hammond ought to stay home more and look after her,' I said to Esther. 'Satan always finds mischief for idle hands,' I said."

"If there's anything really wrong, it's my job to do something about it," Spanger remarked. "Did you actually see Mr. Swink come out of Mrs. Hammond's room?"

"Not *her* room," Sarah Blakely emphasized sententiously. Larson hastened to suggest:

"You didn't really see any definite evidence of an affair between Mrs. Hammond and Mr. Swink, did you?"

"If you mean actual black-and-white evidence that you can swear by and take to court, no," Mrs. Blakely declared. "But there was a whole lot more going on than was apparent on the surface. My friends say I'm psychic—"

"Is Hammond a traveling man?" Mack interrupted.

"Yes, he's on the road—I guess that's the way they put it—for some silk hosiery company. No-Runno or something like that, they're called. Mr. Hammond is away most of the time, but he usually gets in on a Friday and stays here over the weekend. That's why I was so surprised to see him this afternoon. I don't ever remember that he came in on a Thursday before. And he always goes out real early on Monday morning." Mack continued to prime the pump. "You're pretty well acquainted with your neighbors in this corridor, aren't you, Mrs. Blakely?"

"I think it's my Christian duty to be neighborly. Although I must say there's some of them that don't feel the same way about it. Now, Mr. Westborough is a nice quiet, friendly little man, and Mr. Devon is real cheerful, but that Mrs. Graham is a regular iceberg. I simply won't speak to her any more. She paints her fingernails red, too, just like a heathen that doesn't know any better. As I said to Esther Hatteras, 'If the Lord had wanted us to have red fingernails, He'd have given 'em to us. It isn't Christian for us to go against His will.'"

"What does Mr. Graham do for a living?" Mack catechized.

Sarah Blakely sniffed again. "He's an artist. He has a studio down in the Loop. He calls it an office and says he's a commercial artist to make it sound more respectable, I suppose. You can't tell me, though, that he doesn't have models in there just the same. And how Mrs. Graham can stand for her husband painting a lot of shameless nude hussies is more than I can see."

"Graham specializes in mechanically accurate pen-and-ink drawings of machinery," Westborough volunteered timidly.

"Humph!" Sarah Blakely snorted. "Whoever heard of an artist that didn't draw nude women? And how he makes a living at it is more than I can see. It must cost a lot for the three of them to keep an apartment in this hotel. Of course it isn't much of an apartment—just two rooms and a kitchenette—but for the same money they could get a nice house in the suburbs. And it would be much better for them, too. It's shameful to keep that boy cooped up like a pigeon in a cage, as I told Esther Hatteras. No wonder he gets into mischief with his chemicals and so on. Of course, he isn't Mr. Graham's boy. Maybe that makes a difference."

"He isn't?"

"No. The Grahams haven't been married more than three years. Cedric is her child by a former husband who died six years ago, she told me. I must admit that Mr. Graham always treats him just like a real son, although of course it isn't the same as having one of your own. 'Mr. Graham,' I said to him once, 'there's no sensation in the world so comforting as to have your own flesh and blood playing around the house. I've got three,' I said, 'and I know what I'm talking about. You and Mrs. Graham ought to get busy and have one of your own, and then you'll see if I'm not right.' "

O'Ryan guffawed.

"Well, that's telling him, anyway! How'd he take that crack?"

"He got red in the face and told me to mind my own business. We haven't been very friendly since."

"Were Graham and his wife acquainted with Swink?" Mack inquired.

"No. I saw them meet him face to face in the hall one day, and they didn't even nod. But then that Mrs. Graham always was an iceberg."

O'Ryan's huge body quivered with repressed laughter.

"Just to keep the police records straight, Mrs. Blakely, can you tell us what Mr. Graham's middle initial, 'E,' stands for?"

"Egbert," she returned promptly.

O'Ryan made a wry face and took two quarters from his pocket. "I owe you four bits, Johnny." Mack pocketed the money carelessly.

"What do you think of Mr. Devon?" he continued.

"I don't know him very well. He always seems pleasant, although he does use rather peculiar language now and then, I've noticed, and makes mistakes in his grammar. But it's not everybody who can have a college education, and thank goodness I'm no snob. 'Live and let live' is my motto." She pointed the sentiment with an appropriate pause and then continued, "I believe he sells vacuum cleaners."

"He does," Spanger confirmed. "I checked that up the day after he'd registered. Devon didn't look quite right to me, but as far as I can make out he's on the level. Travels light, but he pays his bill in advance, and that's all the hotel can ask."

Mack wrote again in his notebook. "Mrs. Blakely, we appreciate your help. Now tell me what you know about Miss Gant."

"Humph!" Sarah Blakely sniffed again. "I was wondering if you were going to ask about her. She used to have a roommate, but the roommate moved out on her last Sunday and left her with the whole week's hotel bill to pay. I don't think she could do it, or if she did she had a hard time of it. Though why she wants to live beyond her means is more than I can see. I know it sounds big to be able to tell everybody, 'I'm staying at the Equable,' but if I were a stenographer and making a stenographer's salary, I would certainly hunt myself a more inexpensive boarding place. One of these clubs for girls would be a deal more suitable, I believe, only of course they wouldn't allow her to have men in her room."

The woman's tongue was tinctured with venom. Larson said hotly:

"I know something about that. Swink, so drunk he could hardly see straight, blundered into the wrong room. Miss Gant had no more idea that he was in there than you have of working a problem in differential calculus, Mrs. Blakely."

"A likely story," she sneered. "How could he get into her room unless she let him in? These doors lock, don't they?"

Larson explained with a patience which he was far from feeling. "Miss Gant's door stuck a little in the door jamb, and didn't always close tight enough to work the spring lock. The hotel carpenter fixed it, and he'll verify everything I'm saying about the condition of the door."

"Yes, I saw him working on it the next day," Mrs. Blakely admitted. "He'd probably say anything you told him to, wouldn't he?"

Larson, flushing angrily, curbed a hot retort in answer to Mack's question, "When did this happen?"

"Day before yesterday—Tuesday evening."

"You didn't say anything to me about it, Larson," Spanger reproached.

"I didn't think it necessary," Larson defended himself. "Swink was drunk, and the condition of the door was obvious. Miss Gant cried out as soon as she found him in her room, and I came at once and escorted the man to his own quarters. The whole matter was trifling."

"It's my business when people start getting into wrong rooms," Spanger bristled. "You're taking too much on yourself, Larson."

Mack put in quietly, "Did you see Miss Gant open her door and find Swink, or did she tell you about that afterwards?"

"She told me about it afterwards," Larson was forced to admit.

Mrs. Blakely leered knowingly. "A man will believe anything a good-looking girl tells him. My George was a regular child as far as women were concerned."

Spanger, still nettled, returned to his grounds of complaint. "Send for me the next time you find a fellow in a girl's room," he ordered peremptorily. "The hotel pays me to look after these cases, not you. You weren't even on duty then, were you?"

"No."

"Couldn't have been, or you wouldn't have been right there when the girl screamed. Come on now, how did she look? Clothes torn? Hair mussed?"

"Spanger, you have a filthy mind," Larson accused with insulting slowness. "I suppose it's your rotten profession."

Spanger clenched his fists and took a step forward. "Squarehead, another crack like that out of you and I'll—"

"You'll what?" Larson demanded, his temper rising to meet the other's. "I'm ready any time you say!"

O'Ryan stepped between the two men. "Shut up, you two," he growled, "or I'll lock up both of you. Yes, I mean you too, Jerry."

Mack, who had escorted Mrs. Blakely, rather against her will, from the room, returned to close the door behind him.

"Larson," he began quietly, "it's time for you to talk turkey with us. What's between you and the Gant girl, and what'd you do to Swink the other night?"

VII

LARSON, his cheeks flushed and his voice quivering with suppressed resentment, wheeled to face the detective.

"I don't know what you mean."

"Oh yes you do," Mack contradicted in a tone of deadly calm.

"What's going on between you and the Gant girl?" Larson scowled savagely.

"I scarcely know Miss Gant."

"Never saw her before the other night, I suppose?"

"Certainly I have. It's my business to know who the guests of this hotel are, and Miss Gant is one of them. That's all."

"So the Gant girl was just another guest to you?" Mack said sarcastically.

Larson's voice retained its coolness. "You are attaching far too much importance to the incident. Swink was obviously drunk. Not an ugly drunk, but stupid and vacuous."

"What'd you do to him after you found him in her room?" Mack demanded. "Take your time and give us all the details, Larson."

"I helped him to his feet and out the door."

"Which door?"

"The door to the corridor, of course."

"Not the connecting door between the two rooms?"

"It was locked."

"Try it to see?"

"Didn't even think of it. The connecting doors are always locked unless the office orders them opened."

"A passkey would open it."

"I don't carry a passkey around with me."

"No?"

"Not when I'm off duty."

"Who does carry 'em?"

"There're two of them down at the desk. Sometimes a bellman has to take a package to a room when a guest is out or something like that. Mr. Swann has a passkey and so does Spanger. And the maids have floor keys. But I can't think of any others."

Mack made additional notations in the black book. "All right, Larson. Get back to your story. Was the door to Swink's room from the hall open?"

"No. Closed and locked."

"Who opened it?"

"I did—Swink was too far gone. I reached in his pocket and found his key. Then I helped him over to the bed, took off his shoes and coat, opened the window, and left him."

"You didn't undress him?"

"No. I didn't feel that my duty to the hotel involved playing nursemaid to drunks."

Mack was rummaging through the little heap of articles which had been taken from the dead man's clothes and were now lying upon the bed in a neat, orderly pile. A sterling silver cigarette case. A tooled leather billfold. A fountain pen of green onyx and pencil to match, both gold-trimmed. A match box. Two handkerchiefs: one crumpled and the other an obvious "spare." A leather key case. A thick gold watch and a watch chain terminating in a gold pocketknife. A pile of silver and copper coins. And a key to which was attached a large tag with the notation, "If carried away by mistake, please drop into nearest mail box. No postage is necessary."

Mack snatched the last article at once. "Let's see if this will open the connecting doors."

He tried it on the door to Yvonne Gant's bedroom, then, with an equal lack of success, on the door to Hammond's room. Finally, he carried the key out into the hall and returned, a minute or two later, saying, "It won't open the Gant girl's front door either. Swink must've had some other way."

"I told you how he got in," Larson insisted.

"You told me how you *thought* he got in," Mack corrected.

"Did Miss Gant find her door locked or open that night?"

"I didn't ask her."

"Why hadn't she said something before about the door sticking?"

"I don't know."

Mack took a threatening step forward. "Seems to me you're holding out on us, Larson."

The night clerk met his gaze squarely until O'Ryan, with a good-humored laugh, broke the tension.

"Johnny, there's one thing I can't get through my skull. Larson's probably telling us the truth about the Gant girl's door, or he's just a plain damn fool, because all we have to do to check his story is to talk to the carpenter. But what's really important is how the guy who planted the tube got into the room —and how he got into Graham's room."

"That," Mack admitted, "is bothering me, too."

"Swink's door doesn't stick, does it?"

Mack shook his head. "Nope, I tested it, and it works perfectly O.K. The spring locks the door every time you close it."

"He might've used a passkey," Spanger cogitated, "but it's beyond me how he got hold of one. As Larson told you, there aren't many of 'em, and we keep a close check on where they are. If a passkey was missing I'd know it immediately, but there's been no such thing reported."

"I have a conjecture which I offer to you for what it is worth," Westborough interpolated in a timorous voice.

"Would it be possible for someone to borrow surreptitiously an employee's passkey and retain it sufficiently long to have a duplicate made?"

Spanger shook his head decisively.

"That would take an hour or so. No one could sneak a passkey away for that long without it being noticed."

"But it would take only a few seconds to secure a wax impression," Westborough persisted. "It's conceivable that this might have been done without exciting undue suspicion. With such an impression, it would be, I believe, a simple matter to secure a duplicate key."

"The wax mold is a good dodge for fiction writers," Mack retorted. "Did you ever see a key made from one, Westborough?"

"But metal can be cast from wax with no particular difficulty. In Italy I observed very handsome bronzes produced by the *cire perdue*—literally lost wax—process. A wax model is covered with a prepared mixture of plaster, silica, and, I believe, other ingredients, which hardens in a few minutes and is able to withstand high temperatures. Then the wax is melted away and the molten bronze poured into the resulting mold."

"You might do it by electro-deposition, too," Larson suggested. "First you'd have to make the wax conductive by coating it with graphite, and then you'd hang it from the cathode in a plating solution."

"Maybe so," Mack rejoined noncommittally. "I don't know anything about your seer purdoo or electro-plating. But all the locksmiths I ever met have to have the original key to work from. They take a blank of the proper size and shape and file it."

O'Ryan, who had taken little interest in this discussion, now contributed an idea of his own.

"He might've picked the locks."

Spanger jumped up with the eagerness of a small boy to recite a well-learned lesson. "I don't say it can't be done, see? When I was on the force, I learned there's hardly a lock made that some guy can't pick—if you give him enough time and the right tools. But I will say this: the hotel spent a lot of dough putting good cylinder locks on every door, and picking them is no job for an amateur. I've opened up several kinds of locks myself: Johnny knows that. Well, just for my own information, I experimented on my own door when I first came here. I couldn't get to first base."

"Dear me!" Westborough broke in excitedly. "The dilemma is really baffling. On the one hand the difficulty, apparently insurmountable, of securing a passkey; on the other the extreme improbability that the two doors could have been opened by other means. Perhaps the solution lies elsewhere. Mr. Spanger, doesn't the hotel keep a complete set of duplicate keys to every room? I mean, of course, in addition to those distributed to guests."

"Sure," Spanger confirmed. "Hugh Clark, the carpenter, has them. Clark also does the locksmith work," he explained. "He has a full set of dups in his workshop and a lot of blanks. When a key's reported missing—and you'd be surprised to learn how many are carted off and disappear during a year—he files another in twenty minutes. The system saves a lot of time because otherwise Hugh'd have to take off the lock and turn the tumblers till he got the right combination."

"What about someone getting into Clark's shop?" O'Ryan wanted to know. Spanger laughed.

"Hugh keeps that set of dups in a steel case padlocked with two of the meanest-looking padlocks you ever saw. One padlock isn't enough for Hugh. No sir, he has to have two of 'em. He takes better care of his dups than they do the originals in the key rack upstairs."

"What about the key rack?" O'Ryan queried. "Graham's key was there, you remember. Maybe someone sneaked up, grabbed both keys, and then managed to put 'em back again without being seen."

"No," Larson objected. "He couldn't do that without hitting Larry Collins over the head. You're forgetting that the key rack is a good four feet back of the counter, and there's no way on earth of reaching it from the outside. Even if Collins had happened to leave his post for some reason, the bellman's bench faces the key rack, and someone's nearly always on duty there."

"Collins didn't leave the desk any time in the evening," O'Ryan declared after consulting again the report he had received from Phelan.

"Besides, you forgot something, Terry," Mack put in jocosely. "It's a great idea, all right, but Swink's key wasn't in the rack. Graham's, yes, but not Swink's. Take another look at Phelan's dope, and you'll see I'm right. Swink got his key from the desk after dinner, but he never put it back again."

O'Ryan, referring once more to his list, agreed that this was correct, and Mack suggested that Hammond be the next one brought in.

"I want to find out if he heard Mrs. Blakely and her crony talking about his wife and Swink. We need more facts and less guesswork about these people in the corridor."

Ever since Sarah Blakely had dripped her poison, Larson had been battling with his conscience. Or rather the battle had been between an innate sense of conduct becoming to a gentleman and the loyalty one owes to an impersonal abstraction called the "law." Should he or should he not reveal a certain memory? A lonely woman stealing furtively to her room in the quiet hours of the night. Unfair to throw her to the wolves? Yes, he told himself, but this is a murder case. "Murder most foul," even though Swink was a pig. "You haven't the right to shield anyone—even Yvonne Gant." But to throw into the discussion a morsel of gossip whose choiceness would do credit to Mrs. Blakely? Well, there didn't seem to be any help for it.

"Something happened last night which I think you ought to know," he began. "It was probably about two-thirty or going on three. Mrs. Hammond came into the lobby in full evening clothes. Alone. She asked for her key and went on upstairs. About ten minutes later Swink came in and asked for his key. And he was in evening dress, too."

"Great Scott!" Mack ejaculated. "Why didn't you tell us that before?"

O'Ryan had opened the door to the corridor. "Phelan, bring in Mrs. Hammond. No, alone. We'll get her husband's story later."

VIII

"TWENTY MINUTES to two," Mack declared, consulting his watch. "I could use a good strong cup of black coffee. How about you, Terry?"

"Sounds O.K."

Larson picked up the telephone. "I'll see what can be done about it." He spoke into the transmitter, then hung up. "You'll get your coffee in a few minutes, and I told them to send up some sandwiches."

Mack grinned appreciatively. "That's the ticket!"

A patrolman ushered in Norah Hammond. Her flaming scarlet negligee clung closely about her slender figure. Cloudy blue-black hair tumbled in bangs far down on her forehead, and her eyebrows were two dark and narrow lines against the creamy white skin. Her mouth, friendly and unmistakably Irish, was a trifle too large for the other features.

"Mrs. Hammond?" Mack asked.

"Yes." Her eyes were fixed downward on her small red slippers. "I was certainly sorry to learn of Mr. Swink's death, but I doubt if I am able to tell you anything useful. You see I was away from the hotel the entire evening."

"We heard about it," Mack drawled. "Away last evening, too, weren't you?"

"Yes, why?" Her voice was casual and apparently uninterested. Yet Larson could see her fidgeting with the small platinum circlet on her left hand.

Mack answered curtly, "You had a date with Elmo Swink last night, sister."

She flared defiantly, "And if I did?"

Mack's voice lashed like a whip. "If you make a fool of your husband, that's none of my business. But it is my business to find out why Swink is dead. Get that? Somebody killed a man, and we've got to find out why."

Norah Hammond nervously twisted at the ring. "I'm sure I don't know how I can help you."

"All right, you asked for it." Mack's tone was bald, brutal. "Your husband learned how you double-crossed him. He stayed home from the show tonight to kill Swink."

Her hand fluttered like a pale moth against her slender throat.

"Oh, my God!"

"So this is police third degree!" Larson thought angrily. "For just one lousy little cent I'd knock your face in, Lieutenant Mack." O'Ryan's voice, calm and kindly, drove away the red mist.

"Better ask the lady to sit down, Johnny."

Mack pushed a chair forward, and Norah Hammond sank into it, her face chalk white.

"That isn't true!" She shuddered. "Oh, it isn't! Fred—oh, you don't know my husband! He couldn't do such a thing!"

"That's what you say!"

Her quick Irish temper kindled. "It's what I know! It's what anybody but a stupid policeman would know!" Her eyes, blue and vivid, flamed at the detective, and Mack drawled, "Steady, sister." Suddenly Norah Hammond laughed, and the flame died down. It was a short laugh without mirth, a laugh of sheer nervous relief.

"How dumb of me not to think of this before! Fred didn't know about Mr. Swink."

Mack's "No?" was doubtingly sarcastic. "Didn't know you were out with Swink last night?"

"He didn't!"

"Expect us to believe that?"

"It may be true," O'Ryan put in, his sympathies plainly with the Irish. "After all, the Blakely woman didn't know this girl had been out with Swink."

"I wonder," Mack speculated.

"You wouldn't expect her to keep a scandal like that from us, would you?" O'Ryan continued.

Spanger guffawed. "That hen could no more stop from yammering about a bit of gossip than a bird from gulping down a worm!" Mack was silent, and Westborough ventured timidly, "I believe Mrs. Hammond is telling us the truth."

Norah Hammond, with quick Gallic insight, had sensed O'Ryan's friendliness. "Officer"

"Captain O'Ryan," he corrected.

"Captain O'Ryan, I have never mentioned one thing about Mr. Swink to my husband. I intended to—Fred is so fine himself that it wouldn't be fair not to—but—you see he just got home today—I couldn't tell him about it."

"Swink was pretty fresh," O'Ryan surmised shrewdly.

"He was a beast!" she flashed. "A nasty fat beast. It served me right for going out with him. But I didn't know he would be that way."

"His kind are," O'Ryan pronounced paternally.

"Tell us about it," Mack ordered.

She appealed to O'Ryan. "Must I?"

"Yes. Where did he take you?"

"To the Club Baroque."

"That joint isn't so bad," O'Ryan declared.

"You met him out of the hotel?" Mack conjectured.

80

"Of course. I had to. There are always so many gossiping old ladies around in the lobby." Spanger grimaced.

"That's putting it mildly."

"Of course, I had no business going with him—I really do care a lot for my husband. But Fred is away most of the time, and there have been so many lonesome evenings. Sometimes I'd get so bored with myself I'd want to scream."

"You had dinner together?" Mack probed. "A cocktail or two first, I suppose?"

"Yes. The dinner was very nice. Mr. Swink knew how to order, and he was an entertaining talker. We danced between courses. Even that wasn't so bad. For a fat man he was comparatively light on his feet. Not such a good dancer as Fred, of course, but far from being a poor one."

"How did Swink's liquor affect him?" Mack wanted to know. Norah Hammond raised her head and laughed.

"Funny you should ask that! We had several highballs during the course of the evening, and I never saw a man get so tight on so little."

"Some people can't carry any liquor," Spanger commented. "Thin walls to their stomach or something, I heard."

"You got in pretty late," O'Ryan interjected. "Why didn't you break away from him earlier?"

"I tried to, but he kept pulling me down to my chair again. I didn't want to raise a scene. You see," she confessed, "there was a friend of Fred's across the room, and I was petrified. He didn't see me, thank goodness, but I didn't want to do anything that would attract attention."

"How did you manage to get away?" O'Ryan asked.

"Mr. Swink slumped forward in his chair and went to sleep. He snored so loudly everybody in the place turned around to laugh at him. I was never so embarrassed in all my life! Fortunately, Fred's friend had gone by that time."

"Seems to me," O'Ryan commented parenthetically, "that friend Swink put in most of his time in getting drunk. Night before last, last night, and tonight."

"He was a disgusting pig!" Norah Hammond exclaimed indignantly. "The waiter woke him up finally and made him swallow some coffee. After that we managed to get him into a taxi. Ugh!"

"Tried to kiss you, did he!"

She shuddered. "If that were all! Well, I slapped his face as hard as I could, and after that he stayed on his own side of the cab. But the things he kept saying! The cab pulled up before the Equable, and I said, 'Nothing on earth can make me walk into this lobby with you. Either you go first or I will.' He tried to put his hat on—he had sat on it all the way home, and it was a terrible mess—and said, 'All right, baby. I'll wait out here. But leave your door open tonight 'cause I'm coming in to see you.' I slammed the door of the cab and walked into the lobby. Fortunately, there wasn't anybody there but Mr. Larson. He's awfully nice, and I knew he'd never tell on me." Chris, shamefaced, stared down at the carpet as Mrs. Hammond continued her story. "I got to my own room and locked the door. I was never so mad in all my life—I simply trembled with rage. Honestly, I believe that if Mr. Swink had tried to get into my room that night I would have shot him. Fred has a revolver, you know, which he leaves with me when he goes on the road."

"Swink didn't try it, then?" Mack inquired.

"Thank goodness, no! And I sat up for a long time worrying about it. I was actually afraid to go to bed until I heard him snoring from the next room. I thought his snores were disgusting when I heard them at the Club, but last night they were the sweetest music I ever listened to. This morning I said to myself before I got out of bed, 'Norah, that's what you get for two-timing the best husband a girl ever had. Never again.' "

Mack scratched thoughtfully at his chin. "So your husband has a gun?"

"Yes," she admitted. "I suppose I shouldn't have blurted that out."

"All right so long as he doesn't walk around with the gat in his pocket," O'Ryan informed.

"Oh no, he never did that."

"A gun," Mack pronounced slowly, "has got about as much to do with this case as my aunt Harriet up at Niles, Michigan. And yet I'm thinking, Mrs. Hammond, it's mighty lucky for you that Swink wasn't shot. Also that you were away from the hotel all evening." He turned on her abruptly. "You were gone all evening, weren't you?"

She started. "Why, yes, of course."

"Where?"

"To a movie with Mr. and Mrs. Graham."

"They left their little boy alone here, didn't they?"

"Why, no, we took him with us."

"See a good show?"

"Not very."

"What was it about!"

"I don't remember the name. It was about secret service men, and there was a lot of shooting. I don't care much for that sort of picture, and neither does Luella. Mr. Graham and Cedric liked it though."

"What did you do after the show?"

"Had some chop suey at a Chinese restaurant. Ronald—Mr. Graham—insisted upon taking us."

"You're sorta thick with the Grahams, aren't you?"

"They're a lovely couple," she exclaimed. "Lu's one of the best friends I've got. I don't know what I'd do without them when Fred goes out on the road."

"Your husband got in today, didn't he?"

"Yes."

"And he goes out on Monday as usual, I suppose?"

"Why, yes. Why?"

"You've only got three more days with him. Seems rather funny you'd want to chase out tonight with the Graham pair and leave your husband at home alone."

"He had a headache," Norah Hammond answered hotly. "I didn't want to go, but he insisted. Said he felt so rotten he'd be poor company, and he felt he ought to be left alone. I could see he meant it, and I didn't want to stand there arguing with Mr. and Mrs. Graham right in the room."

Mack asked irrelevantly, "Was Mr. Hammond in bed when you got back?"

"No, he was up waiting for me." She laughed. "Men sometimes do such silly things. I counted six separate cigar butts in the ash tray, and the room was simply reeking with smoke. I scolded him properly about it. The worst possible thing he could do for his head."

For so large a man O'Ryan moved with surprising alacrity.

"Clancy," he called to the patrolman in the corridor. "Bring in Hammond right away, and keep Mrs. Hammond apart from her husband until we've had a chance to get his story."

IX

A KNOCK REVERBERATED from the door. "That must be Hammond now," Mack conjectured. Larson awaited the salesman's entrance with misgivings. He didn't like to think that he had been instrumental in focusing police attention upon the genial knight of the road. Yet he was forced to admit that both Mack and O'Ryan were sharply distrustful and perhaps you couldn't blame them. Hammond's headache, for example, had sounded decidedly fishy. Men like Hammond acquired headaches only after a night of wholesome carousal, not suddenly and opportunely like a swooning Victorian virgin. Also he could not believe that Mrs. Hammond had been telling the entire truth. If she had informed her husband about her evening with Swink—

Larson's lips pursed in a soundless whistle. Yes, the situation should prove interesting, he concluded, as he watched the detective cross to the door.

But it was only a bellboy with a well-loaded tray, which he set upon a night stand adjacent to the bed. Mack, who took his coffee strong and black, had gulped the last of the cup and was thoughtfully munching a chicken sandwich by the time the patrolman brought in Hammond.

Hammond's pajamas were partially obscured by a dressing gown of brocaded purple silk. "What you been saying to my wife?" he demanded, infuriated and plainly caring little about hiding it.

Lieutenant Mack, as Larson had already observed, knew when to bluster and when to be calm. The more agitated his adversary appeared, the more placid Mack's demeanor. His eyes were now quietly fixed upon the salesman, but he said nothing. Not until he had relighted the stubby cigar which he had been smoking or chewing most of the evening. Then:

"I don't like your attitude, Hammond."

Hammond slammed his fist against the night stand so hard that the dishes on the tray clattered. His hand was a wide, muscular one, its back covered by short black hairs, Larson noticed.

"I should give a damn what you like!" The dishes clattered again. "I know a few people down at the City Hall, and I'm telling you I won't stand for any of your goddam third degree. Try it, and I'll get your shield."

Mack said without rancor, "If it was a question of going through a stop sign, your pull might work. But you're up against a murder rap."

"Murder rap?" the salesman echoed, his voice softened several decibels.

"Not even the Mayor is big enough to pull me off this job," Mack boasted. "Not till I get the truth out of someone. Sit down, Hammond."

Hammond plopped into a chair while Mack coolly tilted the shade of the floor lamp. The salesman's lower jaw was sagging. "What you mean murder rap?"

The time was ripe for the detective to bluster, Larson predicted, and he was right. With disarming suddenness, Mack snarled:

"You killed Swink because you caught him playing around with your wife."

"It's a damn lie!" Hammond shouted, springing to his feet. "My wife wouldn't have looked twice at the swine."

"Sit down!" Mack barked. "We know differently. She just admitted going out with him last night."

"Christ!" Hammond's hand plowed feverishly through his sandy hair. "Norah said *that?*"

Mack continued the inquisition. He was as relentless and as impersonal as a physician dissecting with his scalpel.

"Why didn't you go out with your wife tonight?"

"I had a headache."

"And smoked half-a-dozen cigars? Queer sort of headache medicine."

"Had to do something to calm my nerves," Hammond mumbled.

"Upset about your wife, weren't you?"

"No! Oh, damn it all, I guess I was!"

"And yet you sit there and say you didn't know she'd been out with Swink!"

Hammond growled, "Think I'd have stayed quietly in my room if I'd known that?"

"No?" Mack prompted. "What would you have done?"

Hammond leaned back dejectedly against his chair. "I don't know. I think I'd have beaten him within an inch of his life."

"Big he-man, aren't you?" Mack sneered. "What you meant to tell us was that you'd have taken that gun of yours and shot him."

"Christ, I don't know!"

"You didn't shoot him," Mack continued, his eyes fixed hypnotically upon Hammond's. "You didn't shoot him because you thought of a better way." He paused portentously. "Hammond, what made you smoke so many cigars tonight?"

"I—I told you. I was nervous, and—"

"Yes, a cock-and-bull story, and not even very good cock-and-bull at that," Mack derided. "Why don't you admit the truth? You smoked all those cigars to cover up a smell."

"A smell?" Hammond repeated.

"The smell of bitter almonds," Mack flung at him.

"Bitter almonds?" Hammond's bewilderment was apparently genuine—or was it? Larson couldn't tell, and he wondered if Mack could. The detective went on like a shipping clerk hammering one nail after another into a packing case.

"You don't know that hydrocyanic acid smells like bitter almonds?"

"No."

"You didn't sneak across the corridor to Graham's apartment? You didn't steal a test tube and some sulphuric acid from his kid's chemical set?"

Beads of sweat stood on Hammond's forehead. "No."

"No?" Mack echoed in a silky voice which all but purred. "And you didn't put the acid in the test tube? And didn't add potassium cyanide to it and cork up the tube? And didn't let yourself into this room through the connecting door from your own room? And, without opening the door to the hall, hook the test tube above the edge of the door?"

"I didn't do one of those things," Hammond shouted. "You can't railroad me like this."

"Without opening the door," Mack repeated, his voice rising to a sudden crescendo. "Because you couldn't go out into the hall and close the door after you without disturbing the test tube. But you could go back to your own room through the connecting door. *And you're the only man in the hotel who could.*"

"See here," Hammond protested, completely unnerved. "I don't know what you mean by a test tube and a connecting door. I was in my own room every minute of the evening. Didn't even go down to the lobby for a cigar."

"Can you prove it?"

"You know damn well I can't. I was there alone."

Mack said sternly, "A short time ago you referred to Swink as a swine. Why?"

"I—I overheard some gossip," Hammond confessed, his eyes fixed upon the floor.

"About your wife?"

"Yes."

"Who was talking?"

88

"The Blakely woman to one of her cronies. In the lobby." With a burst of sudden anger he added, "The old vultures spread scandal the whole day long. Goddam'em!"

"What were they saying about Mrs. Hammond?"

"That I ought to stay home more because Norah was having a flirtation with Swink."

"Did you believe that?" Hammond spoke with entire frankness. "I didn't think I did. I kept telling myself I knew Norah and could trust her." He hesitated. "The worst part of gossip like that is that it gets under your skin. You can't keep from wondering if maybe there isn't something to it."

"And that's all you heard them say?"

"Every bit, and I just caught that by accident. The two women saw me and shut up."

"And that's what worried you so that you wouldn't go out with your wife!" Mack exclaimed sarcastically. Hammond cupped his chin in the palm of his hand.

"If you don't see it, you won't. But Norah means a lot to me. Everything, I guess. I'm on the road a lot of the time. A fellow gets plenty of opportunities for hellraising, but I've played square with Norah. Up to today I didn't know she hadn't been doing the same with me." His words came thickly, hesitantly. "I used to wonder how a fellow would feel when he learned his wife had been playing around. Now I know. And I tell you it hurts like hell!"

"You can stop worrying about your wife," O'Ryan interrupted in his bluff fashion. "We've heard her story, and the worst thing she did was to have dinner with Swink."

"You mean that?" Hammond's voice betrayed his eager desperation.

"Straight stuff!" O'Ryan heartily testified. "That girl's all right, Hammond."

Skepticism warred with relief in the salesman's eyes. "Officer, it's decent of you to say that. I appreciate it."

O'Ryan, with pretended brusqueness, advised, "Forget it," but Mack hastened to take full advantage of Hammond's softened mood.

"Are you willing to help us out by giving the straight answers to a few questions?"

"Sure—if I can."

"Well, then, did you hear Swink moving in his room tonight?"

"Yes. I could hear him talking to another fellow about eight-thirty or so."

"What about?"

Hammond shook his head. "I couldn't distinguish words."

"How long'd they stay in the room?"

"Maybe twenty minutes. But Swink came back later."

"He came back at ten minutes to eleven," Mack pronounced.

Hammond gestured his dissent. "I don't mean then. Earlier than that."

"What?"

"Sure. I heard him moving about the room."

"My God, when?" Mack ejaculated.

"I'm not quite sure of the time. I'd say it was nine-thirty or so."

"You're sure Swink was alone?"

"It sounded like it."

"When did he go out again?"

"Now that I think of it, I don't ever remember hearing his door close. He walked about the room for five, maybe ten minutes, and then I stopped hearing him. I wasn't paying any particular attention, to tell the truth."

"Are you sure it was Swink?" Mack asked quietly.

"Eh?" Hammond blinked rapidly. "I can't swear that it was. He had rather a heavy tread and walked like Swink. That's all I could tell."

Mack declared with impressive solemnity, "If you haven't been lying to me, Hammond, the person you heard was Swink's murderer."

X

"IF THAT BIRD told the truth, how did the killer get out?" O'Ryan meditated after Fred Hammond had been allowed to return to his room. "Through the Gant girl's room?"

Mack consulted the omnipresent notebook. "He could've if our dope's right on the time. Hammond claims he heard the guy moving around here about nine thirty. The girl, according to the Colmar dame, doesn't go into her room until nine-forty-five."

"If she had been in her room earlier than that, we'd have had a real Chinese puzzle on our hands," O'Ryan pondered. "In that case our fellow couldn't have gone out the door to the hall without knocking down his tube and couldn't have gone through either of the adjoining rooms—unless he lived in one of them. Of course, there's the window." He turned to Larson. "You opened the window when you first got here. Was it locked or unlocked?"

"Locked from the inside," Larson rejoined promptly.

"Just like one of the 'murder in a sealed room' things that you read about in detective stories," O'Ryan proclaimed. "But as the Gant girl wasn't there he simply walked out through her room."

"I'm not so sure," Mack dissented. "I put it strong about not being able to open the door, because I was trying to break Hammond down." He picked up the broken top of the test tube and held it by the wire, which was still hooked into the string around the rim. "Let's see if a fellow can plant this dohinkus and close the door from the outside while he's doing it."

With the door ajar, Mack suspended the fragment from the top edge. Holding the other end of the wire, he stepped into the hall and began to pull the door shut. As it closed, he was forced to slide the wire toward the hinges to avoid catching his fingers. Finally, he released his hold; the wire, pinched between the door and its frame, held the tube firmly. Mack finished closing the door. His muffled voice penetrated through the barrier.

"Did it stick?"

"Yeh. It's up there O.K."

"I'm coming back in. Catch the thing, somebody, I don't want it smashed any more than it is."

He opened the door gradually. The wire, released from the pressure of the door frame, allowed gravity to take its course. O'Ryan caught the fragment of tube deftly in midair. "Well, that settles one thing, Johnny," he pronounced as Mack reentered the room. "Anybody in the corridor could've done that trick."

"Anyone could," Mack agreed. "Let's talk to Devon."

O'Ryan started toward the door when he was interrupted by the appearance of his two subordinates.

"We're through with the rooms, chief," vouchsafed Patrolman Phelan.

"Find anything?"

"Nothing that looked particularly screwy." Phelan hesitated. "Say, potassium cyanide's a white powder, isn't it?"

"Yeh."

"Well, we found white powders in two or three people's medicine cabinets, but they were all labeled something else." He paused again. "I didn't taste any of 'em to find out if the labels were lying."

"Pick 'em all up," O'Ryan directed, "and we'll send 'em down to headquarters."

"I've got 'em here," Phelan replied. "All marked up to show which belongs to who." He delivered several packets and pillboxes. "You were looking for a passkey, too, weren't you?"

"Yeh," O'Ryan admitted. "I forgot to tell you about it."

"Well, I went down and borrowed one from the room clerk so I'd know what it looked like. Then I compared every key I found with it." He sighed regretfully, "It seemed like a good idea, but it was a dud. There wasn't another passkey anywhere."

Mack said, "Terry told me you were looking for a transfer to the detective division, Phelan."

"Yeh. Don't suppose it's any use, though."

"I'll put in a word for you any time you want," Mack exclaimed heartily.

"Gee, thanks!" Phelan shuffled embarrassedly. "That's sure white of you."

O'Ryan's ham of a hand clapped the patrolman's shoulder. "And I'll add a good word too! By the way, you didn't happen to see anything that looked like sulphuric acid—or maybe another acid?"

Phelan shook his head. "I took special note of everything liquid. But all the liquids I found were the ink in the inkwells, mouth washes, and such junk, and a pint of Old Apple in Hammond's room."

"He can keep that," O'Ryan chuckled. "Have you gone through any of the vacant rooms?"

"Not yet."

"Well, make that the next job. If the bird we're looking for could get into this room and Graham's apartment, he might get into any of those."

"O. K." The two patrolmen started from the room; then Phelan turned back. "Gee, Captain O'Ryan, I almost forgot. A guy by the name of Swann insists on seeing you. Says he's manager of the hotel."

"Tell him he can come in."

Victor Swann was in full evening dress, complete even to the shiny silk topper he carried in his hand. A bald head, singularly flat upon the top, and a jutting aquiline nose were his most prominent features. He was a middle-sized man, forty-five to fifty, and he began talking as soon as he entered the room, omitting all formalities of introductions.

"This is terrible—worst break I ever got, and I've been in the hotel business twenty years." Swann's speech was a crisp and rapid staccato. "One of those things that can't be helped—'act of God,' my lawyer will probably say. Well, the staff will cooperate. Anything you want, say the word."

O'Ryan ostentatiously referred to a huge gold watch.

"Twenty of three. Out rather late tonight, Swann, aren't you?"

"Reception. Lyttelyous'. Scads of dough and daughter homelier than mud fence. Trying to buy a man for her, but there're worse things than poverty." He reached into his pocket for a pack of much advertised cheap cigarettes and pressed the spring of a hammered silver lighter. "Had His Highness Prince Abdul of Muckamuck on hand tonight. Two or three hundred people. Regular three-ring circus. Too amusing to break away from, and the hotel runs itself."

"Prince Abdul of Muckamuck?" Mack repeated skeptically.

"Sounded like that, anyway. Prince's black as a nigger, and a lot of damn silly women were kotowing to him all over the place. They'll get their pictures in the paper tomorrow. So will we, worse luck." He

94

broke off abruptly to glance sternly at the room clerk. "Larson, why aren't you at the desk?"

"I asked him to stick around," Mack replied before the other could answer.

"Still want him?"

"I don't think so."

"Better run on down," Swann advised. "Collins is supposed to leave at eleven, and it's going on three now."

Chris departed regretfully. It was like having an exciting serial break in the middle with a "To be continued in our next" line. He signaled for the elevator and went down to the office. The lobby was deserted except for the room clerk.

"What's the dope?" Collins asked as Chris went to his place behind the counter. Larson shook his tawny head.

"If they know, they're not saying anything about it. Swann's up there now."

"Yeh, he blew in about ten minutes ago. You should've seen him hit the roof when I told him the news." Collins opened a penknife and began to clean his nails. "Funny part is, the boss came back to the hotel around ten."

"The hell he did!"

"Yep." Collins finished his manicuring and proceeded to run a comb through already smooth and glossy hair. "I saw him come in and go upstairs."

"That's damn peculiar! Did he tell you why?"

Collins shook his head. "He never tells me anything."

He started toward the employees' entrance. "Fellow, the next time you stage a murder call your shots. I had a date tonight with one of the keenest-looking blondes you ever saw."

95

"Gee, Larry, I'm sorry! I'll come down two or three hours early tomorrow."

"Forget it." Collins stopped and looked back over his shoulder. "There's one thing about this business that tickles me. I've got the swellest little alibi you ever saw: didn't leave the desk from three o'clock on, and somebody or other to prove practically every minute of it."

Chris said, "I wish I had one like it. Well, so long, Larry."

Meanwhile, in the room that had been occupied by Elmo Swink, Mack was continuing his cross-examination of the hotel manager.

"So you were gone all evening?"

"Right. Even got away for dinner. Met some friends in the Loop." He continued his rapid-fire patter. "This is bad business—smart-aleck reporters snooping around— smear it all over the front page— what time'd it happen, anyhow?"

Mack said, "Swink was alive until ten minutes to eleven."

"Who did it?" was Swann's next question.

Mack shrugged his shoulders. "If I knew, I'd sleep better tonight."

"Unsolved mystery, huh?"

"It is—yet!"

"Hum!" Swann appeared thoughtful. "Well, I hope you don't bother the guests any more than you can help. Some of them are touchy."

Spanger at once told about the search, and Swann was prompt to protest.

"See here, you can't go poking around private rooms without a warrant!"

"No?"

"No."

"Are you going to cooperate or aren't you?"

Swann swallowed hard two or three times. "Might as well make the best of it, I suppose. Especially since you've already done it." He closed the subject and asked, "Was Swink the fat, flabby fellow?"

"You've placed him all right," Spanger grinned.

Swann beamed complacently. "Can't know all the guests of course. Impossible in a place this size. Try to remember all I can though. Good memory for names, fortunately. You have to have in this business."

Mack glanced up quickly. "Go on, Swann, spill it. What do you know about Swink?"

"I? Name on the room rack. That's all. Saw him in the bar this evening, though."

Mack's broad thumb rapidly flicked the pages of his notebook. "What time'd you leave the hotel, Swann?"

"Eight. Maybe five or ten minutes before. Don't remember exactly."

"And you saw Swink in the bar?"

"That's what I said."

"Swann, you're lying. We've a complete record of Swink's movements tonight."

The hotel manager frowned. "See here, I don't like being called a liar. If Swink was the fat, flabby fellow, I saw him in the bar."

"He was in the bar—yes. But not until nine. At eight o'clock he was either in the dining room or in the lobby."

"Well, who said I saw him at eight?"

"You did."

"I beg your pardon?"

97

"You said you left the hotel at eight."

"Didn't I tell you? I came back at ten."

"You what?"

"Lyttelyous mailed out pretty engraved cards—ticket of admission. Nobody can go in without 'em. Ex-prize fighter in knee breeches near the door. Probably would've thrown out Prince Abdul himself. Had to come back. Rotten nuisance, but wife wanted to see the prince."

"How long'd you stay?"

"Long enough to go up, grab tickets, and come down. Wife waited in the car."

"Ten minutes?"

"Five's nearer. Took the elevator right to top floor and kept the pilot waiting while I collected the cards." He looked quizzically at the broken fragments of glass on the writing desk. "What's all this stuff?"

Mack told him.

Swann's comment was, "Eight years building up this place. Give 'em more service for their money than any hotel in Chicago. Now this happens. Guests will be moving out in droves." He crushed out his cigarette in the ash tray and lit another. "If you're through asking questions, I'm going down and stall off reporters. Get 'em to play down hotel angle—if it can be done."

Swann plunged abruptly from the room. O'Ryan observed sympathetically to Spanger, "It's a tough break for him at that."

"One of the worst possible," Spanger agreed solemnly. "I don't think he's right about the guests leaving in droves, but new ones will think twice before registering here."

"What kind of fellow is Swann?" Mack inquired.

"He's O.K. Bit of a slave driver, but a square shooter. And he drives himself harder than he does anyone else. I've been here four months now, and this is the second time I can remember he's ever taken a night off."

"What kind of hotel does he run?"

Spanger grinned. "You've been here two or three hours. You ought to know."

"The rooms are nicely furnished," Mack commented, "and things seem to run along pretty smoothly. That's not what I meant. Who does he cater to? Permanents? Transients, or what?"

"We do quite a bit of transient business," Spanger rejoined. "Lots of people like to stay in a hotel that's outside the Loop but not too far away. But Swann's big play is for permanent residents. We treat 'em right here, and we can give 'em most anything they want. Single and double rooms—everyone with private bath. Two- and three-room kitchenette apartments like the one the Grahams have. Or we can give 'em as large a place as they want up to anything they want to pay." He paused. "We've got people—the old Blakely dame is one of 'em— that have been here for five years."

Mack smiled. "You seem to be pretty well sold on the place, Jerry."

"I'll say I am!" Spanger agreed enthusiastically. "Swann gives 'em their money's worth—and about fifty percent more. That's why it's such a rotten shame that a thing like this had to happen."

"If we clear it up in a hurry, people'll forget about this in a month," Mack observed. He took from his pocket the list he had prepared earlier in the evening and made several additional check marks. "Two more to see, Terry, before we get to bed. Let's have Devon in."

Devon, a small, weazened man of uncertain age, possessed a shock of coarse hair and shifty, lusterless eyes. He had a crooked nose and small, pointed ears which lay flat against his head.

"I don't know nothing about it—see?" he began sullenly. "I was in my own room, and I don't know nothing about it."

"Big hurry to tell us that, aren't you?" Mack sneered. "Where were you tonight?"

"In my own room, I said."

"When'd you go there?"

"How should I know? Think I keep looking at my ticker all the time?"

"You got some idea, haven't you?"

"It might've been around ten," Devon admitted grudgingly. "I'm not saying it was—see? But it might've been."

"Oh, it might, huh? Well, where were you before ten?"

"That's my business."

"Refuse to talk, huh?"

"I know my rights—see? You can't make me answer no questions."

Mack said, "Oh, we can't, eh?" and Devon answered, a shade less defiantly, "No." Mack shot a quick glance at O'Ryan.

"Guess we'll have to take him down to the station, Terry."

"Sure," O'Ryan agreed genially. "We've got the right medicine there. It's just an ordinary garden hose, but when we jam it down his throat and turn on the water he'll talk all right. I never knew a guy yet could hold out more than two minutes. It's kinda rough on the stomach," he concluded with a chuckle.

Devon's face broke into a profuse perspiration. His eyes darted to the door, but O'Ryan's broad back thoroughly blocked that method of exit.

"I'll talk," he conceded sullenly.

"Thought you'd be sensible," O'Ryan said mildly. "What's your name?"

"Ben Devon." He pronounced it Dee-von, with the stress on the first syllable, and not in the accepted English manner of rhyming with "seven."

"That's a street," O'Ryan objected. "That's no name."

"It's my name."

"Where you from, Devon?"

"San Francisco."

"You sure?"

"Sure I'm sure. Born and raised in Frisco."

"What you doing in Chicago?"

"Selling vacuum cleaners."

"Not much dough in that, is there?"

"If you're any good there is."

"You're pretty good, I suppose?"

Devon failed to notice the sarcasm. "I'll say I'm good!"

"What's the name of the outfit you work for?" Mack questioned.

"Feenix Distributors, Inc."

Mack snatched a sheet of paper from the desk. "Feenix?"

"Yeh. P-h-o-e-n-i-x."

Mack's countenance was a perfect blank. "Oh, hell, sit down and write it out for me, will you?"

Devon seated himself at the desk and scrawled the name in a large irregular handwriting. Mack folded the paper and placed it in his breast pocket. "Thanks! So you didn't go up to your room until ten?"

"Yeh, that's right."

"Can you prove it?"

"Sure I can prove it. I was out working my territory—see? You got to make a lot of call-backs at night on account of the frails not wanting to buy till the old man says it's jake."

"Know the names of the people you called on?" Mack inquired.

Devon answered indignantly, "Fine salesman I'd make if I didn't!"

"Well, who were they?"

"Waller, Dawson, and Fremont. I was over last at Fremonts', an old hen living on Thorndale Avenue. She kicked in for a Feenix at about a quarter of nine, and I took the 'L' to the Randolph and Wells Street station. Then I walked along Randolph to Michigan and caught a northbound bus up here."

Mack wrote the names in his notebook. "Why didn't you tell us this in the first place?" he admonished. "Do you realize that if Mrs. Fremont verifies your story, you're completely cleared?"

"Jeez, that a fact!" Devon exclaimed.

"Surest thing you know. The dohinkus that killed Swink was planted at nine-thirty—while you were riding on the 'L' from Rogers Park, if you're giving us the straight story."

"It's the real McCoy. Call the Fremont dame and ask her if she didn't sign up for a cleaner tonight. Her husband and two kids were there, too." Devon produced a battered cigar from his vest pocket, offered it to Mack, and when the latter declined, inserted the stogie in his own mouth at a rakish angle. "Well, if you guys are through shooting questions I'll hit the hay. I'm all petered out."

Cigar jauntily protruding from the corner of his mouth, he swaggered out of the door, and O'Ryan said:

"He looks like a grifter to me, and I don't make many mistakes on them."

"That's what I thought, too," Spanger put in, "so I checked up on him. He works for Phoenix Distributors on a straight commission basis, and they told me he's making good at it. Keeps his bill paid, too."

"I'm going to shoot his prints to Washington," Mack declared. "If he's got a record, we'll know about it in a couple of days or so."

"Too bad you let Jimmy Selzer get away," O'Ryan remarked. "Well, I'll sign an order, and you can have him taken down to headquarters tomorrow."

"I don't want to put him on his guard," Mack demurred. "Besides, it won't be necessary. I think I've got his prints on this." He tapped the pocket containing the paper upon which Devon had written.

XI

"THE GANT GIRL," Mack observed, "is the only person left to talk to tonight. Let's have her in and get it over with."

"If it's O.K. with you," said Spanger, "I'm going to call it a day now. My dogs are killing me."

"They always did," Mack asserted unsympathetically "Well, so long, Jerry."

Westborough peered through his gold-rimmed spectacles at the retreating figure of the hotel detective. "There goes a hell of a good guy," Mack remarked to O'Ryan. The giant nodded assent, and Westborough ventured timidly:

"Evidently you have had prior dealings with Mr. Spanger."

Mack said, "Huh? Oh, yes, I used to know Jerry on the force. He was a sergeant in charge of the jewelry detail, and believe me, that's a job. There're more crooked schemes cooked up to get hold of sparklers than I could tell you about if I talked from now to Christmas. If it wasn't so late, I'd tell you a real story about Jerry Spanger."

103

The diminutive Westborough looked up at the detective's face with an eager interest. "I should like very much to hear it."

"Hell, what's another five minutes or so!" Mack exclaimed with an amused glance. "Well, a year ago Jerry was looking for a guy named Jake the Gent. Finally, a stool tipped him off that Jake was hiding in a rooming house over on North Clark Street—not more 'n a mile from where we are now. So Jerry goes up to get him.

"Jake was a smooth bird." Mack paused portentously. "So far as I know he had only one weakness. He couldn't keep his head when he was stewed. And he was all liquored up when Jerry got there.

"Jerry rang the doorbell, and the landlady let him in. She was on the level and didn't know what kind of customer she had upstairs. The place wasn't a regular hangout; Jake worked by himself and didn't mess up with any mob. Well, Jerry hasn't any more than got inside the door when a gun goes off and a slug just misses his ear. Jake is on the upper landing, and he has a forty-five in his hand and a smile that's none too pleasant on his face.

" 'Turn around, dick, and march out that door, or I'll plow your goddam brains out,' he says.

"Just to show he means business, he shoots again and pots Jerry in the shoulder. And a forty-five can leave one nasty hole! I'll tell the world it can! Jerry flops to the floor, and Jake probably thinks he's done for him. But he hasn't—not by a long ways. Jerry picks up his own gat—he'd dropped it when Jake's shot hit him—and lets Jake have it. Jake fires again, but this time he misses and Jerry don't. Jake tumbles all the way downstairs—deader 'n a mack'rel. Jerry was in the hospital for six weeks, but he got a hundred-dollar check from the *Daily Trumpet* for 'heroism under fire.' "

"A reward that he richly merited," Westborough commented warmly.

O'Ryan chuckled. "You don't often get gabby, Johnny, but when you do, you can shoot off your mouth worse 'n that Blakely hen. You've wasted ten minutes rehashing ancient history."

"Let's talk to the Gant girl," Mack rejoined with a wry smile.

Bronze highlights glinted from the hair of the tall girl whom Patrolman Clancy ushered in. "If I had a daughter," Westborough reflected with a touch of wistfulness, "I should wish her to be rather like Miss Gant." The girl's presence, he fancied, cast a glamour about the room. He was conscious of the ivory pallor of her skin, the faint scent of gardenia perfume. Westborough was no romanticist but a dealer in dry-as-dust facts. Natheless, his mind insisted upon painting her against a medieval tapestry, her hair streaming, Mélisande-like, from the casement of a darkened tower. . . .

With a shrug of his slight shoulders he dismissed the vagary. Yet, as he was being whisked again to the twentieth century, he noted with approval that her slender, tapering fingers were devoid of the murderous-looking red polish so commonly affected nowadays.

"Good-evening." Miss Gant's voice had a vibrant timbre which made even simple utterances musical. Westborough hastened to present a chair.

"Won't you sit down, my dear?"

She smiled her thanks and turned to the two policemen. "I suppose you want to find out what I knew about Mr. Swink?"

"Not so fast, miss." Mack had again produced the inevitable notebook. "We want to find out a few things about you first. Your full name, please."

"Yvonne Gant."

"French name, ain't it?" O'Ryan remarked jocularly.

"My father was French, yes."

"Well, Miss Gant, where do you work?"

"I don't, unfortunately." Her smile was a trifle wan. "Until the beginning of this week I had a job with the Merdock Company as secretary to one of the vice-presidents."

105

"The sheriff annexed that outfit," O'Ryan remarked. "Tough on you, wasn't it?"

"Does it cost a lot to stay here?" Mack wanted to know.

"Not a great deal, but more than I was justified in paying even when I had a job. I won't be high hat and say a position, because it wasn't. It was just a job."

She started quickly at his next question. "It's rather uncanny the way you find out things."

"That's our job."

"Yes, I did have a roommate, I'm sorry to say."

"Why sorry?" Mack inquired.

"Because that young lady left me in the lurch. She pulled out bag and baggage, and I had to pay her bill as well as my own."

"A dirty trick!" O'Ryan declared indignantly.

"I thought so too." She laughed. "Oh well, I guess I can take it."

"You're a game kid. How old are you?"

"Twenty-four."

Mack relit his cigar soberly. "My advice to you is to go home to your folks. Some people say we're having a boom, but it looks like the same old depression to me."

The girl shook her head.

"Your advice *is* sensible, but I've no home to go to. Dad married again, and I'm *persona non grata* with friend stepmother. No, I'll have to take Grant's tip and fight it out on this line." She laughed: her laughter was genuine, hearty. "But I hope it won't take all summer." She shivered and adjusted her flimsy blue negligee more tightly about her. "Brr! It's cold in here."

Mack went toward the window, which nobody had thought to close since Larson had first flung it open, and banged it down. "We sorta let the place air out, I guess," he apologized.

"Where is it—I mean he?"

"Morgue," Mack said succinctly.

"Oh!" She lapsed into silence, and Mack launched into his cross-examination.

"How well'd you know Swink, Miss Gant?"

"I? Scarcely at all."

"You moved into the room next door the first of the week?"

"Yes."

"Did you know Swink before that?"

"I never saw him before then. I was on a different floor."

"When'd you first speak to him?"

"It would be more correct to say when did he first speak to me."

"Well, when did he?"

Her forehead puckered. "It must have been on Tuesday morning. We rode down on the elevator together."

"What'd you talk about?"

"What does one talk about with a person one meets for the first time? Always and invariably the weather. We agreed perfectly that it was a fine day, although it wasn't. It was drizzling."

"When did you see him after that?"

"The same evening."

"Where?"

"In my own room." She paused to scrutinize his expression. "That doesn't seem to surprise you very much. I suppose the old Tabby across the hall has been talking."

"Do you mean Mrs. Blakely?"

"Is that what she's called? I never did know, and I've a beastly memory for names, anyhow."

"What did you do when you found Swink in your room?"

"To my own surprise I went completely Victorian. It was such a shock to see him sitting there that I even shrieked."

"And what happened then?"

"You know, don't you? There really isn't much point in my telling you."

"Maybe we do and maybe we don't," Mack said noncommittally. "Anyway, we want your own account of it."

"Mr. Larson came out of his room."

"What time was it?"

"I'm sorry, but I haven't the faintest. I was ready to turn in, which means anything from nine o'clock on."

"What'd Larson do?"

"He took Swink by the arm and said, 'Let's go to bed,' or something like that, and helped him back to his own room."

Mack said casually, "He used the connecting door into Swink's room, didn't he?" Westborough sensed the tension underlying the detective's assumed indifference and felt that the answer to this question was very important to him. But Miss Gant seemed not to notice.

"The connecting door? Is there—oh, I see what you mean! I had forgotten there was such a door."

"He didn't use it, then?"

108

"No, he used the hall door, of course."

"But he tried the connecting door to see if it was locked?"

"I am sorry to disappoint you, officer, but he didn't go near the connecting door."

"Did you examine it?"

"Of course not. Why should I?"

"Might've been curious to see how Swink got in your room."

"At that particular moment the fact of paramount importance was that he was there, not his manner of effecting entrance."

"Carpenter was up the next day to fix your door, wasn't he?"

"Mr. Larson said he would be, but I didn't see him. However, the door certainly locks all right now."

Mack's eyes were riveted upon the girl's face. "How well do you know Larson?"

She returned his stare with a cool shrug. "As intimately as I knew Mr. Swink, or, for that matter, anyone in the hotel. In short, not very well. However, I must except Mr. Westborough, to whom I am indebted for an excellent breakfast and for still more entertaining conversation."

Westborough regarded the floor in an embarrassed manner. Mack said gruffly:

"We were talking about Larson, not Mr. Westborough. What's your opinion of Larson?"

This, Westborough conjectured, was another question of importance to the detective. Miss Gant's answer came without reservation.

"What I have seen of him I liked very much. He certainly handled my little difficulty in a tactful and efficient manner."

Mack abandoned the rapier and took up a bludgeon. "Ever go out with him?" he demanded abruptly. Her eyes—violet and expressive—widened in astonishment.

"No."

"Nor have any long talks with him?"

"No."

"Practically a stranger, then?"

"You could call it that."

"Miss Gant, where were you this evening?"

"In the lounge room on the mezzanine."

"All evening?"

"Until I came to my room, yes."

"What were you doing there?"

"Playing the piano."

O'Ryan, plainly nettled, advised, "Don't get funny."

"I'm not trying to. That's really what I was doing."

"What's a piano doing in the lounge?" O'Ryan wanted to know.

"That's a question to ask the manager. All I know is that it's there."

"What sort of music do you play?" Mack questioned. Westborough answered:

"I have heard Miss Gant play Chopin. If I remember, one selection was the very lovely Nocturne in E Flat, an old favorite of mine. That same evening she played, I believe, another Chopin number, the Ballade in A Flat."

Yvonne Gant smiled. "Yes, I do play Chopin, Liszt, Mozart—a smattering of everything and nothing particularly well."

"I thought your touch quite professional," Westborough demurred.

Mack returned at once to the question before the house. "What time'd you leave off playing?"

"I never play after ten, so it must have been around that time. Perhaps a little earlier."

"And you went upstairs right away?"

"Yes."

"Did you see anyone in the hall?"

"I don't believe so. It seems to me now that it was completely empty."

"Did you hear anyone moving about in this room—Swink's?"

"I didn't notice."

Yvonne Gant was allowed to leave, and Mack grinned at Westborough. "There you are. It's like that problem that was going the rounds a while back. Smith, Brown, and Robinson are the engineer, fireman, and conductor on a train, and you found out which was which through a lot of idiotic statements like 'Smith played billiards with the fireman' and 'Brown's great-aunt lived in a suburb fifty miles from Evanston while Smith's great-aunt lived with the engineer.' "

"I never could work that one," O'Ryan admitted.

"The killer's got to be someone in this corridor," Mack analyzed, sitting down at the writing desk. He took a sheet of stationery from the drawer. "Anyone else would've had to pass either the linen room or the Colmar dame's room, and no one else did. Do you check with that, Terry?"

"Sure," the giant agreed, "but we know all that already."

"All right," Mack assented, "now let's make a timetable of what each party we've talked to did tonight. Assuming that no one was lying, it ought to tell us who are Smith, Brown, and Robinson."

He consulted the habitual notebook and began to write while Westborough and O'Ryan glanced over his shoulder.

"Chilton: In lobby with Swink eight to eight-thirty. Went to Swink's room at eight-thirty, left at eight-fifty-five. Left bar sometime after ten—gone fifteen minutes. So far as known did not go to west corridor of third floor at this time. Went up there with Swink at about a quarter to eleven.

"Larson: In own room all evening. Slept until nine.

"Westborough: Went to own room at seven-thirty.

"Colmar: With sister in her room from seven on. Left about a quarter to eleven; met Swink and Chilton in hall.

"Chambermaid: Visited Swink's room at nine.

"Graham, Mrs. Graham, Cedric Graham, Mrs. Hammond: Left hotel at eight-thirty, returned at quarter to twelve.

"Mrs. Blakely: Went to own room at nine-thirty.

"Hammond: In own room since dinner.

"Swann: Left hotel at eight, returned at ten, and stayed five or ten minutes. So far as known did not go into west corridor of third floor. Did not return to hotel again until two-thirty.

"Devon: Did not go to room until ten.

"Miss Gant: Went to own room at nine forty-five or so.

"Murderer: In Swink's room at nine-thirty."

Mack finished writing and restored his fountain pen to his pocket. "Well?" he challenged. "What do you think of it?"

"Dear me!" Westborough ejaculated. "It is a remarkably thorough analysis indeed. In fact, there is only one person whose movements you have failed to account for."

"Who's that?" Mack demanded, bristling.

"Mr. Spanger."

PART TWO: *From the Notebook of Theocritus Lucius Westborough*

XII

MY MIND, like a machine, mills incessantly over tonight's events. I turn to the pen as the only possible method of exorcising these thoughts. Moreover, the written word will remain—*littera scripta manet.*

A detective, I have discovered, is not unlike a historian in his mode of working. A detective garners facts—so does a historian. A detective endeavors to arrange such facts into a semblance of logical continuity—likewise a historian. A detective discards, or should discard, the nonessentials in order that the residuum may stand in its true significance with the stark reality of a monolith. And should not a disciple of Klio follow the same procedure?

Let us, then, begin with the facts. Let us set them down in irrefutable black and white. Later, perhaps, I shall find it possible to add, as Browning puts it in "The Ring and the Book," "something of mine which, mixed up with the mass, makes it bear hammer and be firm to file."

The facts which appear of greatest significance are those which drove—if I may use such a conclusive word at such an inconclusive moment—that the murderer cannot have come from outside the hotel. The *causa sine qua non* is that he must be one of the persons rooming off the west corridor. Furthermore, he must have been in the west corridor by nine-thirty and not have left it since that time.

Quaeritur: Can one be sure that the murderer was in Swink's room at nine-thirty? Only the word of Mr. Hammond establishes this important point. If Hammond lied, the reason is obvious. But

115

there is also the inevitable human factor to consider: Hammond may be mistaken. Some people, and I must include myself among them, can only make inaccurate guesses with regard to the passage of time. Others have an innate time sense which functions with almost watch-like precision. Psychological experiments seem necessary to determine in which category Hammond belongs.

This brings to mind the same doubt with regard to the accuracy of other sections of Lieutenant Mack's timetable—those based upon the opinion of Miss Colmar. Nevertheless, it is best to be logical even in the treatment of the illogical. Since we must make a starting point of some kind, let us assume that the entire timetable, including Hammond's contribution, is approximately correct. Who, then, was physically able to have been in Swink's room at the proper hour? Who are the "X's," "Y's," and "Z's" to this human equation?

Myself
Larson
The Colmars
Miss Kriskrowski
Mrs. Blakely
Hammond

And no others.

At this point, I shall risk a digression from the strict realm of fact. Some conjecture is, I believe, fully justified. "Fancy with fact is just one fact the more," to use again the words of that profound logician, Robert Browning.

So now for the fanciful. Is it significant that Chilton and Devon are able to produce seemingly ironclad alibis for nine-thirty but no alibis for ten? Both of these gentlemen, as I recall, aroused the suspicions of the police. Neither seemed to be speaking with entire frankness.

James Chilton! The name strikes a responsive chord in my memory, yet to my chagrin, I am unable to recall in what connection

I have heard it. I am acquainted with no Chiltons; nevertheless, the name is oddly familiar.

Let us venture even further upon fancy's unmapped sea. Was Swann telling the truth about the reason for his return to the hotel? That return, as I recall, was also at ten o'clock. "A strange coincidence, to use a phrase by which such things are settled nowadays," said Lord Byron. And Miss Gant? Not in her room at nine-thirty, but there shortly before ten. Again that curious recurrence of the hour. Can it be altogether pure coincidence?

The motive is a question of even greater perplexity than the opportunity. No one in this microcosm of suspects had—apparently—more than a cursory acquaintance with the murdered man.

Quaeritur: Have any guests secured their rooms since the advent of Swink two weeks ago? Yes, Chilton, who registered last Monday, and Miss Gant, who on Sunday moved to her room from another part of the hotel. Is it possible that either of them selected rooms in order to be near Swink?

Apparently the motive is well concealed, and yet surely there do not exist many motives sufficient to induce one human being to take the life of another. Indeed, I am unable to think of more than four.

Greed: The smell of money is good whatever its source, states the proverb, and man is undoubtedly wolf to man. Yet Swink's diamond stick pin was left intact upon his bureau. Moreover, logic irresistibly forces the conclusion that Swink could not have been killed to secure any object upon his person. The murderer did not have, and probably could not have had, access to Swink's person after his death.

Unless it is later shown that one of the suspects has a financial stake in Swink's property—if indeed he has property—the broad motive of greed may be safely omitted. My second motive, however, is not so easily eliminated.

Sex: Jealousy is a possible motive for Hammond. Larson, obviously interested in Miss Gant, must also be included under this category. I regret that lack of data compels me to dismiss this important question in so few words.

Fear: The unknown person whom I heard Swink address last Monday? Mrs. Hammond, perhaps? In strict justice, I must state that such a motive for Mrs. Hammond would be a weak one. Moreover, she is definitely known to have been out of the hotel at the time of the murder—no matter whether it was at nine-thirty or at ten.

Revenge: My fourth and last motive seems, perhaps, the most likely. The deceased did not look like a gentleman with an altogether unblemished past. Perhaps one of his dupes—"suckers," to use the colloquial term—had emulated the proverbial worm in turning upon his deceiver.

N.B.: Swink had attempted to interest two people of the group in his financial schemes. However, both of these—Chilton and Mrs. Blakely—denied actual investment in the enterprise.

To summarize: I am forced to the conclusion that no adequate motive for Swink's death is as yet known. Undoubtedly such a motive existed, but whether its roots were embedded deeply in Swink's supposedly unsavory past or shallowly in the two weeks he has spent at this hotel, I can only conjecture.

Passing now from the questions of opportunity and motive to that of method, it is fairly obvious that Swink's murderer must meet three other requirements in addition to those I have already outlined. He must have at least a smattering of chemistry, access to a cyanide, and a means of opening the doors to Swink's room and to the Graham apartment.

Larson? He possesses the necessary knowledge, yes, but it would be a *non sequitur* to assume for this reason that he is the guilty party. A complete chemical engineering course is not necessarily needed to learn how to produce hydrocyanic acid.

The *mot de l' énigme* is undeniably the cyanide. Police routine indubitably is thorough, and the police should have no difficulty in tracing its purchase, since such purchase could not have been made prior to the advent of Swink at the hotel two weeks ago.

Dear me, there is already a fallacy in my reasoning! I am assuming that the murderer evolved his scheme subsequent to the arrival of Swink and then purchased or procured in some manner the cyanide in order to carry out his plot. Such an assumption is not necessarily valid. The entire crime may have been built around the fact that *the slayer already had the cyanide in his possession.*

Let us see to what such ratiocination leads. Why would a person have cyanide in his possession? The most probable answer is that he is engaged in an occupation requiring the use of the chemical. Let me list the vocations of the west corridor's guests.

Christopher Larson: Night clerk, chemical engineering student.

James Chilton: Broker (supposedly).

Sarah Blakely: None.

Yvonne Gant: Stenographer in search of position.

T. L. Westborough: Archaeologist and historian.

Ronald E. Graham: Commercial artist.

Mrs. R. E. Graham: Housewife.

Fred Hammond: Hosiery salesman.

Mrs. Fred Hammond: Housewife.

Benjamin Devon: Vacuum cleaner salesman.

The only one of these occupations which provides access to a cyanide is Larson's. Yet I must delve below the surface. Although I have never worked in a chemical laboratory, it does not seem that such dangerous poisons would be kept on open shelves. I deem it more probable that they would be locked in a storeroom and could be secured only upon application to an instructor and then only for the purpose of a specific experiment. If such should prove to be the case, then Larson's difficulty in securing the toxic agent would be as great as that of any of the others. I must regretfully admit that this line of thought, upon which I embarked so hopefully, has terminated in another blind alley.

Large, however, as the cyanide must bulk in the solution of the crime, it was not the only ingredient required. The author of this crime must have had some kind of acid. Two possibilities arise immediately. Either he knew of the sulphuric acid contained in the Graham boy's chemical set or he did not. Could he have known? Well, Mrs. Hammond, at least, was probably informed and she might have imparted the information to others.

Quaeritur: In the event he provided his own supply of acid, what means of disposal was used for the excess or for the container? I cannot believe that the negative results of the police search may be taken as conclusive. The bottle may have been hidden in a place where the police failed to look. But I confess that I am unable to surmise where such a spot might be.

N.B.: Children and fools tell the truth, according to the Spanish proverb. In the opinion of Cedric Graham none of the acid had been used from the bottle contained among his chemicals.

To consider now the manner of effecting ingress into the Swink and Graham rooms. Two chambermaids and Swann, Spanger, and Larson possess the means of opening the two doors. Larson, however, denied that he carries a passkey while off duty, and no such key was found upon his person or in his room.

Larson! Strange how inevitably his name occurs in my every list. He was among those in the west corridor at nine-thirty. His interest in Miss Gant betrays at least a suspicion of a motive. He is thoroughly conversant with the science of chemistry. He possesses the most likely opportunity to secure the cyanide. And, finally, he has ready access to a passkey. Dear me, the situation is very similar to the Smith, Brown, Robinson problem which Lieutenant Mack mentioned. Larson and Larson only meets every qualification. *Ergo,* Larson is the only possible solution.

Yes, but why should Larson put his information so readily at the disposal of the police? Candor deliberately assumed to disarm suspicion? That would imply a degree of subtlety which I do not think Larson possesses. Or does he? In such deep psychological waters I sink over my head rapidly.

While on the subject of psychology, however, what can one glean of the murderer's? His plot shows at least one glaring weakness. Swink, had he not stooped toward the floor at the moment the test tube shattered, would probably not have succumbed to the vapor.

Quaeritur: Did the murderer take into consideration the physiological fact that reason is one of the first faculties of the mind to be inhibited by alcohol? Did he know of Swink's habitual intoxication (since it occurred upon three successive nights, I dare say it may be termed habitual), and count upon the befuddlement of his victim's brain?

Also, did he know—or care—that his trap might close upon an innocent victim? The chambermaid, for instance. Or did he make sure that she had already left the corridor before he arranged his pitfall?

On the positive side, I find much to commend in the scheme. "The greatest crimes are perilous in their inception but well rewarded after their consummation," as Tacitus aptly observes, yet the slayer of Swink took comparatively few hazards.

Point No. 1: The ingredients were easily prepared, the tube inserted with little difficulty in its position above the door, once the murderer had secured access to the room. Far less risk was involved than in an attempt to poison Swink's food, which would have been difficult and nearly certain of detection.

Point No. 2: "If it were done when 'tis done, then 'twere well it were done quickly." A slower poison would have allowed Swink a chance to make an accusation. But the deadly swiftness of hydrocyanic acid rendered this danger negligible. (The vapor, introduced through the lungs, would act with even greater rapidity than if the poison were swallowed, if I am not mistaken.)

I am unable to resist the temptation to observe parenthetically that prussic acid, prepared by an easy process of distillation from a water in which crushed peach stones had been soaked, was known and dreaded far toward the beginnings of civilization. Witness the inscription upon an Egyptian papyrus which I have seen at the Louvre, "Pronounce not the name under the penalty of the peach." "The peach" is, of course, an obvious reference to the method of manufacture.

Undoubtedly the same baneful drug, or at least one of the cyanides, was in use among the Romans. Tacitus mentions several illuminating incidents in the *Annals*:

Vibulenus Agrippa, after being accused of high treason, snatched a dose of poison from his robes, drank, and fell dead *immediately* in the Senate chamber.

The Empress Agrippina, deliberating upon a method of killing her husband, Claudius, reflected that "the deed would be betrayed by a poison that was sudden and *instantaneous*" and employed the skilled poisoner, Locusta, to concoct "some rare compound which might derange his mind and delay death." This drug seems to have been ineffective, and Claudius was on the verge of recovery when his physician, Xenophon, under pretense of assisting the emperor to vomit, inserted in the imperial throat, a "feather smeared with some *rapid* poison."

Nero was assured by the same Locusta that the death of Britannicus "should be as *sudden* as if it were the hurried work of the dagger." Tacitus' account confirms the correctness of the prognostication. Britannicus is said to have lost *instantly* both "voice and breath."

In each of these three incidents I have underlined the words which refer to the action of the toxic agent. I can think of no poison other than the cyanides which would take effect with the promptitude of the drug swallowed by Vibulenus Agrippa or that employed in the murder of Britannicus.

It is growing late, and I have strayed so far from the *mise en scéne* that I fear I shall never be able to return tonight. Besides I am so sleepy that further reasoning is out of the question. But—what appalling secrets the next few hours may unfold . . .

PART THREE: *Friday Morning*

XIII

VICTOR SWANN closed the door of his office, and the noise from the lobby diminished to a scarcely audible hum. Mack regarded appraisingly the oak-paneled wall, the heavy velvet drapes masking the windows, and the antique bronze lighting fixture. "Must've cost a pile to fix up this joint," he mused.

He settled himself in a green-leather upholstered chair of comfortable proportions as Swann began the conversation.

"Wanted to see you—soon as you came in. Queer things went on in the night."

Mack's eyes were inquisitive narrow slits. "What things?"

"Tell him, Jerry," Swann directed.

The house detective cleared his throat with two or three rumbling coughs and reached in his vest pocket for a cigar of slender dimensions.

"Stogie, Johnny?"

Mack replied with a disdainful glance at the proffered smoke, "I'll stick to my own, thanks. What did go on last night?"

Spanger decapitated his ladylike cheroot and spat the end with commendable accuracy into the sand of an urn-shaped receptacle. "Someone got into Swink's room."

Mack leaped to his feet in one quick motion. "The hell you say! Who?"

Spanger calmly lit his cigar and flicked the match at the urn. His aim was poor and it fluttered down to the heavy carpet. "You tell me. Whoever it was, he wrecked the furniture."

Swann commenced an indignant inventory of the damage. "Mattress has to be restuffed and two chairs reupholstered. God knows what else. Room's a mess."

Mack said, "I hope you didn't try to clean it up."

"Go up and take a look," Spanger retorted. "It's just the way we found it."

"Who found it?"

"Maid," Spanger replied curtly. "Half an hour or so ago. The Blakely woman saw something, too," he added, "but we haven't been able to get anything from her. She's in her room having hysterics."

"Humph!" Mack's snort might have expressed any emotion. "Somebody must've been looking for something."

"You don't say so!" Spanger drawled sarcastically. "I thought he was hell-raising out of pure spite."

"I tested that door before we left last night," Mack recollected. "It was locked then."

"Locks don't mean anything around here now," Spanger gibed. "We gotta guy can melt right through walls."

"Well, get a blotter and blot him up," Mack advised on his way out. He stopped as his hand was about to close over the door knob. "Where'll I find the housekeeper?"

"Room 503—Mrs. Simmons." Swann's usual laconic manner changed suddenly into an earnest pleading. "See here, Lieutenant Mack, I've got to get this thing cleared up. Six permanents have already given notice."

Mack answered, "You don't want it cleared up any more than we do," and left the office without waiting for Spanger, who was engrossed in conversation with the hotel manager. He stepped into a waiting elevator, and the steel doors clanged shut behind him.

"You on duty last night?" he inquired of the pilot.

"No sir. My shift's from seven to three. What floor, sir?"

"Third." The pilot shifted a lever, and the car shot upward. "When does the next shift go off duty?" Mack asked.

"Eleven tonight."

Mack left the car. He made another notation in his notebook as he walked toward the west corridor. The door to Swink's room stood ajar, and he whistled upon catching his first glimpse of the interior.

A ruthless hand had torn the covers from the bed, ripped open the inner spring mattress, and scattered tufts of black horsehair in several piles. Mack inspected the damaged mattress and observed that it had been slit in three distinct places. He turned his attention to the chairs. Denuded of their upholstery, they stood in naked shame like a woman caught unawares in the bathtub. One had been tipped on its side, Mack noted.

The detective's restless eyes flitted to the top of the writing desk. "Humph!" he ejaculated. He walked over to the desk and pulled open the drawer. His face wore a perplexed expression as he examined the interior. Then he stepped across the room to the closet. Swink's two extra suits and a pair of silk pajamas were still hanging there, and a large tan Gladstone bag was toward the back. Mack dragged it into the room and jerked it open. He was regarding its contents with a thoughtful air when Jerry Spanger came in.

"You might wait for a fellow," he grumbled and then asked, "Well, whatta you make of it, Johnny?"

"Something damn queer."

"Whole thing's queer!"

"I don't mean that. Look at this bag."

"What about it? Nothing in it to get excited about."

"Doesn't look like anybody had pawed through it, does it?"

"Can't say that it does."

Mack gestured toward the dresser.

"I haven't looked inside the bureau yet. But the drawers are closed the way we left 'em last night."

Spanger pulled open a small top drawer while Mack watched over the house detective's shoulder. "Socks and hankies," he pronounced. Spanger opened another drawer. "And here's a pile of shirts. None of this stuff's been disturbed."

"Well?" Spanger questioned, lifting his bushy eyebrows.

"Go over and take a look inside the desk drawer," Mack directed.

Spanger did so. "Nothing here."

"Except a penholder, letterheads, envelopes, an inkwell, and a Gideon Bible," Mack corrected.

"That junk's in every desk in the hotel."

"Sure it is. But see how neat the inside of that drawer looks. And the chambermaid hasn't touched it since yesterday morning."

"I get it," Spanger said. "This punk didn't search Swink's belongings."

"If he did, he was mighty careful not to disturb anything. But he didn't give a damn about the mattress and—" Mack brought his hand against his thigh in a resounding slap. "Say, here's an idea. Why didn't this guy look through Swink's stuff? Because he'd already done it—see? Last night when he was in the room at nine-thirty. But last night he didn't have time to find what he wanted so he sneaks in again and goes over the place with a fine-tooth comb. He's got nerve, that fellow!"

Spanger regarded the torn chairs with a rueful expression. "He musta thought Swink had done a man-sized job of hiding his thimble. What the hell do you suppose he was looking for?"

"Westborough heard Swink try his hand at blackmail," Mack reminded.

Spanger chuckled. "I see—the good old letters."

"Letters, pix—oh, hell! What would a guy be apt to hold as evidence?"

"A raised check or a marriage certificate, maybe," Spanger contributed. "Think this mug found it?"

Mack shook his head. "If I were Swink and wanted to hide something the last place on earth I'd pick would be the inside of a hotel mattress."

"Why?"

"Some houseman might change it to another room. And that goes for the chairs too. They look just like the chairs in a lot of other rooms, and once they were out of here it'd be a devil of a job to trace 'em."

"What makes you think a houseman is suddenly going to decide to shift furniture?" Spanger questioned.

Mack shrugged his shoulders. "How should I know whether he would or not? But if I was Swink and wanted to hide something, I'd think that maybe he might. See? I wouldn't hide it in anything portable."

Spanger grimaced. "You talk like the country boy who found the horse because he thought where he'd go if he was one of 'em. Just where would you hide the papers if you was a horse?" he demanded with a chuckle.

Mack's eyes shifted absent-mindedly from one wall to another. "Damned if I know!" he exclaimed. "I think I'd rent a safety deposit box under a fake name and put 'em in there. And I'll bet ten bucks that's what our fat friend did."

"Maybe you're right."

"Well, we've got to get more facts," Mack went on. "You said the Blakely woman heard something, and the Gant girl might've too. So might the Hammonds and even Westborough." He crossed the corridor and knocked on Sarah Blakely's door.

"Who's there?" a muffled voice asked.

"Police. We want to talk to you."

"You'll have to wait a few minutes. I'm taking a bath."

"Hell," Mack muttered under his breath. He turned to the house detective. "Keep an eye on this door, Jerry, and don't let the old dame sneak out on us."

He tried a door across the corridor, and the pleasantly modulated voice of Yvonne Gant answered, "Who is it?"

"Police," Mack said again. There was the noise of a bolt being unfastened, and the door was flung open.

"Good-morning," Miss Gant called cheerfully. "Lieutenant Mack, isn't it? Won't you come in?"

Mack stepped over the threshold. The chambermaid had paid her matutinal visit and the room was immaculate. Mack noted a pile of library books on the writing desk and flipped the top one open. It was by Aldous Huxley, a name which conveyed to Mack exactly nothing. The second volume was an anthology of modern British poetry. Mack took one look and abandoned literature for his hostess, who had seated herself at a dressing table and was putting the finishing touches to her bronze-colored hair. She was wearing the skirt of a tailored suit and a little gray sweater.

"How'd you sleep last night?" Mack asked abruptly.

Her glance switched from the mirror to his face.

"Very soundly—as I always do. Why?"

"Hear anything going on next door?"

"I heard a lot of talking all evening. Finally, it quieted down and I was able to get to sleep."

"Hear anything after that?"

"Nothing at all. Sorry I can't help you."

"That's all right. Good-bye."

"Good-bye."

Mack closed the door and called to Jerry Spanger in the corridor. "What about it?"

"She's still in there."

"Well, keep her there till I get back."

He sauntered down the corridor and knocked. Fred Hammond, clad only in gaudy yellow-striped pajamas, opened the door.

"Be quiet, can't you? My wife's asleep."

"Come out here, then."

"Be with you in a minute." He slipped a dressing gown of Tyrian purple over his pajamas, and Mack escorted him to Swink's room.

"Know anything about this?"

Hammond shook his head. "Someone sure made a mess, didn't they? Who was it?"

"If I knew I wouldn't be asking you."

"Well, I can't help you."

"How'd you sleep last night?"

"Like hell! How'd you expect anyone to sleep with the racket you were making in here?"

"So you heard us?" Mack glanced up with quick interest. "How late did we keep it up?"

"How should I know? I kept dozing off for a few minutes and then waking up again all night long." His forehead puckered. "I did look at my watch once, though, when I got up to go to the bathroom."

"What time was it?"

131

"Few minutes past five."

"And the noise was still going on?"

"Worse if anything."

"People talking?"

"No, it didn't sound like that. More like furniture being moved."

"And you thought it was the police?"

"Who else could it be?"

Mack said slowly, "We were all out of here before three-thirty. Hammond, that makes the second time you heard the murderer!"

XIV

THEOCRITUS LUCIUS WESTBOROUGH peeped from his bedroom. "Good-morning, Lieutenant Mack," he began as he glimpsed the detective. "I have made an analysis which I should like to have you read."

Mack waved the proffered papers impatiently away. "Some other time. What I want to know right now is if you heard anything fishy going on across the corridor about five this morning."

Westborough reluctantly restored the sheaf to his breast pocket. "Dear me, I'm sorry, but I heard nothing. I am afraid that I was paying profound allegiance to the goddess of Sleep at about that hour."

"You can come in now," Mrs. Blakeley's muffled voice sounded from the door of the next room.

"May I accompany you?" Westborough inquired.

"Sure." Mack stepped into Mrs. Blakeley's room followed by Westborough and Jerry Spanger. The irate dowager glowered at the house detective.

"Mr. Swink's room is haunted, and I don't intend to spend another night in this place if I can help it. And I don't like tobacco smoke, so you'll have to put that thing out."

Spanger laid his cigar at the edge of the writing desk. "Sorry, Mrs. Blakeley. Now what's it all about?"

"Don't put that thing there," she shrieked. "Do you want to start a fire?"

Spanger regretfully went to the window and tossed the butt into the court. "What's this about Swink's room being haunted?"

"An evil spirit has taken possession. A—a—*poltergeist*."

"What?"

"I said a poltergeist."

"In the name of the seven ring-tailed fishes, what's that?"

"Poltergeist," Westborough informed, "is a combination of two German words: *geist*, a spirit; *polter*, to cause a disturbance. I believe that, in the language of psychical research it refers to a spirit addicted to practical jokes. One who causes raps, weird noises, and so on."

"Tripe!" Mack exclaimed contemptuously.

Sarah Blakely, looking at him as though he were a cockroach upon which she was about to set foot, quoted in a sepulchral voice, " 'There are more things in heaven and earth . . . than are dreamt of in your philosophy.' "

"Just the same," Mack scoffed, "I never heard of a spook that tore up furniture."

"That shows how little you know about it," Mrs. Blakely flared indignantly. "There are things in this universe too deep and too mysterious to be understood by our poor earthbound minds. Don't you think so, Mr. Westborough?"

"The phenomena of haunting," Westborough declared, "cannot be laughed entirely away. The French astronomer, Camille

Flammarion, devoted a quarter of a century in collecting several thousand reports dealing with this subject. Most of the instances he cites were, I believe, well authenticated."

"They," Mrs. Blakely proclaimed with an awed emphasis upon the pronoun, "have moved a couch and chairs in a semicircle as though the devil had held a council meeting. *They* have taken down dishes from shelves, emptied boxes of linen, pulled books from bookcases, and lifted a heavy mahogany bed straight up several feet from the floor while a man was lying on it. *They* have rung doorbells, burst open locked doors, turned keys, fired guns, and caused picture frames to fall to the floor. *They* bombarded a house in Belgium with over 300 stones and, at a house in Portugal, even stole a baby from its cradle and stripped off its swaddling clothes. And you say, Lieutenant Mack—"

Mack hurriedly interrupted the discourse. "How do you know there was a poultry-goose in Swink's room?"

She sniffed. "I was not referring to a species of chicken."

"You score a ten-strike there," Spanger chuckled. "Now tell us about it."

In a voice hollow and theatrical, she whispered, "I heard it this morning."

"When?" Mack put in quickly.

"Very early. I believe it was about five o'clock."

"You heard it from here?"

She hesitated guiltily before shaking her head. "No, from the hall."

"What were you doing in the hall at five o'clock in the morning?"

Her voice raised in shrill protest. "I don't propose to be talked to that way. I called my lawyer on the telephone this morning, and he assures me that I don't have to answer any of your questions."

"Just the same," Mack insisted, "I'd like to know what you were doing in the hall at five o'clock in the morning."

"Your lawyer is quite right," Westborough put in gently, "but, Mrs. Blakely, you want to help the police to bring a murderer to justice, do you not?"

"Ye—es," she admitted hesitantly. "That's why I was in the hall this morning."

"To help bring a murderer to justice?" Westborough asked. She nodded, and Mack broke in, a puzzled expression on his face:
"How could you help do that by being in the hall?"

"Well, if you must know, I'll tell you about it," Mrs. Blakely agreed, settling herself in a chair and adjusting the folds of her flowing black skirt. She turned the full battery of her spectacled eyes upon Mack. "People who do not know are always quick to scoff at the things they do not understand," she pronounced. "Lieutenant Mack, will you loan me your pocketbook, watch charm, key case, any little object you have carried and touched?"

With a look of blank incredulity, Mack passed over a fountain pen. She clutched it tightly in her right hand, closed her eyes, and sank back in her chair, her face bearing a rapt expression.

"I see a street," Mrs. Blakely declaimed in a deep, sibylline voice. "It is lined with elm trees. There are rows of little brick bungalows. It is a street in a western suburb. The suburb is called Westmay."

"Well, I'll be damned!" Mack exclaimed. "That's where I live."

"I see a house," Mrs. Blakely's sepulchral tones continued. "It is number—the numbers do not come clearly. A little tot is playing in the front yard. She is about five years old and tow-headed. A woman is sifting flour into a big green bowl. She is a tall woman with yellow hair gathered into a knot at the back of her head. She goes to the front door and calls, 'Ann.' The child enters the house, and I do not see more."

"I'm a son of a sea cook!" Mack declared, his forehead knit in evident perplexity. "My wife and kid to a T. Mrs. Blakely, I don't know what hocus-pocus you're working, but I have to hand it to you."

"Psychometry, isn't it?" Westborough inquired. "I have seen some very interesting demonstrations."

Mrs. Blakely returned the fountain pen to the detective and cackled, in the manner of a hen who has just laid a particularly large and imposing egg, "Do you see now why I crossed the hall this morning?"

"But you couldn't get into Swink's room," Mack objected, his shrewd common sense once more in the foreground. "Don't you need something belonging to a person to work this monkey business?"

"He had touched the door knob," Mrs. Blakely declared impressively, "and so had his murderer. I have secured astonishing results with less upon which to work."

Mack leaned forward eagerly and asked, "Did you find out anything?" His informant shivered.

"It was the most harrowing experience of my whole life. I hadn't any more than touched my hand to the knob when I heard an awful noise from inside the room. At that moment I realized the presence of a poltergeist and that I was in terrible danger. I ran back to my own room and buried my head under the covers. Not that that would do any good, though, if I once came within the sphere of his influence. Fortunately, I don't believe that happened."

"Prune juice!" Spanger ejaculated under his breath. Mack glared at him and asked Mrs. Blakely to describe the kind of noise she had heard.

"Raps," that lady replied promptly. "Now here, now there, now all over the room at once." A shudder ran over her stout body. "Never in all my life have I know such awful terror."

"Well, the what-you-call-it's gone now," Mack said cheerfully. "Wait a minute and I'll bring you one of Swink's hankies to hold in your hand. Maybe you'll be able to tell us who killed him."

"Are you crazy?" she shrieked. "Nothing on earth would induce me to put myself within reach of that evil spirit. There are times when it is a fate worse than death to peep behind the Curtain."

"Well, if you won't, you won't," Mack said philosophically. When the door had closed behind the three men he remarked to Westborough, "Is that old dame loony? Or am I? She had me going for a while."

"Once in a blue moon there appear to be genuine psychic phenomena," Westborough answered. "Whether or not the present incident is in this category I am, of course, unable to say."

"How'd she learn about my house?" Mack demanded. "Even you didn't know that, Jerry."

Spanger's head moved negatively. "You had a flat in Niles Center the last time I heard. Also I thought your kid was called Gertrude."

"I should like very much to have your opinion upon this analysis," Westborough ventured, reaching within his breast pocket. Mack waved him away again and took the elevator to the fifth floor. He found the housekeeper alone in her office glancing over a printed form headed "Service Memo" and so absorbed in her work that she failed to hear his entrance. The report, Mack noted, provided numerous columns to show the bath towels, face towels, sheets, pillowcases, blankets, and what not supplied to each bedroom. His glance swerved from it to Mrs. Simmons, whose sweet, motherly face was surrounded by a cloud of white hair. Mack took one look and mentally removed his headpiece. Here was a real lady, and he knew it.

"Good-morning, ma'am."

The housekeeper said to herself, "She left three bath towels at 406 and it should only get two," and looked up from the report with a slightly puzzled expression. As she saw Mack her face cleared.

"Oh yes, you're from the police force. Mr. Swann warned me."

"Warned you, ma'am?"

"That's hardly the way to put it," she laughed. "I should say he informed me you were going to pay a visit."

Mack said, "Are the mattresses in this hotel ever changed from one room to another?"

"Not unless a guest makes a fuss about his mattress, and that seldom happens. They're the best inner-spring mattresses made. I know because I selected them. No, they are never moved from one room to another, although a houseman turns each mattress over once a week: one week from end to end and the next week from side to side."

"Well, that clears up a point," Mack declared.

"What point?"

"Nothing much. Just an argument I had with your house detective. All the maids carry passkeys, don't they?"

"Floor keys, yes."

"Are they pretty careful with 'em? About opening doors for guests and letting other people handle 'em and so on?"

"No maid is allowed to open the door for a guest," Mrs. Simmons rejoined firmly. "She must tell him politely that he will have to apply to the room clerk. And if a girl loses her passkey it usually means her job, and she knows it."

"Has anyone lost a passkey recently?"

"No."

"What do they do with the keys while they're going through a room?" Mack questioned.

"I don't understand."

"Well, my wife comes home from the store, and she leaves her key in the outside of the lock," Mack explained. "I've given her the devil for it—I beg your pardon, ma'am—several times, but she keeps on doing it just the same. Have you got any girls with that habit?"

"I did reprimand one girl for carelessness of that nature," Mrs. Simmons reflected. "I told her about two weeks ago that I would have to dismiss her if she persisted in leaving her key in the lock while she cleaned a room."

"What's her name?"

"Anna Larson."

"Larson, huh? Any relation to your night clerk?"

"No, indeed. Mr. Larson is an entirely different type."

Mack failed to conceal his eagerness. "Does this girl happen to clean the rooms opening off the west corridor of the third floor?"

The housekeeper replied thoughtfully, "Why yes, she does!"

XV

MACK LOOKED across the room at the chambermaid, Anna Larson, whom he had finally run to earth with the aid of the housekeeper's schedule. She was a plain girl with a rather unintelligent face. "Just a dumb Swede," Mack remarked to himself.

"Are you Anna Larson?"

The maid pulled a chair near the bed and deposited her armful of sheets and pillowcases. It seemed to take several minutes for her slow mind to grasp that she was being addressed. "Yes," she said finally, "but I can't talk to you. We're not allowed to while we're working."

Mack flicked back the lapel of his coat.

"I think you'd better talk to me, sister."

"A policeman!" she gasped. "I haven't done nothing."

"Who said you had? Just want to ask you a few questions, sister. Go right on working if it makes your conscience feel easier."

With deft hands the maid spread a sheet over the mattress pad and tucked in the corners. She shook out the pillows and put fresh pillowcases on them. "What do you want to know?"

"How long does it take to do a room?" Mack asked.

She completed the bed and began to dust the telephone mouthpiece. There was silence for so long that Mack wondered if she had heard the question.

"I have to do sixteen rooms each day," she informed him at length. "That's if they have people in them. For every room with people that I don't do, I have to do three rooms without people."

"Say that again," Mack directed. She did so, her dust cloth flitting across the furniture, and Mack nodded, "All right, I get it. If you didn't do sixteen occupied rooms in a day, you'd have to do forty-eight vacant rooms."

"If I did nothing but vacant rooms."

"Skip it," Mack advised. "How many hours do you work per day?"

"I don't know. I come to work at seven and I go home at three."

Mack did mental arithmetic.

"Eight-hour day, sixteen rooms. That means you're in each room half an hour?"

She dusted the closet shelf, the window sill, the ledge at the top of the sash, the mirror over the dresser, and each picture frame. "No wonder Jimmy Selzer didn't find any fingerprints," Mack mused.

The question had finally percolated. "I guess it's about half an hour," she pronounced.

"You've had some trouble, haven't you?" Mack asked. "Didn't you get bawled out for leaving your passkey on the outside of the door?"

Anna Larson's face reddened. "I forgot about that."

"Ever do that trick since?" Mack wanted to know. "You don't need to worry about me. I won't tell anyone about it." He was forced to qualify this statement, "That is, unless I have to, and then I'll see that you keep your job."

"I keep forgetting," she said sullenly. "I know I shouldn't, but I can't seem to help it. I forget all about that key until I come out and find it sticking in the lock outside."

"Humph!" Mack ejaculated. "How many times a day do you leave your key around like that?"

"Maybe once or twice."

"Ever find your key missing when you came out?" She shook her head. "Come on, tell the truth about it, sister. I'll see you keep your job."

"I'm telling the truth. I never did."

"Oh, you found it again, of course," Mack went on, "lying on the floor or something. But it was gone for a while, wasn't it?"

She shook her head again.

"I'm giving it to you straight, mister. I've never missed the key."

Mack gave it up. He left the third floor and went down to the carpenter shop. From within came the strains of "The Man on the Flying Trapeze," expertly whistled. Mack flung the door open. Sunlight streamed through one of the basement windows to illuminate the tall, gangly figure at the carpenter's bench. He had clamped what appeared to be the leg of a chair in a vise and was sandpapering while he whistled.

Mack inquired, "You do the locksmith work around here?"

The carpenter looked at him suspiciously.

"You'll have to tell it to the room clerk, mister."

Once again Mack jerked back the lapel of his coat.

"I don't know whether you know it or not, but there was a murder in this dump last night."

"Yeh, I heard about it." The carpenter laid down his sandpaper and reached in the pocket of his apron for a stubby, well-caked briar and a nickel sack of tobacco. "Where do I come in?"

"What's your name?"

"Hugh Clark."

Mack jotted it down in his notebook. "Did Larson tell you two or three days ago to fix the door of room 311?"

"Yep, and I did."

"What was the matter with it?"

"It stuck a little against the jamb. Not much, but enough to stop the door from locking when it was slammed shut."

Mack thumbed back several pages in his notebook and made a check mark.

"Do you do the locksmith work?" he again asked.

"Yep. What there is of it."

You keep a supply of blanks here, I suppose?"

"Yep."

"And a set of duplicates for every room?" Clark jerked his thumb toward a large steel cabinet. "In there."

Mack took a close look at it, and saw that Jerry Spanger had been right about the two padlocks. "You take care of 'em all right."

Clark smiled. "I'm responsible for those keys, and nobody's going to get at 'em without my knowing it."

Mack said, "Tell me something about the locks here."

"What do you want to know about 'em?"

Can you open 'em with skeleton keys?"

Skeleton keys, hell!" Clark jeered. "What do you think we have here—warded locks? The key has to push up a row of five pin tumblers in the cylinder, and a variation of even a fiftieth of an inch will stop the plug from turning. What skeleton key would work on a layout like that? You couldn't even get one in the keyhole—it takes a paracentric key."

"What the deuce is a paracentric key?"

"The keyway is corrugated with ridges on both sides, and your key has to be corrugated to fit or it won't go in."

Mack said, "I'll take your word for it. But your corrugations won't prevent a pick being stuck in to force up the tumblers."

"They make it damn difficult. The keyway's pretty small to begin with, and that makes it hard to get a pick in so it can rake the tumblers. I'm not saying it can't be done," Clark mused as though thinking aloud. "God knows any lock with an open keyhole can be picked, given a guy clever enough and with time enough to do it. But I will say this much: opening one of these locks with a pick is no job for an amateur."

"Jerry Spanger said he couldn't do it."

"That flatfoot!" Clark exclaimed contemptuously.

"Two doors were opened last night," Mack said. "This fellow might've gotten hold of Swink's key and slipped the catch so he could open the door later on. That would call for a tricky bit of maneuvering to get it away from Swink and back to him again, but still it might be done. But Graham's door was opened too, and he couldn't get Graham's key because it was down in the key rack all evening, and he'd have to hit the room clerk over the head first.

143

Either he picked the locks or he got hold of a passkey some way. Which do you think?"

Clark hunched his shoulders, "I'm damned if I know."

"Well, there's one way to find out," Mack went on. "I want you to take the locks off both doors—314 and 315. If they were picked, we should be able to tell when we get a look inside the cylinders. Any jigger that forced the tumblers in line would leave scratches on 'em, wouldn't it?"

"Should." Clark took another drag at his pipe. "I've got to have an order from the manager before I start monkeying with those locks."

"You'll get it," Mack promised. He paused on his way out. "Say, how do you master-key locks, anyway?"

"Two or three ways of doing it. The locks here have a second plug that fits around the first like a ring. Then each tumbler is set to line up with either the plug or with the master ring. The passkey turns the plug but not the ring, and the room key turns the plug and the ring together as one piece."

"That should make picking easier," Mack commented.

"Yep, it gives two chances to get the tumblers in line, but it's still just about as hard a job as it ever was."

"You sure know your locks!" Mack exclaimed.

"I ought to. I've taken enough of 'em apart to have an idea what they're like inside."

"Well, I'm coming back here sometime after three. Can you have the locks opened by then?"

"Sure—if I get an order from the manager."

"I said you'd get that." Mack went up to the ground floor and into the lobby. Westborough was in there reading a newspaper which he laid down upon seeing the detective.

144

"Lieutenant Mack, I do not wish to be obtrusive, but I should like very much to have you glance at this analysis."

Smiling at the little man's persistence, Mack took the papers from him and ran through them hastily.

"You've got it all down in black and white. So what?"

"I thought it might prove helpful as a means of approach," Westborough began hesitantly.

"Listen here," Mack scoffed. "You've got a lot of fine four-bit words here—I can't even pronounce some of 'em, let alone tell you what they mean—and it reads swell, but when it comes down to it, what do you say? Nothing that we don't already know, do you?"

"I suppose not."

"Crimes aren't solved by a guy sitting around on his fanny and thinking about 'em," Mack said patronizingly. "You've got to get the facts, and that calls for leg work. Leg work, that's what it takes. An ounce of leg work is worth a pound of theories. Do you know what I'm going to do today?"

Westborough shook his head.

"I've got the whole squad working on this case. We're going to comb every silver platter, every photographer, every steel foundry, and every other place we can think of where a guy might've got some cyanide. If he bought it, someone will remember, and if he hooked it—well, we'll probably be able to get a description of a stranger hanging around the plant that we can tie in with someone in the hotel. And I've got a lot more work to do right in this hotel—see? As soon as the afternoon shift comes on, I've got to have a powwow with the room clerk. I've got to find the chambermaid who turns down the beds in the west corridor and talk to all the elevator operators. Hell, I've even got to see the shine in the washroom who fixed Chilton's panties. That, Mr. Westborough, is the way crimes are cleared up, and it's the only way."

This was one of the longest speeches Mack had ever made, and it was met by the perfect tribute paid to the Gettysburg address—silence. Mack went on in a somewhat kindlier manner. "That wasn't such a bad point you made about Larson's laboratory. We'll have to check that up pretty carefully." He continued to thumb through Westborough's notes. "Hell, what's all this junk about Tacitus?"

Westborough flushed. "I didn't mean to include that sheet. It contains some reflections of my own that are really not germane to the case."

Mack's eyes traversed the paper with an interest far from perfunctory.

"You know a lot about poisons, don't you, Westborough?"

"A little, yes."

Mack loosed a Parthian arrow as he crossed the lobby. "Well, take care that you don't know too much for your own good."

XVI

"REGAL PLATING WORKS" read the legend on the building directory. Mack grinned. "So do I, but I don't have to put up a sign about it."

It was a dingy five-story red-brick building, and it stood in the middle of the wholesale and small manufacturing district just north of the Loop. Trucks rattled and rumbled over the ancient stone pavement of the street outside while the detective waited for the elevator. It descended at last—an antediluvian car with twisted gratings. A crusty old operator was wrangling with a smart-aleck messenger boy as Mack stepped inside the car.

"Them boys are always leaving the doors to the shaft open," he grumbled. "The inspector gives me the old Ned for it, but it ain't my fault. I can't be on every floor at once to watch the kids."

"Tough luck," Mack sympathized. "Four."

146

"That's the Regal Plating Works. They've got the entire floor. Peerless Plating is on the second, and there's still another on the third. You'd think those fellows would spread out a bit over the rest of the city instead of nesting up with their competitors, wouldn't you?"

He canvassed the Regal Plating Works and the plating concerns on the third and second floors with fruitless results. Any worker in a silver-plating establishment, he concluded, would have no difficulty in contriving the demise of his mother-in-law in case the old lady became unbearable. But an outsider—well, that was something else again! The places were all practically burglar proof, and a careful check was kept on the stuff. He called on several photographers and two or three photo-engravers in the neighborhood and reached the same conclusions with regard to these businesses. Clearly the tracing of the cyanide was going to prove troublesome.

He returned to the Hotel Equable and approached the desk. Collins, the room clerk, was for the moment unoccupied.

"Where do you keep your passkeys?" Mack questioned him.

Collins jerked open a drawer. "In here. We only have two of them."

"Keep records of when you let a bellhop or somebody take one?"

"We keep records of just about everything in the hotel business." Collins referred to some reports. "A bellman borrowed a key about four o'clock to take a package to the sixth floor."

"How long'd he have it?"

"Fifteen minutes."

"Humph!" Mack pondered. "Anybody using either of those keys last night?"

"No, both of them were at the desk all evening."

"Are you just saying that, or did you actually see them?"

"I saw 'em several times," Collins bridled. "Last time was somewhere around ten."

"And several times before that, huh?"

"Yes."

"That's that!" Mack exclaimed. He lit a fresh cigar and took two or three meditative puffs. "Did Graham leave his key at the desk last night?"

"Yes, about eight-thirty or so. He was with his family and Mrs. Hammond. If you want to know the time they got back, I can tell you that too. It was a quarter to twelve"

"One thing at a time," Mack cut in. "Where was Swink's key?"

"I don't know, but it wasn't here. He got it early in the evening, and he never did bring it back again."

"That checks with what you told Phelan—O'Ryan's Man Friday," Mack admitted. "Speaking of Phelan, how were you able to remember all the times people asked for keys and so on? I couldn't do it."

The room clerk appeared to be pleased at the compliment. "We've been trained to keep our eyes open, and you have to remember names and faces in the hotel business. I'll admit, however, that some of the times on that list were guesswork."

"Including any of the people in the west corridor?" Mack wanted to know.

"No, I'm pretty sure about those. Most of them have been here for some time."

"How long has Chilton been here?"

"Since Monday, I think." Collins consulted the register and nodded confirmatively. "Yes, that's right. Say, I just happened to think of something about him."

"What?"

"Before he registered he asked if Swink was staying here."

"The hell he did!"

"When I gave him Swink's room number he asked for something on the third floor," Collins went on. "I fixed him up with a room as close to Swink's as I could manage. Figured they were friends."

"I thought there was something screwy about that guy!" Mack ejaculated. "He told us he'd never seen Swink before he came here." He scrutinized attentively the tiers of pigeonholes in the key rack. "Were you at the desk all evening, Collins?"

"I was on duty, wasn't I? In fact, I stayed three or four hours overtime because you kept Larson upstairs."

"If you were away from the desk for even two or three minutes," Mack persisted, "somebody might've borrowed one of the passkeys."

Collins said, "You're barking up the wrong tree this time. I was here every minute, and I could probably prove it if I had to. People were coming in and out of the lobby all evening."

Mack strolled over to the elevators and buttonholed an operator. "Know a guy named Chilton?"

"I do now."

"Take him up last night?"

"Sure. He was with the fat guy that got croaked— Swink."

"Didn't you take Chilton up alone?"

"Not me."

Similar questioning of the other operators yielded equally barren results, and the detective ascended to the upper floors of the hotel in search of a chambermaid. Her name was Irma Egstrom, and she admitted having been in Swink's room at nine o'clock.

"See anything that looked funny while you were in there?" Mack interrogated.

"Not a thing. The room looked just like it always does."

"Was there a diamond stickpin on the dresser?"

"Yes," she confessed. "I should've reported that to the housekeeper, but I forgot about it."

"Did you meet anybody in the hall?"

"Only Mrs. Blakely."

"What time was that?"

"Nine-thirty or so. Just as I'd finished up the last room on the floor."

The girl's story corroborated Hammond's to a certain extent, Mack reflected while riding downstairs. At least it fixed the time of the murderer's visit as definitely after nine o'clock.

An array of white porcelain washbowls gleamed from the lavatory. The nickel-plated fittings were polished to mirror brightness, and the tiled floor was scrubbed immaculately. Mack held his hands under a metal spheroid containing liquid soap and turned on the hot water. A gentleman of African ancestry approached to lay a neatly folded towel beside him.

"Yassuh, boss?"

Mack sloshed his hands about in the bowl and picked up the towel. "You on duty last night, George?"

"Yassuh."

"Know Mr. Chilton?"

"Ah does now, boss."

The elevator pilot, Mack recalled, had said practically the same thing. He wondered by what underground channels of information the account of Chilton's importance in the Swink case had gotten around to the hotel employees.

"Was Chilton in here last night?"

150

"Yassuh, he sure was!" The Negro chuckled throatily. "His suspenders was in a bad way, and Ah had to sew a button on his pants."

Chilton's excuse for leaving the bar was just silly enough to be true, Mack mused, or else he had already bribed the coon. The detective glowered threateningly.

"I'm on the police force, George."

"Thought you was, suh."

"And if you don't come clean with me I'll put you in the pen for thirty years," Mack admonished sternly. "Did Chilton slip you five bucks to tell me he was in the washroom?"

The Negro's consternation was apparently genuine. "No suh! Ah ain't never seen him today. Honest Ah ain't, boss."

Mack said, "All right, George, have a cigar," and left the lavatory. The leg work he had bragged about to Westborough was getting him exactly nowhere, he reflected on his way to the carpenter shop.

Hugh Clark looked up from his bench. "I've got your locks ready for you."

"Which is which?"

"You're looking at Swink's now. Take this magnifying glass and you can see better."

Mack inspected the pile of parts from the lock in the best Sherlockian tradition, and then leaned over to survey those from its mate. He vented a low whistle of astonishment.

"Both of 'em picked, huh?"

"I'd call it that," Clark agreed curtly.

PART FOUR: *Saturday Night*

XVII

JERRY SPANGER, the inevitable thin cigar twisted into the corner of his mouth, looked up from his newspaper as Lieutenant John Mack entered the lobby. He rose to his feet and shuffled toward the desk in time to hear Mack ask Collins:

"Chilton in?"

"I'll have the operator call," Collins replied.

"Wait a minute," Spanger cut in, "Johnny, your friend Chilton was trying to take French leave tonight."

"What?"

"I told him it'd be healthier to ask you before he pulled out as long as he was one of the principal witnesses in a murder case."

"How long ago was this?"

"About fifteen minutes. He had his suitcase packed and wanted to pay his bill and check out."

Larry Collins volunteered further information: "He got a wire earlier in the evening."

"What was in it?"

"How should I know?"

"Thought you fellows opened wires."

Collins flushed. "Why should we? We can tell by the star system just how important the message is. One star is a rush message and two stars—"

"Yeh, I know. How was this one marked?" Mack inquired.

"One star."

"Humph! Tell the operator not to ring. I'm going right up."

Mack rushed to the elevators, Spanger following. A car slowed to a perfect stop at the exact floor level, and Theocritus Lucius Westborough got out.

"Lieutenant Mack, I just saw you arrive from the upstairs window in the corridor."

"Did you see Chilton?" Mack wanted to know.

"Yes, he was standing by the window with me."

"What'd he do when he saw me?"

"He left immediately and went toward his room."

Mack laid plans with Napoleonic celerity. "Can you drive a car?" Westborough murmured assent, and Mack directed, "Get in my car out there and run it around to the alley and park by the fire escape. Keep the engine running till you hear from me."

Westborough took the proffered car keys and dashed for the front entrance. It was a very creditable dash, too, for a man of his years. Mack and Spanger stepped into the elevator, and the car shot upwards to the third floor. Mack ran down the corridor with the speed of a track man, Spanger panting to keep pace with him. He reached the west corridor and glanced toward the end. A tall man who carried a suitcase, was fumbling with the fire-escape door.

"Chilton!" Mack exclaimed and darted after him.

The fugitive had a good start, and, despite his suitcase, was making excellent time in the descent of the fire escape. Mack followed down the steel stairs. At the second floor the stairs swung to the ground under Chilton's weight, and Mack was so close behind that the counterpoise had no chance to get into action. He reached the ground just as Chilton climbed into a cruising Yellow. Gears ground together in a noisy shriek, and the cab was off like a golden streak. But Mack's own car was waiting, with Westborough at the wheel and the engine running. Mack sprang inside and quickly displaced Westborough from the driver's seat.

The Yellow turned the corner, a block in advance of its pursuers, and shot south on Michigan. Mack reached the boulevard just as a green light changed to red. He turned into the boulevard in defiance of the signal, barely escaping collision with an ancient Ford, loaded with five fat Italians, who shrieked anathemas which neither Mack nor Westborough heard. The little man was leaning tensely forward in his seat.

"So this is what a man hunt is like. There is a certain indescribable thrill."

Mack grunted and stepped on the gas. "The fool hasn't a chance. We'll catch him in half a mile."

From ahead came the clamor of a bell. It was ringing steadily and monotonously, and to Chicagoans it meant just one thing. "The bridge!" Mack exclaimed. "Some damn barge wants through. We're sunk if they beat us across."

He held the throttle down and opened the siren. Its shrill, persistent humming tossed the gage of battle to the bell's monotonous dinging, or so Westborough fancied. "Don't let him through," the siren shrieked, while the bell dinned, "You haven't time."

Traffic was heavy on Michigan as always, but Mack wove in and out with the skill of a practiced Chicago driver. Cars gave way on either side for the police siren as the distance between the two cars lessened to half a block. Then Westborough noticed the gates. Pointed wooden barriers descended from opposite sides of the boulevard and from both sides of the bridge, parting the waves of traffic as the Red Sea had been parted for the children of Israel. The bridge, a ponderous, clumsy mass, began to rise.

"We've got him now," Mack jubilated.

It was true. The Yellow slithered to an abrupt stop before the wooden gates as Mack, by a deft motion of the wheel, brought his car alongside.

"Out of there, Chilton!" he commanded.

If Chilton had been contemplating a break on foot he thought better of it and stepped sheepishly out of the cab. The driver apologized, "I didn't know you was cops or I would've stopped before."

"You heard the siren, didn't you?" Mack asked sternly, and turned to Chilton. "Get in," he directed curtly.

Chilton retrieved his suitcase from the taxi, tossed a bill to the driver, and stepped inside Mack's car.

"What's the big idea of doing a sneak on us?" Mack demanded. "Don't you know you're a material witness?"

Chilton, evidently trying to brazen it out, said icily, "I didn't know that I was under arrest."

"You're going to be," Mack reported severely. "Whatever'd you want to do a damn fool stunt like this for? Didn't you know it would be a dead giveaway?"

"I can explain."

"You'll have to—down at headquarters. The New York police talked to Crabb and Cunningham."

"If you go back to the hotel first," Chilton told him, "you'll find a letter for you."

"What?"

"I wasn't pulling out without letting you know who I was. I left it in my room."

"All right, we'll go back to the hotel, but you're going to have to do some tall talking. No James Chilton ever worked for Crabb and Cunningham."

Mack, who drove rapidly at all times, reached the Hotel Equable in a very few minutes. He drew up before the red-and-white striped canopy at the entrance, parking expertly before a sign which plainly read, "No Parking." His hand rested in his coat pocket as Chilton stepped from the car, his shrewd, watchful eyes never for a minute relaxing their vigil over that man.

The newspapers had been generous in the space allotted to the "Equable Murder," and a horde of curiosity seekers had been thronging about the hotel ever since, to the great disgust of Swann, who saw no way to rid himself of these unwelcome visitors. A number of them were now ensconced in the most comfortable chairs in the lobby, having driven away by their presence the regular occupants, even such seasoned veterans as Sarah Blakely. Many inquisitive glances were now directed at the detective and his party, which Mack returned with contemptuous annoyance. He had no patience with busybodies.

"Upstairs," he directed shortly. "We'll talk in your room, Chilton."

Jerry Spanger and other Equable employees, by herculean efforts and with the firm cooperation of the police force, had succeeded in convincing the idly curious that it was healthier not to wander about the upper floors. Hence the west corridor was left severely alone.

Mack opened the door with Chilton's key and they stepped over the threshold. Westborough followed. The detective, who seemed to have a liking for the little man, made no attempt to order him away.

"Well?" Mack demanded and Chilton pointed at the writing desk. Mack picked up an envelope with the Hotel Equable return card in its upper corner. He tore it open and perused its contents in austere silence.

"A fine story, Chilton," he sneered finally. "Can you prove it?"

Chilton reached toward his breast pocket, but Mack stopped him.

"Keep your hands away from there! Frisk him, Westborough."

"Frisk?" Westborough repeated, then his face cleared. "Oh, yes, to be sure."

He patted the outside of Chilton's pockets with his thin white hands. "He doesn't have a revolver."

"Good!" Mack grunted. "Now hand me those papers he was trying to get."

Westborough reached in Chilton's pocket and handed the detective an opened letter together with a billfold. Mack read aloud.

"The Amco Detective Agency—licensed, bonded. Reliable male and female operatives of all nationalities, trades, professions, or occupations. Personal surveillance —with or without autos. Dictograph and wire service. Dependable advice on confidential matters, including patent infringements, blackmail and threatening letters. Escorts or watchmen furnished for all occasions. Call on Amco—days, nights, or Sundays. Not the largest but the best."

Mack put the letter into his pocket. "I've heard of Amco—but these things can be forged. I knew a crook who carried credentials from twenty different agencies. We stopped his racket, though, and he's doing time. Why didn't you bring these out before, Chilton?"

"I would have if they were fakes, wouldn't I?" Chilton demanded belligerently. "But since they're the real thing I didn't want to tip my hand, at least not until I'd given the client a chance to have his say. We claim our investigations are confidential, and we mean it."

Mack thought it over. "That doesn't sound so screwy. Now that you mention it, I remember the crook I was telling you about always used to flash his fake credentials right away. But if I pass that stall, you'll have to still explain why you beat it down the fire escape."

"Same reason."

"You got a wire tonight," Mack reminded him.

"That from the client?"

"No—headquarters."

"What'd you do with it?" Mack demanded.

Chilton took a yellow envelope from his coat pocket. Mack read the telegram thoughtfully.

"Humph! It's signed Amco, but what the hell? Anyone can stick a name on a telegram. They tell you to say nothing unless you can't help yourself. You're in that fix now, Chilton, and I'd advise you to talk. Who's your client?"

"I can't tell you."

"You can't or you won't?"

"Even if I knew," Chilton said emphatically,

"I probably wouldn't tell you. But I don't, and that's straight. The chief got the dope and gave me instructions."

"You didn't see your client?"

"Nope."

"Nor hear his name?"

"No. The chief can be close-mouthed as hell."

"He told you to shadow Swink, eh?"

"It wasn't exactly shadowing—we call it personal surveillance."

"You weren't so clever when you asked for a room near Swink," Mack sneered. Chilton stiffened in the manner of the beggar reputed to have said, "Gentlemen, you can give or not give, as you choose—but don't tell me how to run my business."

"I didn't know Swink from Adam so I had to have his room number. How was I to know the guy was going to be murdered? Ordinarily the room clerk would have forgotten all about it when he saw me chumming with Swink."

"What were your instructions?"

"To register at the hotel, strike up an acquaintance with Swink, and pretend I was a sucker if he tried to sell me anything."

"What else?"

"To get evidence that would stick on a charge of using the mails to defraud."

"What?" Mack exploded, and Chilton repeated his answer.

"What was Swink's racket?" Mack asked.

"As near as I could make out he was on the level. I had the Georgetown mine investigated; we've got a connection with an agency in Denver. They wired on Thursday afternoon the mine was bona fide and Swink an accredited representative."

"Know anything about Swink's past?" Chilton shook his head at this question. "Wasn't that part of the investigation?" Mack persisted.

"If it was, another of our men handled it. As I said before, the chief never tells his operatives any more than he can help. I don't think Swink had been any mama's angel child, though."

"What makes you say that?" Mack inquired quickly.

Chilton shrugged his shoulders. "Call it a hunch if you want to. In this game you get a feeling that tells you whether a man's on the level or a crook. You ought to know that."

"I do," Mack declared, his eyes fixed sternly on Chilton. "Sure you're not keeping something back?"

"I've told you all I know. You'll have to get the rest from the home office."

"Your name isn't Chilton, of course?"

"No, it's Jasper. Robert Jasper. Chilton was one of the guys who came over on the *Mayflower*."

"To be sure!" Westborough exclaimed. "No wonder that the name struck a familiar chord in my memory. James Chilton was one of the forty-one signatories of the historic Mayflower Compact. He died the same month as the landing at Plymouth and left no male heirs but a daughter Mary, who—"

"Anyway," Jasper interrupted, "I figured the name would make a good front." He bent down for his suitcase. "There's just time to make my train."

"Wait!" Mack's voice barked like a pistol shot. "I'm not through with you, Chilton, or Jasper, or whatever your name is. Did we search your room the night of the murder?"

Surprise was written large on Jasper's face. "Why—yes. All of them were searched, weren't they?"

"Your person too?"

"Oh, sure—your men did a complete and thorough job."

"Yes," Mack admitted, "Phelan was in charge, and Phelan is a smart young fellow. He doesn't miss many bets. Not many."

"Well, what of it? He didn't find anything."

"That's just the point!" Mack ejaculated. "He didn't! He didn't find those papers you showed me. Why not?"

Jasper stroked his chin but volunteered no answer.

"Don't tell me you hid 'em under the rug or anything like that," Mack challenged. "Phelan would've spotted any ordinary hide-out. But you had 'em ditched in a good safe place. Where?"

"There's a trick pocket in this," said Jasper, indicating the suitcase. He edged toward the door, but Mack's broad shoulders blocked the entrance.

"Open it up," Mack demanded peremptorily.

"Let me see your search warrant," Jasper hedged.

"Oh, you want one of those, do you? I'll get it all right, but you'll stick in the jug till I do. Now, are you going to give me the keys or not?"

Jasper sullenly took a key case from his pocket. "It's this little one."

Mack flung the suitcase upon the bed and threw out helter-skelter socks, shirts, ties, and pajamas in a way that reminded Westborough of a terrier digging in sand. "Where's the trick pocket?" he demanded.

Jasper pressed an almost invisible bump, and a flap, cunningly concealed within the lid, opened. Mack explored the recess with his hand and whistled. He drew out a curious object which looked like a long curved needle attached to a handle.

"Do you know what this is?"'

Westborough shook his head. "If I might hazard a surmise—"

"It's called a pick," Mack interrupted, "and it's used in opening cylinder locks. Swink's room was entered with one and so was Graham's."

Westborough caught the glint of steel as Mack's hand withdrew from his pocket. The next instant there was a sharp click, and Jasper stood with manacled hands.

"Robert Jasper-Chilton," Mack pronounced sternly, "you may say you're a private dick, but you're just the common or garden variety of killer to me."

PART FIVE: *Sunday*

XVIII

SUNDAY MORNINGS were surprisingly quiet at the Hotel Equable. Most of the guests slept until noon.

Westborough, returning to his room from an early breakfast, noted with approval that the chambermaid had completed her ministrations while he was enjoying his toasted English muffins and marmalade. She had left the windows open, and the morning sun streamed from the court in a blaze of glory. After a week of deluges and drizzles, typical of a Chicago April, it was good for the soul, Westborough reflected, to discover that the sun still existed.

Seating himself at his writing desk, Westborough took a fountain pen from his pocket and several sheets of stationery from the drawer. Despite Mack's scorn of his first analysis, it amused the little man to make a permanent record of his conclusions. He unscrewed the top from his fountain pen and began in a cramped handwriting, which, by no means a thing of beauty, was entirely legible—to others as well as to Westborough.

"Chilton admits to picking the lock of Swink's door and searching his room," he wrote. "This was done, he claims, on Wednesday night, a matter not impossible, since from Mrs. Hammond's story we know that Swink was away the entire evening. Chilton—I must remember to call him Jasper—denies being in Swink's room at any time during the night of the murder other than the period from eight-thirty to eight fifty-five when he was there with Swink. He could not, under any circumstances, have placed the tube above the door then, since the chambermaid entered the room at nine o'clock.

"Jasper's alibi for the balance of the evening remains apparently impregnable. He left the bar at ten o'clock—not at nine-thirty—and stayed in the lavatory long enough for the porter to sew a button upon his trousers—dear me, I should like to know just how long that operation takes. I must remember to ask the porter to perform that office for me. At any rate, Jasper was not gone from the bar for longer than fifteen minutes which, deducting the time spent in the washroom, leaves an extremely scanty margin in which to climb the stairs to the third floor (no elevator operator remembers taking him up), pick the lock of Swink's door—I understand that this undertaking is difficult—cut from the floor and fold back the carpet, and insert the test tube above the door.

"Jasper, naturally enough, denies picking the lock of the Grahams' apartment. Yet it was undoubtedly entered in that manner. Can there be another pick or similar implement belonging to a guest in the west corridor? But if so, where and how was it concealed during the exhaustive police search.

"Lieutenant Mack, clear-sighted and shrewd as he is, does not seem to realize the full significance of the poltergeist which so terrified our worthy Mrs. Blakely. Jasper's employment terminated automatically with Swink's death, and he could have had no further interest in Swink's private papers. Hence, having already searched the room, as he himself admits, *before* Swink's death, he would scarcely search it again *after*. Ergo, Mrs. Blakely's poltergeist was other than Jasper.

"Jasper, of course, may be lying, but that is a matter readily susceptible to verification when—"

At this point Westborough's fountain pen ran dry, and he refilled it from the inkwell. But the interruption to the continuous flow of words had destroyed his trend of thought. He could not recall exactly just what he had been going to say next.

Absent-mindedly he fumbled with the drawer of the desk. A pipe might help to collect his now random and scattered ideas if anything could. His pipe was amber-stemmed with a bowl carved to resemble a human skull. Westborough had found it in a little shop in a side street in Rome, and, despite its grotesque shape, was singularly attached to it, as the well-bitten mouthpiece and heavy caking of the bowl would have told even an amateur disciple of the gentleman from Baker Street. Westborough's hand continued to explore the recesses of the drawer until it encountered the second object of his search—a yellow oilskin tobacco pouch.

Westborough, to whom smoking was a rite and not a pastime, unwrapped it with great care. "Dear me!" he exclaimed in vexation upon seeing that only a few scattered grains of tobacco remained in the bottom of the pouch. Although Westborough's scholarly pertinacity had collated such an enormous volume of scattered references to Trajan as to evoke the admiration of historical authorities, the little man was singularly incompetent when confronted with life's minor crises. He debated now whether it would be better to call the desk or whether he should descend to the cigar counter in person for a can of tobacco. Either alternative offered objections. He did not wish to leave his room now, but on the other hand the bellboy might not bring the right brand and it would be necessary to order him to return. Moreover, Westborough did not like bellboys. He felt that they were laughing at him behind their uniformed backs—as they usually were.

A third alternative presented itself, enabling Westborough to cut the Gordian knot. He knocked at the domicile of his next-door neighbor, and the tall form of Ronald E. Graham appeared in the doorway. Graham had a good briar pipe in his mouth, and the air was filled with the fragrance of tobacco smoke, which Westborough sniffed appreciatively.

"My tobacco is exhausted," he began with his habitual hesitancy. "I was upon the point of descending to the lobby when I remembered that you and I are devotees of the same brand. If you will be kind enough—"

165

"Fill your pouch," Graham interrupted heartily. "Just opened up a new pound can this morning."

The familiar blue-and-green-striped can was on the smoking stand. The smoking stand was near the window and beside a portable drawing board. There was a drawing tacked to the board, and Westborough's curiosity vanquished his manners.

"Do you object to my examining your drawing?"

Graham smiled. "Look all you want to, but there isn't much to see. I'm doing a pen-and-ink sketch over a photostat."

"Is that what you call a photostat?" Westborough questioned. "But why do you make your drawing upon it? Your lines are scarcely visible to me."

"Tricks to all trades, Westborough," Graham laughed. "I order the photostat for any size I want, and the proportions are fixed automatically—no scaling and no pantograph work. The photostat was, of course, ordered from a photograph of the original object, so my drawing will be right in every detail. When I'm through I have the photostat bleached, and there'll be nothing left upon this paper but my India ink lines."

"Most ingenious," Westborough muttered. "Do you do much of this sort of work?"

Graham shook his head. "Only occasionally now. I used to do quite a bit, though."

Turning away from the drawing board, Westborough remembered his manners. "I certainly am indebted to you for the tobacco. Is Mrs. Graham out? And I do not see young Cedric either."

"Lu took the kid down to Elgin for a few days," Graham explained. "Norah Hammond invited her. Norah's folks have a big house there and are always glad to have company. It will do both of the girls good to get away from here."

Filling the death's-head pipe with grave deliberation, Westborough agreed with his host. "The atmosphere of this hotel during the past few days is scarcely the environment for your young son," he pronounced. "I must go now, as I do not wish to keep you from your work."

"Don't rush off," Graham protested. "I can go right on working. You won't bother me any."

Our social amenities, Westborough reflected, can cause an endless amount of red tape and useless persiflage. He was quite ready to depart to his own room, and his host was undoubtedly just as eager to get rid of him. Nevertheless, social usage decreed that Graham should protest against Westborough's departure and that Westborough should appear to take his host's protestations as genuine. Graham settled back to his drawing board upon Westborough's urging, and the little man touched a match to the death's head as he watched the artist fill his pen from a bottle of India ink.

Under Graham's skillful hands simple black lines grew into live things. It is always a pleasant experience, thought Westborough, to watch while someone else does creative work. What was the word so much in vogue today? The word with the peculiar German sound— yes, kibitz.

"Has Mr. Hammond gone to Elgin also?" Westborough inquired because he could think of nothing else to say.

Graham nodded. "He drove them down early this morning. Fred won't stay any longer than he can help, though. From two or three things he's dropped I gather he doesn't get along any too well with his wife's relatives. Norah's an only child, and her parents think that no man on earth could be good enough for her, as nearly as I can make out."

Further conversation languished, and Westborough announced once more that he must take his departure. He thanked his host again for the tobacco, said he hoped that Mrs. Graham and Cedric would have a pleasant time, advised Mr. Graham not to work too hard, and, the amenities being at last entirely satisfied, returned to his own room.

Back once more at his writing desk, he discovered that the death's head had failed him. His thoughts refused to focus upon the death of Elmo Swink and diffused upon a dozen different topics. Miss Gant, for instance. Westborough was sure that she didn't have a great deal of money. The weekly bills were placed last night in the mail rack. Miss Gant might not be able to pay. She might even be asked to leave the hotel.

"Dear me!" Westborough voiced his favorite expletive and reflected upon the contingency. One couldn't—even if one were an elderly recluse—offer money to a comparative stranger of the opposite sex. One couldn't tell the office that one would stand responsible for her hotel bill— not without creating a juicy topic for Mrs. Blakely and Mrs. Hatteras to discuss. But on the other hand, one couldn't allow a young lady to suffer—not when one had money which one would never miss. "The very thing!" Westborough, beaming like Mr. Jarndyce or the Brothers Cheeryble, suddenly exclaimed.

He stepped across the corridor but checked his fist as it was about to descend upon Miss Gant's door. Most of the Equable guests were in the habit of sleeping until noon on Sundays, he realized.

Somehow, though, he didn't feel like returning to his writing desk. It was a glorious and balmy April Sunday—one of those tidbits which Mother Chicago occasionally tosses her children to make up for too frequent punishment. Perhaps a stroll through Lincoln Park? Later a motion picture or a call upon his sister-in-law? This simple program appearing attractive, Westborough strolled down the corridor, nearly bumping into Mr. Larson on his way out.

Westborough bowed gravely to the night clerk, whom he liked, and Larson responded with a cordial "Good morning!" However, Larson showed no signs of doing anything but continuing to block

168

traffic in the corridor, so Westborough marched alone toward the elevators.

His jaw dropped in surprise as Robert Jasper stepped from an ascending car. Jasper said, "Good-morning," in a tone purposely modulated to discourage further conversation, but Westborough did not allow himself to be discouraged.

"May I congratulate you upon your fortunate release, Mr. Jasper?"

His smile was genuine, and even Jasper unbent. "Thanks." He started toward his own room, but Westborough interrupted once more.

"At the risk of being thought impertinent, I would like to ask what happened."

"The agency put up a bond, and I'm out," Jasper said shortly. "I can't leave town, though, or the bond is forfeited."

"Ah, is not one so bond a prisoner still?" Westborough shamelessly misquoted from *Yeomen of the Guard*. He added, as casually as he could make it, "Did the police learn anything concerning Mr. Swink's past?"

The question wasn't casual enough, for Jasper was on his guard again. He said curtly, "If they did, I didn't hear about it," and went toward his room. Westborough's eyes followed him until he had disappeared around the corner. Then Westborough signaled an elevator and rode downstairs, his face very thoughtful.

Fred Hammond's blue streamlined De Soto purred westward on all six. To Hammond, the exhilaration of eating up the road under his rubber tires was comparable only to the pleasure derived from a "long tall one" or from a game of stud with selected cronies. One of his greatest delights was to pass a car which was doing at least sixty while another car sped toward him at an equal pace. Seeing a chance to indulge in this harmless amusement now, he swerved to the left

169

and pressed down the throttle. For a breath-taking instant the two cars hung neck and neck on the road while the automobile from the opposite direction drew nearer at an ominously fast rate. Then Hammond, forging slightly ahead, jerked his wheel sharply to the right and made it—with inches to spare.

Seated beside her husband, Norah Hammond begged, "Fred, please don't do that again."

"We're still here, aren't we?" Hammond asked.

Norah Hammond, laughing happily, laid her small hand on top of his large and hairy one. Fred Hammond returned the pressure. Two nights ago it had seemed that nothing could be the same again between him and Norah. Then, in a whirlwind of sudden passion, he had swept her into his arms, and their misunderstanding had dissolved into the mists from which it had sprung.

Hammond slowed down as they approached a roadside stand in order to buy ice-cream cones for Cedric and the two women. He preferred a cigar himself and lit one, allowing the motor to die while he waited for the girls to finish their ice cream.

Luella Graham gave the balance of her cone to Cedric, who had already gobbled his. "I still don't understand, Fred, how you were able to persuade the police to let you go out on the road."

"I got to earn a living, don't I?" Hammond demanded with a chuckle. "Besides," he added mysteriously, "I got a friend in the City Comptroller's office."

He started the motor once more and was up to seventy again before they had gone little more than a block. He knew there was no need to hurry, but he couldn't help himself. Speed, a matter of dollars and cents when on the road, had become a confirmed habit when pleasure driving.

However, he slowed down to conform to local speed laws as they rolled over the red-brick paved streets of Elgin. He parked the car before a large frame house, of the bay window and cupola period of architecture, which was built on an embankment about twenty feet above the street level. Hammond was visibly hesitant about leaving the car.

"Your dad always manages to get my goat," he whispered to his wife.

She patted his hand in the manner of a wife when she feels that her husband is no more than a spoiled, sulky boy. "I know, darling, but you will stay for dinner, won't you? Mother will feel so badly if you don't."

Hammond grinned. "Oh, I'll do that, but, for heaven's sake, keep him off of politics." He lifted a bag in either hand and began to climb the long flight of steps. "I'll have to clear out before long, you know, Norah. I've got to get back to the hotel and finish packing—you know I've got a tough day ahead tomorrow."

Norah Hammond smiled in the manner of a wife who is hearing an excuse for at least the hundredth time. "Yes, darling, of course."

Chris Larson intercepted Yvonne Gant in the corridor. Their meeting may have seemed like a coincidence, but it was not. Chris had foregone a whole hour of precious sleep in order to keep vigil beside her door. There were many things he had wanted to tell her, but when he saw her, a piquant vision in blue, he couldn't think of one of them.

She smiled in a friendly manner and said, "Good morning, Mr. Larson."

They walked toward the elevators. Chris Larson's working life had been too full to allow of much time for frivolity, and he had never acquired the free-and-easy manner with girls that he envied in Larry Collins. "Say something, you dope," he told himself angrily.

"This is a pleasant surprise, Miss Gant," he began aloud. "Will you—that is, I wonder if you will—I mean I'd be glad if you will—

have breakfast with me." ("There!" he told himself. "I've done it at last.")

Within the dining room, cool and spacious, Larson ordered a breakfast that would do credit to Gargantua. It started with strawberries, which were just beginning to come into season and were correspondingly costly, and continued through an incredible number of items. Miss Gant ate as though she were hungry, and Chris liked that. He could never abide women who toyed daintily with food.

"How about some more of those rolls and another pot of coffee?" he suggested.

"Gracious, no! I've eaten enough now for a boa constrictor!"

Chris laughed. Laughing was easy with this girl across the table. "If you're not doing anything special, what about a walk to Lincoln Park?" he proposed. "Or I can rent a car?"

"I like to walk," she told him simply.

Jerry Spanger glowered at Chris as they walked toward the front entrance. "He seems to have a grouch at the world," Miss Gant remarked.

"Only at me," Chris qualified. "We had a sort of quarrel the other night, and both of us are too stubborn to apologize." She didn't ask the cause of the quarrel, nor did he volunteer the information.

The lake was a rippling grayish green while a cloudless sky cupped the horizon like the "inverted bowl" of Omar Khayyam. Spring roistered like a hoyden, and Lincoln Park was transformed into a lady in delicate green. Tree and shrub were tentatively donning seasonal finery, and every bend in the curved path upon which they strolled disclosed fresh surprises. Here was an elm, straight and slim, here a dwarfish locust, then a maple and the gnarled bark of a cottonwood. It was good to see these old friends and others: a willow which drooped low over the lagoon and a row of sentinel-like poplars.

"They always remind me of folded-up umbrellas," Yvonne Gant laughed happily.

They reached a concrete bench and sat down. "A perfect day, isn't it?" Miss Gant observed, still thoughtful. "Lovely, but with that undertone of tragedy every perfect day should have."

"You're much too cynical," Larson commented. "And if you're thinking of the hotel—"

"Bother the hotel! This is the first chance I've had to forget that ghastly business."

"I wish you'd change your room," Chris said gravely.

Her hyacinthine eyes issued a cool challenge. "Why?"

"I don't like to think of you next to the room where that—"

"Oh, don't. You're giving me the jitters."

"But will you move, Miss Gant?" he persisted doggedly.

"I don't think so."

"I'd feel better if you would."

"Aren't you taking rather a lot on yourself, Mr. Larson?"

Chris flushed. "Probably I am. I beg your pardon."

"You clumsy oaf!" he said bitterly to himself. "Of course she resents being ordered around by a stranger."

"I'm sorry," she said in a softened voice, moving a perceptible trifle toward his side of the bench. "Just one of my silly moods. Pay no attention to it—*Chris*."

Their eyes met. For years Chris was to remember the glance which passed between them. It was like—he could think of no adequate simile. . . .

Hours later he said huskily, "I suppose we'd better have something to eat and get back."

She stirred lazily. "It couldn't last, of course. Minutes like these never do. You know that thing of Eugene Lee-Hamilton's? 'The present is mere grass, quick mown away; the past is stone and stands forever fast.' "

"I never got beyond Gunga Din in poetry."

"Such a solemn, serious Chris!" The laughter in her eyes changed to swift alarm. "Where is our sun? The sky is a smoky opal, and it terrifies me. I have a feeling something is due to happen tonight." A drop of rain splattered on the concrete path. "Something pretty awful," she continued, unheeding. "Silly, isn't it?"

Larson, his face very grave, shook his head. "That's why I wish you'd change your room."

"I can't! No, I can't tell you why, either. Maybe sometime, but not now." The rain spattered with increasing volume, and she caught his arm, lamenting, "We'll have to run, or my hat'll be ruined!"

Benny Devon, who had been away from the hotel the entire Sunday on errands of his own, returned to his room early in the evening. It was quiet there—quiet and private—and both of these virtues appealed to Benny Devon at that minute. He had a problem he wanted to think out.

He fumbled for a cigarette, but found the pack empty. He didn't have a cigar, either. Well, let it go. He had other things to think about. "It's a sweet racket," Devon said aloud. "I've got to prove it, sure, but that ought to be a pushover if that mug did what I think he did."

He tiptoed to the door and opened it an inch at a time. The corridor was deserted. "All downstairs, I guess," Devon thought. "Christ, how do I know there isn't a bull in one of those rooms?"

His forehead broke into a sweat as he slammed the door hastily shut. Eventually he summoned sufficient courage to open the door for a second look. He found the corridor as lonely and deserted as before.

"I don't like it," thought Benny Devon. "Something tells me I'm going to get a bad break, but, Christ! if I don't do it tonight, I may never get another chance. Pull yourself together, Benny, you've cracked tougher cribs. It's gravy, kid, just so much gravy!"

His rubber soles were soundless on the carpeted floor of the corridor. It wasn't necessary to move on tiptoes, but Devon took that extra precaution. He stopped before a door to peer once more up and down the corridor. "Jeez! If there should be a bull"

Tense as a coiled steel spring, Devon flopped to his knees. The door was locked, but no lock had been known to stop Benny Devon for long. This one yielded within a few minutes. Devon sighed in audible relief when he was able to step within the room and close the door behind him. For a minute he stood with the stillness of a statue while he strained his little pointed ears. "Coast's clear now!" he decided, slinking toward the window. He took a brief look at the open air. "Still raining! What a lousy burg!"

Moving carefully, slowly, and methodically, Benny Devon proceeded to ransack the room. It didn't take him long. He opened the door of a closet and felt deep within its recess. Then:

"That's it!" Devon exulted. "That's your meal ticket out of Chi! To hell with the bulls now! You've got the gravy, kid! You're sitting pretty—"

With the quickness of a puma Devon stiffened into immobility. He had heard the sharp click which tells of a key being inserted within a lock. Like a trapped beast's, his eyes glared helplessly from one side of the room to another in a frantic endeavor to find a hiding place. "God!" breathed Benny Devon, and for the first time in his life the expletive was a prayer.

He flattened himself behind the door, motionless as a shadow. Only the preternatural stiffness of his back, the tense straining of neck and throat muscles betrayed his desperation. His hand clenched with death-like rigor about the object he had taken from the closet. If his luck held, thought Benny Devon. If his luck held—

"It's me or him now! Me or him. Christ, I've got to—"

The knob turned as the door commenced to swing inward.

XIX

THE CHAIR, a tall one of gilt and needlepoint tapestry, was styled in the manner of a period when wigs were worn high, and the rigid etiquette of the Sun King's court permitted no relaxation. Obviously intended as a decoration for the lobby and not for use, it did not look particularly comfortable. Nevertheless, as it was the only chair available, Westborough seated himself gingerly upon its edge and fell into a study.

"Hi, there. Still solving the crime?" Lieutenant Mack's voice eventually interrupted Westborough's meditations.

"I have made a few more notes if you care to see them."

"I might take a look at them," Mack said good-naturedly. "Have you seen Jerry Spanger around anywhere?"

Upon Westborough's replying negatively, Mack strode to the desk to repeat the question to Larry Collins. "He hasn't been in the lobby for an hour or two," the room clerk said, "but I can have a bellman hunt him for you."

"Do that," Mack requested, "and when you find him, tell him I'll be in Westborough's room—or Larson's." He glanced at the large octagonal electric clock above the desk and set his watch. "Twenty minutes to nine."

Westborough's room was blue with smoke. "I forgot to open the window before I left this morning," Westborough apologized, jerking it up now. Returning to his guest, he brought out the oilskin pouch and offered it to the detective.

"Do you smoke a pipe, Lieutenant Mack?"

"Like cigars better," Mack grunted laconically, bringing one from his vest pocket. He lit it reflectively. "You're a funny little mutt, Westborough, but I think you've got a head on you. What do you think is the next thing to do?"

Westborough suggested diffidently, "Have you investigated the guests' telephone calls? I believe the hotel keeps a record."

"We wouldn't miss a bet like that," Mack declared emphatically. He chuckled. "The one thing I learned was how the Blakely woman got all her dope on my family. Remember the other morning?"

"Oh yes, the experiment in psychometry."

"If that's what you call it. Well, the old girl had called up her niece and talked to her nearly an hour on Friday morning. The niece lives in Westmay, and the world doesn't hold a bigger gossip monger. She knows more about what her neighbors are doing than they do themselves."

"Most psychical experiences turn out like that," was Westborough's comment. Mack puffed thoughtfully at his cigar. "The trouble with this mess," he said, "is there isn't a motive worth a damn. I never heard of a murder without a motive, but what is it?"

"Swink's past, perhaps?" Westborough volunteered.

Mack shook his head. "No, we've checked that angle. Swink was a slimy animal, but what the hell? Nothing we've uncovered ties into anyone here. In fact, as nearly as we can make out, he hasn't been in Chicago for about twelve years. There's an interesting story about his reason for leaving this town, but it's got as much to do with this case as my aunt Harriet up at Niles, Michigan."

Westborough bent forward avidly. "I should like very much to hear it."

"Well, Swink—he was using his real name at that time, and he's never used it since—got hitched on the fifth of July to a girl named Mary Winters. They were married at noon and about three o'clock Mary Winters was killed."

"Killed?" Westborough echoed.

"I know what you're thinking, but you're dead wrong. The jane or the fellow she was with drove through a streetcar tunnel—some nut tries that stunt every once in a while. A streetcar was coming hell bent the other way, and you can guess what happened. After they'd picked up the pieces—"

"You referred to the fellow she was with," Westborough expostulated. "Wasn't her husband—"

"If he was, he got clear. And if he did, he must've evaporated, because there isn't much room for pedestrians in those tunnels. Funny, isn't it? Jane gets married at twelve and at three is killed riding with a man not her husband. What do you make of it?"

"I suppose," Westborough hazarded, "that there is no doubt about the girl really being Mary Winters?"

"Her own mother identified her. The fellow who was killed with the girl was a friend of Swink's, but up to that date we could find no connection between him and Mary Winters. The girl's parents had never heard of him or Swink either, but that doesn't prove a thing. After that accident Swink faded from sight, and there's a hi—hi—what's the word I'm trying to say?"

"Hiatus?" Westborough suggested.

"Yeh. Good word if I could only remember it. Anyway there's a gap of about a year in his record, and then he shows up in Seattle under a different name as a fake check artist. Next we know he turns up in New York—"

"Did you learn the reason for Jasper's errand?" Westborough queried.

"Got all the dope," Mack informed cheerfully. He paused to look at his watch. "Funny, they haven't been able to find Jerry Spanger yet!"

"It is peculiar," Westborough agreed.

178

"Well, we'll give him a few more minutes. Do you know what happened this morning? Amco got in touch with their client, and he sent his secretary out by plane to talk to us. He gave us an interesting yarn, but, hell! unless I miss my guess, it's got about as much to do with this case as my aunt Har—"

"Someday I hope I shall have the pleasure of meeting your elderly female relative," Westborough interposed.

"One up for you!" Mack chuckled. "Well, Swink—he used half-a-dozen other names, but that's as good a handle as any—worked the good old estate racket on an old dame and extracted practically every cent she had. When she learned that the man she'd taken for a nice friendly lawyer was a fake, the old girl killed herself with an overdose of digitalis. But she had one mighty good friend—they were childhood sweethearts in fact—and his name was Ezra Whittington."

"I've heard of Mr. Whittington."

"Who hasn't? He's got the reputation of being a fighter and is one tough guy to buck. He put private detectives on Swink's trail. They collected a lot of dirt about the fellow all right but failed to get their man. Swink—he was going by another name then—had faded clear out of the picture as far as Whittington was concerned until about three weeks ago. Then one of Whittington's friends asks his advice on a letter he'd got about this Colorado gold mine. The letter was signed Elmo Swink, a name which didn't mean a thing to Whittington, but the way some of the sentences were strung together made him think of the fake lawyer who had swindled his old girl. He gets handwriting experts to work on the signatures, and when they tell him Swink is the guy he's after, he sics Amco on him. However, he's afraid he might not be able to get a conviction on the old charge, so he instructs Amco to dig up dope that will make Swink take the rap for using the mails to defraud."

"Have you seen Whittington?" Westborough inquired. Mack shook his head. "Or a picture of him?" Westborough persisted.

"He won't let them be taken. Smashed two or three cameras for newspaper men, if I remember."

"Then you don't know what Whittington looks like?"

"Haven't the faintest idea," Mack began, but stopped abruptly and exclaimed, "Whew!" He thought intently for some seconds, pacing the floor while he cogitated. Finally, he shook his head. "I get your drift all right, and it's a big idea. But it's no go. I just remembered that Whittington was in Washington Thursday night— with one of these business men's groups conferring with the President."

"The President of the United States is certainly an unimpeachable alibi," Westborough agreed. "I suppose there is no doubt but what Whittington was there?"

"I don't think so," Mack answered, "but it might be worth checking up." He seated himself in a chair and tilted it backwards at a precarious angle. "Funny it should take 'em so long to find Spanger!" he exclaimed again.

"Have you been able to trace the source of the cyanide?" Westborough asked.

"No. We've about finished checking, and so far we haven't found a soul buying a small quantity of cyanide recently."

"Perhaps it was stolen."

"Maybe, but there haven't been any strangers hanging around the places we visited, and there's no evidence that any of them were broken into."

Westborough volunteered another suggestion. "Perhaps one of the workmen abstracted the cyanide and sold it without the knowledge of his employer?"

"That possibility's got me screwy," Mack admitted. "It could happen all right, and if it did, we'll never know about it. Naturally, the guy that supplied the cyanide will keep still about it." He paused and added as an afterthought, "We haven't found any trails yet that lead from a business using cyanide to the Equable."

"Let us discuss another aspect of the problem," Westborough invited. "Have you thought of Colmar?"

"What about him?"

"Leaving the hotel before your search, he would have been able to carry away the objects which are apparently missing."

"What objects?"

"If you will refer to the notes I have made on the subject, you will recall that I discussed the relative chances of the murderer's knowing or not knowing of the existence of the sulphuric acid in the Graham boy's chemical set. If he didn't know, another bottle of acid should have been found somewhere."

"That's an interesting little point," Mack agreed. "I talked to Mrs. Hammond on Friday. She remembered Mrs. Graham mentioning the acid, but it didn't make a very deep impression on her. She is almost sure she didn't tell anyone else about it. Almost but not quite."

Westborough sighed regretfully. "That information, I'm afraid, isn't very helpful."

"No," Mack assented, "but you can't get all the breaks. Say, you said objects and not object. What else would you say was missing?"

"An instrument similar to the one you found in Jasper's suitcase."

"A second pick, eh?" Mack grew suddenly thoughtful. "How do you make that out?"

"Very simply. Jasper may be telling the truth about not opening Mr. Graham's door."

"I must be getting dumb," Mack ejaculated, crushing his cigar butt into an ash tray. "If Jasper didn't do for Swink, he didn't pick Graham's lock. That's A-B-C stuff. Then there'd have to be a second pick hidden somewhere around the corridor. But who hid it? And where?"

"Colmar," Westborough suggested again.

"Sure, I thought of Colmar," Mack exclaimed savagely. "It's my business to think of everybody. But he couldn't do it unless his sister was an accessory. And she's harmless, or I'll buy you a dinner at the Villa Venice. She's taught kindergarten for five years."

"It would be difficult for Colmar without his sister's knowledge," Westborough admitted, "yet it might be possible. He may have left her alone for a few minutes upon some such pretext as the purchase of a pack of cigarettes. May I ask what is Colmar's profession?"

"He's a lawyer," Mack stated. Westborough's face fell. "And from what the force at Springfield told us, he's a smart one," Mack went on. "He's got a pile of friends in the state legislature and is supposed to be some sort of lobbyist. However, that's no crime!"

"My theory that the criminal is engaged in an occupation requiring the use of a cyanide is refuted at every turn," Westborough lamented.

Mack clapped his shoulder consolingly. "Cheer up! You're doing pretty well for a rank amateur." The forelegs of his chair descended to the floor in a noisy thud. "Westborough, there's one guy who had both the method and the opportunity and even a motive—at least, it's as near to a motive as any I've been able to dig up so far." He rose to his feet. "I've been stalling around here waiting for Jerry Spanger. He phoned me a piece of news this morning, and I want to get his slant. But I'm not going to wait any longer."

"Your suspect is, of course, Larson?" Westborough inquired.

"Why not?" Mack growled.

"I believe that every human being is capable of murder given sufficient provocation," Westborough answered slowly. "But for a big, easy-going man such as Larson the provocation would have to be extreme."

"He's hot tempered," Mack reminded.

"But not underhanded," Westborough added. "Moreover, Larson is a man of too much intelligence, I believe, to plot a crime the very nature of which would point directly at him. At least, not without the arrangement of some sort of alibi."

"I don't agree with you," Mack said. "Any alibi that Larson arranged would look phony, and he has sense enough to know it. He's always in his room up to eleven o'clock, and he has to be there because it's his only chance to sleep or study. No alibi at all is a damn sight better than a screwy one." He paused and added with deliberate emphasis, "Westborough, in ninety-nine times out of a hundred, the obvious answer to a case is the right one. It's only in books that the nice old gentleman who was supposed to be up at Lake Delavan the day of the crime turns out to be the murderer. Well, I'm going to put the screws on Larson now. Do you want to sit in on it?"

Westborough accompanied the detective across the corridor. Mack rapped, and Chris Larson came to the door, in his shirtsleeves and smoking a straight briar.

"What can I do for you?" he asked.

"Plenty," Mack snapped, closing the door and standing with his back against it. "Larson, we had that stuff in the tube analyzed."

"The salt?"

"That's what the chemist called it. It's not my idea of something to put on hamburgers. Anyway, it was potassium sulphate. That mean anything to you?"

"Potassium cyanide with sulphuric ac—" Larson began.

"You telling me?" Mack's eyes were piercing gimlets. "Larson, you worked with some potassium cyanide two weeks ago—about the time that Swink first came to this hotel."

"Yes," the night clerk admitted, "I did."

"Jerry Spanger called me this morning to tell me that he had seen you on very friendly terms with Miss Gant. You took her to breakfast and afterwards left the hotel with her."

"Spanger's a meddlesome old woman," the night clerk fulminated. "Is it any of your business if I did ask Miss Gant to breakfast?"

"The other night you said you knew her only as a guest in the hotel."

"That was true—then."

"You're crazy about that girl, aren't you?" Mack sneered.

"That's my business," Larson answered sullenly.

Mack pounded his fist against the desk. "Of course you are! Anyone can see it. And there's your motive, Larson. Swink didn't get into the wrong room by *mistake*. He had relations with Miss Gant and—"

He got no farther. Larson lunged forward in a blaze of sudden fury. "It's a filthy lie! Get out, or I'll throw you out!"

Mack's eyes glinted in amusement. "I doubt if you could manage that job, Larson." The tinkling of the room telephone broke the tension. Mack picked it up, saying, "We'll argue this later." Larson's fists unclenched. Westborough, with his odd characteristic of remaining aloofly impersonal, noted this fact and remembered his earlier conversation with the detective. Larson was hot tempered, yes, but his anger cooled quickly.

In a bored voice Mack said to the telephone, "Yeh, you're talking to him," and then, with quickening interest, "Yeh, read it." The voice at the other end of the wire muttered something, and Mack ejaculated, "The hell you say! What's the rest of it?" The rest of the conversation was a long monologue from the other end of the wire which Westborough found unintelligible. At length Mack hung up the receiver with an elation which he did not try to conceal.

"We've got the dope from Washington! Devon's got a record as long as your arm. It even includes murder." He picked up the telephone again and conversed with the room clerk. "Collins thinks Devon is in his room," he told Westborough, his hand over the mouthpiece. "He saw him come in between six and seven, and he hasn't left the hotel since." He replaced the receiver on the hook and volunteered additional information. "Jerry Spanger seems to have dropped clear out of sight for the last two hours." He stared inquiringly at the night clerk. "What the devil am I going to do with you while I pick up Devon?"

"Mr. Larson might be of assistance in that matter," Westborough suggested. Larson gave the little man a grateful look and concurred in the suggestion. "If Devon's the fellow that's caused all this trouble, I'd sure like a chance at him," he said. Mack scrutinized Larson's face intently for perhaps a minute. "All right," he said finally. "I may be a damn fool, but I'm going to trust you. Come along."

The upper sides of the corridor were spotted with alternate patches of light and obscurity. A lighted splotch above Westborough's door reminded him that he had forgotten to turn off the switch. The transoms of Miss Gant and Mrs. Blakely were dark, and so was that of the vacant number 315. But light shone from the Hammond and Graham transoms. . . . Westborough glanced backward . . . there was also a gleam of light above Jasper's door. He turned his head and peered down the corridor. Devon's transom was dark.

Mack knocked on the door, but there was no answer. He waited for a moment before rapping his knuckles for the second time against the wood. Still no stir of life from within. Larson volunteered to fetch a passkey, and Mack nodded. The night clerk disappeared around the corner of the dimly illuminated corridor.

Regarding the silent and darkened door, Westborough experienced a sudden chill. The stillness was oppressive, abnormal. There should be conversation, bursts of laughter from at least one of the lighted rooms, but there wasn't even a radio playing.

Westborough recalled that the third floor was by now largely deserted, but the explanation did not entirely allay his uneasiness.

"Better stand to one side of the door," Mack advised grimly. Westborough shuffled uneasily as he obeyed the detective's orders. A trapped criminal, prepared to shoot it out with his captors, would be human, understandable. But the austere and awful silence of the room beyond— Anything might happen there, Westborough told himself. Anything and everything. Anything except the bald and simple fact that Devon was out.

Mack, waiting for Larson to return with the passkey, lounged against the wall, his lynx-like eyes riveted upon the doorway. His right hand was buried beneath his coat. Westborough remembered the missing Spanger and shuddered. Devon's record included murder. One murder had already been committed at the Hotel Equable. The chill terror of death, which at some time or another visits every man, came to Westborough now. Spanger, so unaccountably absent from his usual haunts, was a shrewd and capable detective. Suppose that he had conducted an investigation of his own, had penetrated the killer's secret?

"My God!" Westborough exclaimed aloud. "Mr. Spanger!"

"I've been thinking the same thing," Mack answered in a harsh whisper. "If this bird's done for Jerry, I'll—"

Muffled footsteps sounded at the end of the corridor. Westborough twisted his head and saw Larson walking toward them. The flat and shining pate of the hotel manager accompanied him.

"What's going on here?" Victor Swann demanded. Mack motioned him to silence and demanded the passkey from Larson. He inserted it in the lock without turning it.

"Westborough, Swann," the detective barked authoritatively, "get out of the line of fire. Larson, when I give the word turn that key, push the door open, and jump out of the way like billy-be-damned. There may be some shooting here." He jerked his right hand from the holster beneath his coat as he spoke.

"Must you shoot up my hotel?" Swann asked with gloomy resignation.

Mack growled, "Shut up!" and gave the signal to Larson. The night clerk opened the door and sprang to one side as Mack had instructed.

Mack's voice rang out deep and threatening, "Out of there, Devon." But if Devon was within he made no answer. Holding his revolver in readiness Mack dashed towards the room. He stopped suddenly upon the threshold, "He's here all right! My God!"

Westborough, deliberately disobeying the detective's orders, shifted his position to look within the room. He noticed first a large armchair. It had been drawn to face the doorway, and in it a man was seated—with a start Westborough realized that the motionless figure was a man no longer.

Benny Devon's blackened and bloody tongue lolled grotesquely from between purplish lips, while eyes wide and staring greeted his visitors.

XX

LARSON'S PIPE clattered to the floor. Westborough, in the remote corner of his brain which remained ever aloof, observed the gray smear which the ashes left against the dark carpet. Mack left the figure in the chair to dart to the telephone, issuing curt commands with the swiftness of decision which characterizes the seasoned executive.

"Horrible!" Swann gasped and added a naive and brutal afterthought, "This will about do for my hotel."

The motionless form might have been something from Madam Tussaud's waxworks. Westborough averted his eyes. His stomach felt queasy, and he leaned against the wall. "Dear me!" he gasped. "I hope—I'm not—going to be sick!" He glanced about the room, making an effort to comprehend what his eyes were seeing.

First the bed. The covers had been torn off and were lying in a tousled heap on the floor. "It doesn't make sense," he could hear Mack saying—in his mind, of course, since the detective was still busy at the telephone. Something else appeared to him as odd, but his eyes had made a second circuit of the room before he recognized what it was. Stacked against the wall was a vacuum cleaner, and beside it, flat on the floor, a leather case—open!

The case, of course, was used for vacuum cleaner accessories, but why was it open? Why was the bedclothing disarranged? Trifles these, but they concealed a message—if his brain was able to unravel the enigma. Westborough inspected the room for a third time, forcing himself to see every detail—the thousand and one trivialities which are ordinarily never noticed.

The blotter, pen, and inkwell upon the writing desk. They were placed with a neat precision which suggested they had not been disturbed since the advent of the maid that morning, the ash tray beside them. Westborough almost missed the fact that it was empty. Almost but not quite. He turned to it again. Not one cigarette butt, not a burnt match, not even a fleck of ash. Furthermore, the matches in the pack attached to it were intact. Westborough ascertained that before directing his attention once more upon the leather carrying case.

He made a mental inventory of its contents. A hose, eight feet long, and coiled like a big striped snake. Duraluminum nozzles of assorted sizes and shapes. A moderately large and a very small brush. A bottle of moth spray. A roll of black electrician's tape and a screwdriver. Several small circulars, all the same, of the kind which manufacturers, for no reason at all that a sensible man can fathom, refer to as "literature." Westborough picked up one of the circulars and noted that it contained a detailed description of the functions of these various gadgets. He read it carefully:

"Doc Hildreth'll be up before long, and O'Ryan's on his way here now," Mack declared, replacing the receiver of the telephone. "Swann, will you tell everyone on this floor not to leave their rooms?"

The hotel manager, his face as pallid as though he had received a death sentence, shuffled out the door. Larson mumbled something about a drink of water and started to follow. "Stay here!" Mack's voice cracked like a pistol shot. "What do you know about this?"

Larson deliberately turned his back upon the detective and went toward the window. "What should I know about it?"

"I'm asking you, not answering riddles."

Larson continued to regard the asphalt three stories below. "This is as big a surprise to me as it is to you," he said. "Maybe bigger."

"What do you mean by that last crack?" Mack demanded irately.

Larson failed to answer, and the detective decided not to press the point. Instead he made a quick scrutiny of the room and remarked upon the very questions which Westborough had observed earlier.

"What's the bed doing all messed up? Why is this junk spread out on the floor?" He supplied his own answer. "Looks like there'd been a roughhouse."

"I don't think so," Westborough demurred.

"Why not?" Mack snapped, his voice tinged with suspicion.

"Nothing else in the room has been disturbed," Westborough elucidated. "If there had been a fight, you would expect a chair, a lamp, or some other light object to be upset."

"Maybe," Mack grunted, "and maybe not. It's easy to straighten those things."

"Then why not close the case of cleaner tools?"

"Maybe Devon left them that way. He might've been out making a call."

"On Sunday?"

"Hell, that's right!" Mack exclaimed. "It is Sunday." He turned belligerently upon Westborough. "All right, Mr. Wise Guy. You tell me what you make of it."

Westborough pointed to the cleaner case. "An article belonging in that case is missing."

Larson, who had left the window to join in the inspection of the tools, rejoined, "Yes, it's the extension pipe."

"I don't know the name of the article, but there is a picture in this circular of an object not in the case. The manufacturer says that it is used for cleaning draperies and curtains."

With an abrupt, "Let's see," Mack jerked the circular from Westborough's hand. "It's a metal pipe about two feet long, I'd say." His eyes flicked rapidly about the room. "I don't see the damn thing anywhere around, either." His eyes came to rest upon a closed door. "Maybe it's in there."

Action invariably accompanied speech as far as Mack was concerned. His fingers had closed about the closet doorknob almost before he completed the last sentence. "It's locked," he said, "but the key's right here."

Westborough was not prepared, could not anticipate the next event. He heard a sharp grunt of surprise as Mack tugged at the door, and the second following, the bound figure of a man tumbled into the room.

Mack braced himself and eased the helpless being to the floor. "Jerry Spanger! My God!"

Westborough and Larson rushed to the side of the house detective. Spanger's arms were pinioned behind his back with strips of linen, obviously torn from a sheet. His feet were likewise tied together, and his mouth gagged with a handkerchief held in place by black tape. Mack carried him to the bed and listened for his heart. "Thank God! It's still beating."

"Brandy might help," Westborough interposed, "I have some in my room." Mack nodded, and he hurried to procure it. When he returned, Mack had untied Spanger's hands and feet and was about to rip off the tape fastening the gag. Spanger moaned as the adhesive was wrenched from his skin.

"Trying to yank out my whiskers?" he demanded weakly.

"Why, you old son of a gun, you're just too tough to kill!" Mack exclaimed delightedly. "Here, take a nip of this, fellow, and you'll feel better." Supporting Spanger with one arm, he helped him to swallow a generous portion of Westborough's brandy. The house detective smacked his lips and essayed to sit up. "Take it easy," Mack advised, propping him with a pillow.

Victor Swann returned from his errand. "Told everyone on floor," he began, then stopped short in bewilderment. "What the devil happened to Spanger?"

"You tell me," Mack drawled. "Feel like talking, Jerry?"

Spanger raised a hand to his head. "I guess so. Head aches like the dickens, though."

Mack examined the house detective's cranium. "Yeh, you got a nasty crack, all right. Who did it, Jerry?"

"I wish I knew," Spanger ejaculated. "I didn't see the bastard."

"Didn't see him?"

"No. Last thing I remember is hearing a step behind me. I started to turn, but I guess I wasn't quick enough. There were about a million stars . . . Maybe I better begin at the beginning."

"Feel up to it, old man?"

"Give me another snifter of brandy and I will." Mack handed over the bottle, and Spanger took a deep gulp. "Well, I was coming down the corridor—"

"Which corridor?" Mack interrupted.

"Let me think—the old head isn't functioning the way it ought— the south corridor, I guess. Anyway, I saw something shiny on the floor. I got down and picked it up, and it was a cigarette lighter. I took it under a light where I could get a better look at it, and I'll be hanged if I didn't recognize the thing. It was Devon's. So I thought, 'Well, I'll just give that back to you, fellow, before you start a rumpus over losing it.' I knocked on the door, but Devon didn't answer, so I waited a while and I knocked again. Still no answer. Then I thought, 'Well, I'll just open the door and leave it in his room.'"

"You know that's a direct infraction of the house rules, Spanger," Swann admonished severely. "Any articles found about the hotel are to be turned in at the desk."

"Sure I know the rule," Spanger admitted. "Ninety times out of a hundred I'd go by it." He rubbed his head ruefully. "I wish now I had."

"What happened after you opened the door?" Mack asked.

"It was dark, and I didn't see a thing for a moment. Not until I got well inside. Then I saw Devon laid out cold in that chair." He pointed to the tall armchair, only the back of which was visible from the bed. "Is he still there?"

"Yeh," Mack grunted laconically.

"God, what a sight that was! I'm pretty hardboiled, but this was so damn sudden, staring right out of the darkness at me, that I was all bowled over in a heap. I never stopped to think that there might be someone else in the room—not until I heard that step I told you about."

"What kind of step?"

192

"Just a step. I didn't get a chance to tell what sort of guy was making it. I started to turn around, and then, zowie! I always thought the star business in the funny papers was a gag, but I saw them all right."

"What time was it?" Mack inquired.

"Somewhere around seven. I wouldn't swear any closer than that."

"Any idea who hit you, Jerry?"

"No more than a babe unborn. I didn't see a soul, I tell you. I can't even guess what he did it with unless he had a blackjack."

"I think I can tell that," Mack said, stepping inside the closet. He came out almost immediately carrying a duraluminum pipe, about two feet long and an inch and a half in diameter. Mack held this very delicately by means of his handkerchief. He laid it on the writing desk. "What the devil!" Spanger ejaculated as he slid off the bed. He walked shakily across the floor. "No, don't bother," he said as Larson made a move to support him. "I can make it all right. What's that thing, Johnny?"

"One of the dohinkuses Devon carried around for his cleaner. Here's the way I've got it doped out: stop me if you don't check. The guy that choked Devon was still in the room when you knocked. He scurried around and looked for something to slug you, then he thought of these cleaner tools. He had plenty of time—see—because you knocked twice before you got out your passkey. He crouched behind the door—it opens inward—so you didn't see him. Then he sloughed you, ripped up a sheet, and tied you up. The tape he used for the gag was also among Devon's junk. But I don't know why he stuck the pipe in the closet instead of putting it back where it belonged."

"Possibly," Westborough suggested hesitantly, "he wanted to— give Mr. Spanger a break—I believe you would put it. He reasoned that the absence of the pipe would induce us to search the closet before Mr. Spanger would suffocate."

193

"Maybe. If he thought all that out, he's got a head on him!"

"The fact that he grasped so quickly the potentialities of the vacuum cleaner tools as a weapon indicates a mind that reacts promptly to emergencies."

Psychological analysis was not Mack's long suit. "Whoever he was, he's a dirty killer, and I hope I can pin this job on him if it's the last thing I ever do." He glanced toward the form in the armchair. "What do you suppose he had against Devon?"

"Wasn't Devon also of the criminal element?"

"Yeh," Mack agreed. "We got plenty on him. But I never could see him as the guy that did for Swink. That sort of job takes brains."

"Swink and Devon might have been working together," Larson suggested. "Maybe the murderer killed Devon for the same reason he killed Swink."

"Maybe," Mack agreed without enthusiasm. He turned to the house detective. "Jerry, what became of Devon's lighter?"

"Maybe I've still got it." Spanger reached into his coat pocket. "Yes, here it is." He handed Mack a silver lighter, and the detective inspected it closely.

"How did you know this was Devon's?"

"I kept a close watch on that bird. I've seen him flash it several times, and besides, it had his initials on it."

"If Devon wasn't the gentleman's real name—" Westborough interposed.

"How did you know that?" Mack asked quickly.

"I—I guessed it. When you informed us that Devon had a police record."

"Well, you guessed right. You were about to say you wondered why this had the initials B. D., weren't you?"

"Yes, that was my thought."

194

"Well, why shouldn't it have? He might have bought this after he took his new name and naturally wanted to keep in character."

Spanger was looking intently at the ash tray. "You know, here's a funny thing."

"What?"

"This ash tray. Devon was the kind of bird that could never do without a smoke for more than a couple of minutes. 1 never saw him but what he didn't have a cigarette in his mouth."

Mack's hands skillfully explored the dead man's pockets. "No cigarettes here either. That's funny!"

"Could he have just changed his clothes?" Westborough suggested.

"Now you're talking! Two bits that's just what he did. I'll take a look and see!"

There was a gray suit on a hanger in the closet, and Mack rummaged through the pockets. Suddenly he gave vent to a low whistle.

"Find 'em?" Spanger asked.

"No, but just look what I did find."

The object which he held out for inspection looked to Westborough like a small, long-necked pair of pliers. "What on earth are those?" he asked.

"Nippers," Mack replied succinctly.

"Nippers?"

"Yeh. They fit right into a keyhole and grab hold of the point of a key. When the key's in the lock, you can turn it from the other side of the door."

XXI

"WOULD THIS instrument enable," Westborough glanced nervously toward the corpse, "Mr. Devon to open the doors of this hotel?"

Spanger shook his head. "Nope. Nippers can't get inside a cylinder lock. Besides, these doors lock automatically, so why should anybody leave a key on the inside?"

"I see," Westborough pondered. "I wonder—"

Captain Terence O'Ryan, his jaw set at a grim angle, appeared suddenly from the corridor. Behind the blue-coated figure of the giant officer were Patrolmen Phelan, McCarter, and other satellites. To Westborough the room seemed to pullulate with police, all large in bulk and vociferous in exclamations. The little man took occasion of the confusion to study the actions of his fellow civilians.

Swann, as nervous as a racehorse before the starting gun, was tapping the point of his shoe against the floor. Westborough could see the perspiration gleaming from his bald cranium and would have wagered any reasonable sum that the palms of his hands were equally moist.

Larson, who came from a more stolid race, had resumed his fixed stare from the window and seemed entirely absorbed in a world of his own.

"Peter man," Mack was explaining tersely to O'Ryan, and Westborough inferred that the detective was speaking of the figure in the chair. "Known to the trade as Vacuum Benny. Had a habit of selling vacuum cleaners in between jobs of safe-cracking."

("So that's what a peter man is," Westborough reflected.)

"There wasn't any dope at headquarters, of course," Mack went on. "He never worked Chi. Stuck to small burgs, mostly in Ohio, and specialized in groceries, meat markets, and other dinky businesses. A good plain cracksman without frills. Got his soup the usual way by soaking sawdust in alky—"

196

"Sawdust?" Westborough queried.

Mack smiled in amused condescension. "Dynamite. Soup's nitroglycerine, if you want to know, and that's the way the yeggs make it. Devon was soaping a box—"

"Soaping a box?"

"Yeh! Stopping up the crack around the safe door with laundry soap. The soup's poured in at the top and works its way all around the edge of the door. Then you light a fuse, and bingo! Off comes the door from the hinges as slick as you please."

"Never mind the kindergarten class," O'Ryan interrupted. "What were you going to say about Devon?"

"He was soaping a box in a grocery store when a night watchman breaks in on him. Devon splits the fellow's skull with his jimmy and then gets rattled and leaves the jimmy behind with his fingerprints on it. He'd done a stretch before, and they had his prints at Washington."

"Why at Washington?" Westborough inquired, conscious that he was making a nuisance of himself yet unable to restrain his thirst for information.

"National Division of Identification," Mack explained. "Several million prints on file and complete records"

He checked himself at a look from O'Ryan. "How does this tie into Swink?" the latter asked.

Mack shook his head. "Damned if I know. They both had records, but they weren't in the same racket. Swink was a con man and a high-class one, while Devon cracked safes. Swink stuck to the big time, and Devon played the one-night stands. If you ask me, I'd say they didn't even know each other."

"They didn't as far as I know," Spanger confirmed.

"Did you give this room a good workout the other night, Phelan?" Mack wanted to know. The patrolman nodded emphatically, and Mack pointed to the nippers which he had laid upon the writing desk. "Know what those things are for?"

"Sure I know," Phelan declared in a hurt voice. "If they'd been here the other night we'd have found them. I tell you we went over the whole place with a—"

"What about the trick pocket in Chilton's suitcase?" Mack reminded.

Phelan's face fell. "We did slip up on that, I guess."

"Hell, anyone would!" Mack consoled. "But I don't think Vacuum Benny had a grip with trick pockets." He jerked his thumb toward the case of accessories. "Did you go through that junk?"

"Took every one of 'em out," Phelan answered confidently. "If there's a thing in the room we missed, I'd like to know what."

"Well, something's screwy," Mack deliberated. "Unless he got this little toy since Thursday. But why—"

"Does that thing have to stay here?" Swann interrupted with a grimace at the corpse.

"It does, but you don't." The hotel manager breathed a sigh of relief and started toward the door. "You can clear out too, Larson, but stick in your room. We'll be talking to you later," Mack added, the barest suggestion of a threat in his inflection.

Larson raised his head, looked scornfully into the detective's face for half a minute, and left without speaking. The genial and rotund Dr. Hildreth appeared in the doorway.

"My God, another! Swann been killing off his customers?" The doctor inspected the corpse with a cheerful professional interest. "Pupils dilated, lips and tongue livid—it's not hard to say what happened to this guy."

"I could've told you, and I'm no medico," Mack put in. "He was strangled."

"Throttled," the doctor corrected.

"Hell, what's the difference?"

"To strangle a guy you apply the constricting force by a ligature all the way round his neck, and to throttle him you go direct for his windpipe with your fingers. This bird was throttled."

"In other words he was choked," O'Ryan grinned.

The doctor pointed at the dead man's throat. "You can see the marks of the fingers on one side and thumb on the other. He was grabbed from in front—"

"For God's sake, Doc, don't smudge 'em!" Mack broke in. "Those marks might be prints."

"The thumb mark is on the stiff's right," the doctor went on, "and that means the killer used his right hand, if that's any help to you."

"Sure, that's a big help!" Mack groaned. "So few guys are right-handed." He glanced inquiringly about the room and remarked, "Devon doesn't seem to have kicked up much of a rumpus."

"Why should he?" countered Dr. Hildreth, who was taking a thermometer from his bag. "Given a grip sufficiently powerful, insensibility follows almost immediately. It's even more rapid than if a band were twisted around the throat."

"He died right away, then?" Mack asked thoughtfully.

"I should say that."

"How long ago?"

"Well, there aren't any signs of rigor yet." He jerked a watch from his vest pocket. "It's a quarter to ten now. My guess is that he was killed from seven to seven-thirty: that's based on the drop in body temperature and should be reasonably accurate."

"Seven to seven-thirty," Mack repeated, writing in his notebook. "Thanks, Doc."

The doctor resumed his inspection. Presently he called:

"Here's something else funny."

"What?"

"Cut on his face. It hasn't been cleaned up, but it didn't bleed."

"So what?" O'Ryan asked sarcastically.

"Don't you guys know anything?" Dr. Hildreth demanded irately. "Why do you bleed?"

"I'll bite, why?"

"Because the heart is a pump which keeps up the pressure in all parts of the body. But after the heart action stops there's no more pressure."

"I see what you're driving at," Mack interpolated. "A guy doesn't bleed after death."

"Not in the upper third of the body. Of course, gravity—"

"Here's an idea!" Mack ejaculated. "Suppose that the strangler was real close to this guy and that he was wearing a stick pin—"

"Not a stick pin," the doctor snapped. "Too sharp. Something more blunt— "His glance fell for the first time on the hotel detective. "Good Lord, what happened to your head, Spanger?"

"I got slugged."

"Evidently. Well, come over to the light and I'll take a look at it."

"Something blunt," Mack repeated. He brought his hand against his thigh in a vigorous slap. "By God, I've got it! How's this, Doc. You know those silly little buttons on coat sleeves? I never could understand why they put them there."

"A survival of the time when the sleeve was buttoned back to give the sword arm full play," Westborough explained.

"Suppose one of those buttons was broken," Mack conjectured. "Would the edge leave that kind of mark, Doc?"

"Possibly," the doctor stated in a noncommittal manner, his fingers probing the back of Spanger's head. "I'd have to see the button first."

"You'll see it," Mack promised. "We'll check up on the coat of every guy in the hotel if we have to. When we find a broken button on a sleeve, we've got our man."

"You and the Northwest Mounted," the doctor jeered. "Hey, hold still, Spanger. What's the matter with you?"

The house detective had leaped suddenly from his chair. "That crack on the head must 've knocked the sense out of me. I forgot all about seeing Colmar."

"Colmar? You don't mean the dame?"

"Naw, her brother. The guy from Springfield."

"The hell you say! Where was he?"

"He got off the elevator with his sister, and they went out together."

"What time was this?"

Spanger scratched his head. "Some time after seven," he pronounced.

"Humph!" Mack pondered. "Twice Colmar visits this place, and each time somebody's killed. It may be pure coincidence."

O'Ryan was bellowing instructions to his henchmen. "If he comes back, they'll bring him in right away," he promised.

"All through, Doc?" Mack inquired.

"Yeh! You got off pretty well, Spanger. That tough knob of yours can stand a lot of cracks."

"It's had to," Spanger grinned.

The doctor lifted his bag from the floor. "Shoot the stiff to the morgue when Selzer gets through checking for prints. I've got an idea."

"It'd be the first," Mack chuckled as the doctor went out the door. "Let's go to your room, Westborough," he suggested. "Jimmy Selzer ought to be here any minute now." They filed across the corridor to Westborough's bedroom, and the little man offered chairs. Mack, restless as a caged tiger, elected to pace the floor, chewing viciously at a cigar stub.

"If this is tied in with the Swink job," he said, "it means somebody in this corridor. And one killing is pretty apt to breed another."

"That's a large order at that," O'Ryan drawled from his chair at the writing desk. "The last time I was here it took till after three—"

"Not the women," Mack put in. "A woman might've pulled the other job, but the women are out now. It'd take a mighty husky baby to choke a man, I'd say." He tolled off names on his fingers. "Larson, of course; he's plenty big enough to do it. Hammond's no lily either. Jasper looks like he could give a good account of himself in a scrap, and then there's Graham and you." He paused thoughtfully. "What were you doing with yourself all day, Westborough?"

"I went to a motion picture," the little man began slowly. "I left about four-thirty, I believe, and called upon my sister-in-law, Mrs. James Westborough. She invited me to dinner, and I did not leave her apartment until after eight. I had been in the hotel only a few minutes when I met you."

Mack whipped out his notebook and asked the address of Westborough's sister-in-law.

"Dear me, am I suspected?"

"Why should you be? Just a matter of routine to check up on everyone. If I were a right smart murderer, I'd manufacture myself a nice little alibi for seven to seven-thirty. Wouldn't you? Wouldn't anyone? That's why we got to be careful about checking up on 'em all."

"You think, then," Westborough summarized in his precise fashion, "that the murderer left the hotel to establish an alibi?"

"What do you think?" Mack countered.

"I—I really don't know."

Mack said, "Well, from now on I'm going to be suspicious of birds with alibis for seven to seven-thirty. Who's at home now, Jerry?"

The hotel detective sauntered to the door and made a hasty survey of the corridor. "Looks like everyone is," he reported, "except Miss Gant and the Blakely hen."

"Women are out," Mack declared again. "Let's begin with Larson."

The night clerk strode into the room. "What'd you do today?" Mack demanded.

Larson glowered at the house detective. "I thought you learned all about it from your stool pigeon."

Spanger growled, "One more crack like that, squarehead—"

"Shut up!" Mack barked. "When I want to see a fight I'll pay to see Joe Louis. Now, Larson, where were you?"

"Lincoln Park."

"I won't ask what you were doing, because I can damn well guess. Take your jane to dinner?"

Larson answered coldly, "If you're referring to Miss Gant, your manner's offensive."

"Well, I'm a monkey's uncle," Mack crowed. "Listen, you! This isn't a tea party. What time'd you get back to the hotel?"

Larson took an angry step forward, but fell back as he met Mack's eyes.

"A quarter to eight," he said shortly.

"And Miss Gant was with you all the time?"

"Yes."

"You sure of that?"

"Yes," Larson repeated, glaring as though he wanted to kick someone. Mack allowed him to return to his room, and O'Ryan chuckled.

"Alibi number one."

"Two," Mack corrected. "You forget Westborough's."

"Oh, him!" O'Ryan ejaculated with a derisive glance at the author of *Trajan: His Life and Times.*

Graham was the next to be examined. The tall artist shuffled from one foot to the other and seemed to be ill at ease.

"Good-evening, gentlemen. Another terrible tragedy—"

"What you been doing today?" Mack asked abruptly.

"Trying to forget that damn ditty that goes, 'Boots, boots, boots,' " Graham replied smiling.

"Boots?" Mack repeated, his face puzzled.

"Boots is right. To be exact, forty pen-and-ink sketches of women's shoes. Ordered by a tight Scotchman named McClay, who'll only pay three bucks apiece for them. I've been trying to sandwich the job in at odd times, because there's no profit in a drawing at that price—even if it's nothing but copying a photograph."

"Were you working here?" Mack wanted to know.

"Yes. Mrs. Graham and the kid are gone, and I didn't want to waste the time it'd take to go down to the office."

"Where were you from seven to seven-thirty?"

Graham rubbed his cheek. "Let me see. I went out to a French restaurant and had frog legs and a bottle of claret. That was about six, and I wasn't gone more than an hour—if I was gone that long."

"You came right back to the hotel after dinner?"

"Yes."

"Hear any sort of rumpus going on anywhere?"

"Somebody's radio going full blast, but that's all."

"Radio, eh? Do you know where?"

"It sounded like it came across the court. I didn't pay much attention."

Graham was dismissed and Jasper called in. "Amco's ace," Mack greeted sarcastically. "Been picking any more locks today?"

"See here," Jasper began, settling himself in a chair and crossing his legs coolly, "I thought we'd settled all that business this morning."

"This is something brand new. Didn't Swann tell you about it?"

"All he said was that I'd better stay home so you fellows could have a chin-chin. Well, what's on your mind?"

"Plenty. Another guy was killed here tonight."

Jasper whistled. "What is it, a habit? Who was it this time?"

"An ex-con known as Vacuum Benny. He registered under the name of Devon. Know him?"

Jasper said, "If he's the little squirt who carried a vacuum cleaner around, I've seen him in the hall two or three times."

"Know anything about him?"

"Not a thing." Jasper took a cellophane-wrapped package from his pocket and tore off the end. "Smoke?"

205

Mack shook his head and asked the inevitable question. "What were you doing today?"

"I called on an old pal, fellow that used to be with Amco before he set up his own agency. I stayed with him until five or so."

"What'd you do then?"

"Came back to the hotel and shot Vacuum Benny, of course."

"How'd you know he was shot at five?" Mack asked quickly, and Jasper answered, "Was he? Well, I hate to disappoint you, but I didn't do the job because I was at the Oriental theater watching a new super spectacle called *Three Men and a Cobra*. It took about three hours to sit through the show, so I didn't get back to the hotel much before eight."

"Can you prove that?"

"Probably not. You don't suppose the ushers in the big Loop movie houses remember all the faces they see, do you?"

"Well, that's all I want from you, Jasper—now." The Amco man started toward the door when Mack halted him. "Wait a minute, you. So Devon was shot?"

"How the hell should I know?" Jasper exclaimed and disappeared down the corridor. Mack said thoughtfully, "Larson, Westborough, and now Jasper. Don't tell me Hammond will have an alibi, too."

Hammond's first words were, "Well, I'm damned. You fellows are working overtime, aren't you?"

"Yeh, we get around," Mack said. "Hammond, what'd you do today?"

The salesman grimaced. "Had a hell of a time, if you want to know. Got into a row with my father-in-law. Norah took his side, and the old lady took mine, and there was the devil to pay all around."

"Your father-in-law's in Elgin, isn't he?"

"Sure, that's what I told you before."

"Have dinner there?"

"Yeh, they always eat about three o'clock on Sundays. Then we sat around and chewed the fat. Everything would've been O.K., but the old man got started on politics. He's—"

"What time'd you leave?" Mack interrupted.

"About five-thirty. I couldn't stick any more of his"

"Never mind that. What time'd you come in the hotel?"

"Eight fifteen or so."

"Take you over two and a half hours to drive forty miles?"

"I had tire trouble. Picked up a nail near Bloomingdale and had to change to the spare."

"How long'd that take?"

"Fifteen minutes or so. But I stopped at a joint farther down the road and had the tube patched. That killed more time."

"What joint?" Mack wanted to know.

Hammond shook his head. "You can't prove it by me. It was just a garage along the road, not so very far from Oak Park. I could probably find it again, but that's all I can tell you now."

"Know what time you were there?"

"Yes, at seven-thirty. I remember looking at my watch while they were working on the tube."

"And then you came straight to the hotel?"

"Yes."

"No more stops along the way?"

Before Hammond could answer, a patrolman came to the door with a message for O'Ryan. "Colmar and his sister just got off the elevator."

"Well, bring Colmar in," O'Ryan demanded and Hammond was allowed to return to his room.

Colmar, a tall young man in his early thirties, bore little resemblance to the faded spinster, his sister. His hair was coal black and his eyes black and sparkling. He was wearing a double-breasted gray suit with a blue-edged handkerchief protruding from the breast pocket.

"Marcus Colmar?"

"Usually known as Mark," the young man smiled. "Effie's the only one who makes it Marcus."

"You were up here last Thursday night?"

"Yes. Wanted to give Effie a little surprise."

Mack launched into a series of questions which, Westborough could see, were designed to check his sister's account of the persons who passed their door that night. Westborough's memory was excellent, and he soon realized that Colmar's story was tallying in every important detail with that of his sister. He liked the youngster's straightforward manner and his breezy assurance.

"Why did you come up to Chicago today?" Mack wanted to know.

"Business."

"On Sunday?"

"I got a wire last night that a fellow was coming from New York by plane and wanted to talk to me."

"Spend the afternoon with him?"

"Yes, most of it. Later I called for Effie, and we went out to dinner."

"Where?"

"Henrici's."

"Then what? Don't tell me you went to a movie too!"

"That's just what we did do. *Three Men and a Cobra* it was called."

Mack said, "Humph! Who was the fellow you came up to see?"

"His name wouldn't mean anything to you, but he's private secretary to Ezra Whittington."

"Ezra Whittington?"

"Yes, the utility financier. He owns some gas properties in Illinois, and I represent his interests at Springfield."

"Lobbyist, huh?"

"You could call it that, I suppose. I'm a lawyer by profession."

"Whittington your only client?"

"No, I have a general practice in Springfield."

"Humph!" Mack exclaimed again. "Know a guy by the name of Jasper?"

"Never heard of him."

"Maybe you knew him under the name of Chilton?"

"Chilton?" Colmar repeated. "No, I don't know any Chilton either."

"He's staying in this hotel. Didn't Whittington's secretary tell you about him?"

"Not a word. We spent the entire time discussing a bill which is up for passage in the Legislature. It would mean a new and particularly vicious tax on gas companies, and Whittington wanted to find out what chance it had of passing."

"Well, what chance has it?"

Colmar smiled ruefully. "Pretty good, I'd say. It's become the fashion to soak the utilities. There's such a thing as killing the goose that lays the golden eggs, as some of these loud-mouthed politicians will be learning someday."

"Were you going back to Springfield tonight?"

"Yes, I was counting on catching the twelve-thirty."

Mack drawled. "Well, I don't know as we need to stop you. If we want anything else we can always get you at your Springfield address, can't we?"

"Right! And I'll be glad to do anything I can."

Colmar sauntered from the room. O'Ryan demanded:

"I'm with you in most everything you do, Johnny, but why let that guy get out? There's something screwy about this Whittington business."

"Maybe." Mack bit the end off a fresh cigar. "But the trouble is we can't prove it. Arrest a lawyer with pull and there'll be wires yanked all over the state to get him out. We'd just make saps of ourselves for nothing. On the other hand we can always get hold of Colmar, can't we? He isn't going to run away?"

"Something in that," O'Ryan concurred. "It'd be a dead giveaway if he bolted."

Mack had resumed his restless pacing. "Here's a problem for you," he flung over his shoulder. "Which guy had a broken button on his sleeve, Terry?"

"I didn't see any."

"Neither did I. Button, button, who's got the button?" Mack inquired facetiously. He continued in a graver tone, "Of course he might've changed clothes."

"Phelan and McCarter—" O'Ryan began, and then stopped as those two patrolmen burst into the room. "Through already, boys?"

"Yes." Phelan was excited. "Just for good measure we took a peep into the room where Fatty was killed the other night."

"Well?"

"Somebody's turned things topsy-turvy in there again. Even took all the shelves down from the closet."

"Well, I'm a monkey's uncle!" Mack whistled sharply. "What do you make of that, Jerry?"

The hotel detective shook his head. "It's beyond me."

"Check all the coats?" O'Ryan questioned.

"Chief, if there's a suit we missed I'll eat it. Hammond was packing a coat in his grip just as we came into his room. We jerked it out and took a look at the sleeve. There was a broken button on it."

"Hammond!" Mack exclaimed. "What'd I tell you about fixing up an alibi, Westborough? Well, we got him now."

"Perhaps," Westborough ventured, "the scratch wasn't caused by a broken button."

"Now I'll tell one," Mack muttered on his way to the door. "What did cause it, then?"

Westborough shrugged his narrow shoulders. "There are any number of objects sharp enough to cut the skin and yet blunt enough to cause this type of gash. The possibility which recurs to me with alarming persistence is the edge of a door."

"The edge of a door?" Mack echoed. "Why, that might mean—"

"Yes," Westborough finished for him, "I consider it quite likely that Mr. Devon was choked to death in some other room."

PART SIX: *Monday*

XXII

WESTBOROUGH'S FACE was covered with a mask of lather when his brush paused suddenly in midair. "Of course. How stupid of me not to think of that before," he said to the owlish reflection in the mirror and took up his old-fashioned straight razor.

Having completed his toilet, he opened the door of his room. Far down the corridor the chambermaid, Anna Larson, was wheeling her rubber-tired linen cart. "Do your duties include replenishment of articles in the guests' dresser pincushions?" Westborough asked her.

"Replenishment?" repeated the maid with a puzzled look.

Westborough simplified. "I mean do you keep account of the needles, pins, buttons, and what not in the guests' rooms?"

"Sure, I do that."

"Do you remember the morning after Mr. Swink was killed?"

"Sure, I remember it. That detective fellow, he talked to me then."

"Did you find anything missing from Mr. Devon's dresser that morning?"

"Devon? Who's he?"

Westborough patiently indicated the room.

"319, oh, that's the room where the other man was killed! No, I cannot remember."

"Think hard, please," Westborough persisted. "Needles? Button? Thread?"

This last stirred a chord in the maid's memory. "Thread. Yes, I had to put in a new piece of thread."

"Black or white?"

"I remember now. It was black thread."

Westborough thanked her and sauntered up the corridor. He knocked on the door of 311, which Miss Gant opened at once. She was wearing a tailored suit of russet brown and a tiny-brimmed hat of the same material, tipped at an angle across one eye. Westborough was no style expert, but he felt that the general effect was far from displeasing.

"I see I didn't disturb your slumbers," he began.

She smiled. "I'm looking for a job, and an early start helps, they say. So far it hasn't made much difference."

"The Goddess of Luck, then, has not been overly propitious?"

She shook her head. "I've had lots of luck so far—all bad. Well, something should turn up, as Micawber would put it. And the sooner the better say I."

"I am badly in need of stenographic assistance," Westborough informed hesitantly. "Would you be willing to be my secretary until a more remunerative position presents itself?"

"Would you mind saying that again?"

He did so.

"There!" she exclaimed. "I'd almost forgotten what it sounded like to be offered a job. Mr. Westborough, are you any relation to the good Samaritan?"

"None at all, my dear."

"Once, when I was a little girl," Yvonne Gant mused aloud, "I was stuck in quicksand. Did that ever happen to you, Mr. Westborough?"

"I can't say that I ever had the experience."

214

"Well, you flounder and flounder, and the harder you try to get out, the deeper in you sink. Then Father heard my yelling and threw a rope. It was just a piece of rough manila, but— Well, you will gather, Mr. Westborough, that I am trying tell you how grateful—"

Westborough beamed through his bifocals. "My dear, it isn't a question of gratitude but a business proposition. I suppose the management would object if we worked in my room?"

"Heavens, what would Mrs. Blakely say?" she laughed.

"A great deal, I fear, and very little of it germane to the point. Well, I shall speak to Mr. Spanger and ascertain if suitable working quarters can be improvised." Some distance around the corridor, he turned to ask, "Do you object to using a somewhat battered portable? That is until a more suitable machine can be procured."

"You're an old dear," Yvonne Gant called after him, "and I don't object to a thing."

Spanger, however, was far from being as complaisant. He objected to a major item in the Westborough Work Relief Program.

"No, you can't have her typing in your room, and that's that. Yes, I know you're old enough to be her grandfather, but that doesn't make a nickel's worth of difference. Sorry, but you'll have to rent an office."

"Dear, dear," Westborough murmured. "I really would prefer not to leave the hotel this morning. Are you able to suggest a site where my dictation to Miss Gant would not be derogatory to public morals?"

"Not trying to kid me, are you?"

"Such was far from my intention."

"Well," Spanger pronounced at length, "if you want to rent a sample room, I don't see any objection. Salesmen sometimes have a steno in 'em to get out their letters, and I guess you can do the same if you'll fix it up with the room clerk."

The principal difference between a sample room and an ordinary room, Westborough discovered, was that a sample room cost about twice as much. He was learning the lesson the federal government had already discovered: to wit, that work relief is considerably more expensive than direct.

The sample room was, however, hired, Westborough's dilapidated Corona transported to it, and Miss Gant installed, very business-like, behind an array of freshly sharpened pencils and a stenographer's notebook.

"Are you familiar with Trajan?" Westborough inquired.

Miss Gant, evidently quoting from some half-forgotten textbook, replied, "The Roman Empire reached its greatest extent under the Emperor Trajan." Westborough beamed.

"Exactly. An entire chapter of my manuscript upon that personage must be rewritten. I don't believe the publishers will like it—they told me they were setting the book in type—but it must be done just the same." Westborough cleared his throat and began to dictate while Miss Gant's nimble fingers raced across the notebook.

"To erect the Pyramids, to build the Colosseum dash, these were less colossal undertakings—colossal, Colosseum, that doesn't sound so well, does it?"

"Tremendous," Yvonne Gant suggested.

"Tremendous undertakings than to span the Danube River. This giant bridge, completed by Apollodorus of Damascus in the year 105, covered a stretch of 3720 feet —shall we say three quarters of a mile, Miss Gant?"

His amanuensis opining that three quarters of a mile would convey a more definite impression than 3720 feet, Westborough resumed.

"Twenty stone piers, the remains of which are still visible when the river is at low water, supported the giant wooden arches. From a bas-relief, sculptured by the selfsame Apollodorus on the Column of

Trajan, we learn that the arches were composed of a triple course of pieces of concentric curve—"

"Pieces of concentric curve," Yvonne Gant repeated, pressing so vigorously upon her pencil that the point broke. She took a fresh one while Westborough continued, "At this juncture we must pause to say a few words about the architect Apollodorus—yes, take that, Miss Gant."

The few words on Apollodorus stretched into two or three thousand as Westborough went from the Danube bridge to the Trajan column, to the Forum, back again to the bridge, and then once more returned to the column, and many pages of Yvonne Gant's notebook were covered with hooks and scrawls before the historian finally called a halt.

"There!" he exclaimed. "It isn't what I wanted to say, of course. It never is, but I daresay I can work it over when I see the transcription. You won't mind copying this again, Miss Gant?"

"Not at all," she was about to say when Westborough asked, *à propos de bottes*:

"Does anybody in our corridor carry a cane?"

"You do. A gold-headed one."

"Dear me, yes. It was given to me by my brother James. He's dead now, my dear. I was in Paris at the time, and the cane arrived exactly on my birthday—James did so many things for me like that. But that wasn't what I meant."

She said, "I can't think of anyone else."

Westborough strolled toward the window. "A typical Chicago spring, isn't it? Mist and drizzles again today." He wheeled and faced the girl. "Was it raining the night Mr. Swink met his death?"

"Cats and dogs," she answered cheerfully, "It's rained every day for a week now."

"Hum!" Westborough pondered and was on the verge of saying something else when the door to the sample room opened.

"So this is your hide-out?" Mack called jovially. "Can you break off long enough for a few minutes' powwow?"

Excusing himself to the girl, Westborough escorted the detective upstairs to his own room. "Westborough," Mack began without preamble as soon as the door had closed behind them, "you had a brainstorm last night about Devon being killed in somebody else's room?"

"Yes."

"Well, Doc Hildreth had the same hunch. Cagey old bird, the Doc! He didn't want to say anything until he had a chance to prove it. Doc was down at the morgue bright and early this morning, and I guess he did a good day's work. He called me up at headquarters to say there was smoke in Devon's lungs."

"Smoke in Devon's lungs?"

"Yeah, that mean anything to you? It didn't to me either at first, and then I got to thinking. Was there or wasn't there smoke in his room when we opened the door?"

Westborough, remembering the empty ash tray, said, "There couldn't—"

"Funny how a thing like that slips your mind," Mack interrupted. "And it's my business to notice things, too. Then I recalled he didn't have any cigarettes and Spanger saying that was funny. No, it's a real break at last. Somebody gave Devon's neck a squeeze in another room. And it was a guy who smoked."

"I smoke," Westborough returned promptly.

"Pipe," Mack said laconically. "So does Larson. So does Graham. Hammond smokes cigars. Jasper uses cigarettes. A big help, isn't it?"

"Are you sure," Westborough inquired, "that the guilty party is someone in this corridor?"

218

"Hell, yes! Nobody could cart a corpse any distance in the hotel without being spotted. But it'd be a cinch to watch through a crack in the door until the coast was clear and then pop into another room without anyone being the wiser."

"The dead man's cigarette lighter offers an insuperable difficulty to that theory," Westborough pointed out.

"Eh? What do you mean it does?"

"Didn't Spanger say that he found it in the south corridor?"

"By God, he did. Now what do you make of that?"

Westborough replied, "An object like a cigarette lighter might easily fall from the pocket of a body being transported from one room to another. But its position in the south corridor—"

"Yeah," Mack cut in, "but if it didn't fall out that way, how did it get there?" He chewed at his cigar for a few seconds. "I got it now. The lighter's a plant. Some guy wanted to turn suspicion away from this corridor. And why? Because he lives here. That sound reasonable?"

"Unless the murderer actually does live in the south corridor."

Mack said, "There's not many staying there now, and I checked up on those that were. None of them were in last night. Nope, here's how I got it doped out: the guy that bumped off Devon is the same one who did for Swink. But Devon knew who he was—see? Devon goes to his room and wants five or ten grand to keep his mouth shut so the murderer shuts it for nothing. That make sense?"

"A very logical analysis."

"Hell, it's common sense!"

"I don't say that it isn't the true explanation. Nevertheless, there is a fallacy."

"Oh yeah?"

"Devon, I believe you will agree, was a person of limited intelligence. I will grant you that he probably possessed a certain acumen along lines more or less mechanical, but his powers of abstract reasoning were undeveloped."

"If you're trying to say he was dumb, I'll check."

"From my experience with the Chicago Police Department," Westborough went on, "I conclude that the individuals associated with it possess a reasonably high intelligence quotient."

"Thanks for the bouquet!"

"Yet your theory presupposes that Devon had discovered unaided what the united resources of the Chicago Police Department have so far failed to do—the identity of Swink's murderer. In other words, that Devon was, to use the vernacular, smarter than your whole department put together."

"Ouch!" Mack laughed. "Well, this dumb police department will tell you a thing or two. Devon didn't figure it out. Hell, if I can't that punk couldn't! He stumbled on it. He saw the guy doing it."

"You forget your timetable," Westborough reminded. "The murderer was in Swink's room at nine-thirty, and Devon on his way to the hotel at that time." He paused. "Or did you discover that he was lying?"

"No, we checked his alibi, and it was O.K.," Mack admitted. "He couldn't have reached the hotel before ten."

"Unless," Westborough conjectured, "Hammond was wrong about the time of the murder."

"Humph!" Mack pondered. "If I hadn't let Hammond go—"

"You let him go?"

"Yeh. He came to me this morning and put up a song and dance about how he'd lose his job if he didn't get out on the road today. I sent a man out with Hammond to see if he could find the garage Hammond talked about it. If he does and if the garageman checks

Hammond's alibi, then O.K., let him go, I said. Hell! I'm too soft for my own good, I guess."

"If you will pardon the reflections of an amateur," Westborough replied, "I should like to remind you that an alibi is merely a statement of the axiom that one body cannot be in two places simultaneously."

"Yeh, what of it?"

"That axiom will, of course, always remain literally true. Nevertheless, improved transportation facilities tend to mitigate its practical importance. Do I make myself clear?"

"As the Chicago River," Mack grinned.

"As an example," Westborough continued, "by the fastest mode of transport in existence between New York and Chicago, the two cities were prior to the advent of the airplane separated by a time of, I believe, twenty hours. Now they are separated by only five hours."

"What's that got to do with it?" Mack demanded.

"Merely an example. Formerly, a person supposedly in New York during the commission of a crime in Chicago might have an alibi as old as twenty hours and it would be held valid since no physical means of shortening the time gap between the two cities existed. Now the time in which such an alibi would be valid has narrowed to five hours."

"In other words?"

"The better the transportation or the shorter the distance between the two points in question, the more accurately must the alibi be timed to be valid. Now, alibis, unless prearranged by an accomplice, are seldom accurately timed for the reason that their very nature of casual happenings makes them largely a matter of guesswork and belief."

"Humph!" Mack pondered. "You're driving at something important. You mean that Hammond killed Devon, jumped into his

221

car, and traveled out of town as fast as he could go to kid the guy at the garage into believing that he was there at seven-thirty? Say, that isn't such a dumb idea," Mack went on. "Hammond could've stuck a nail in his own tire and said he picked it up on the road and had to change. Who could check that?"

"You are forgetting," Westborough protested, "that Hammond was back here shortly after eight."

Mack came down to earth with a bang. "Right you are. That spoils the whole case. He couldn't have left the hotel at seven, which is the earliest time Doc Hildreth will give him, go out four miles or so west of Oak Park, have a tire vulcanized, and get back here by eight-fifteen. Or could he?" Mack paused to consider this question. "You know, I'll get one of the boys to try it. With the right break on lights—"

A knocking upon the door interrupted further speculation. Westborough opened it to reveal Victor Swann. In his hand he held an object which resembled a thin piece of steel attached to a pistol-grip handle.

"Been hunting all over for you," Swann began in his usual telegraphic manner. "Houseman found this thingumajig while he was baling waste paper."

"A jigger gun!" Mack ejaculated.

"Another implement to pick locks?" Westborough queried.

The detective nodded. "Where was this found?" he asked the hotel manager.

"Basement. Houseman baling—"

"Yeah, I got that. But where does he get the paper he took to the baler?"

"Maids' closets. One on every floor. Maid empties waste paper from rooms into big bag hanging on door of closet."

"Did the houseman tell you which bag this thing came from?"

"Didn't I tell you? The one on this floor."

"He's sure of that?"

"Seemed to be."

Mack began to wrap the lock-picking instrument in a sheet of stationery abstracted from Westborough's desk. "Devon's," he explained laconically, putting it into his pocket. "He used it last night, I'll bet."

"That settles it," Swann burst out angrily. "Locks picked like so much cheese in this corridor. Must have new ones put in tomorrow. Upset master-key system. Can't help it. Guests have to be protected—I'll let 'em know about new locks now."

He stamped hurriedly from the room, and Mack winked at Westborough.

"Clucks like an old hen because one chick's got away somewhere," he laughed. Slowly the grin faded from his face. "Do you know what this means? Devon had to leave traces when he opened that room last night. Scratches on the key way or on the tumblers. This case is just as good as closed now. All we do is open up the locks and we've got our man."

"Suppose," Westborough conjectured, "the murder took place in Swink's room?"

"Why bring that up? You don't think—"

Westborough shook his head. "Not particularly. The point merely occurred to me."

"Well, if you're right, we're out of luck!" Mack exclaimed disgustedly. "Jasper picked that lock before. We'd have made a charge against him for that, but Amco's got too much pull not to get him out of it."

"You examined Swink's lock before?"

"Yes."

"Did you take photographs of the marks on the tumblers?"

"Hell, a fellow can't think of everything!" Mack declared. He wheeled abruptly on Westborough. "What makes you keep harping that Devon was choked in Swink's room?"

"Harping," Westborough replied cheerfully, "is an excellent word. Someone does keep harping on that room; it has been entered twice since Swink's death."

"Yeh," Mack admitted. "First he tore the guts out of the mattress and chair upholstery. Last night he had the bureau drawers on the floor and the shelf boards down from the closets. Doesn't make sense!"

"It would suggest a persistent and continued search."

"For what?" Mack exploded. "Swink's stuff is down at the station, and there isn't a damn thing in the room but the regular hotel furniture." He paced the floor chewing at his cigar stub. "Here's a guy looking for something that isn't there, and on the other hand is a guy hiding something that should've been found." He tapped his pocket. "What'd Devon do with this the other night? What'd he do with the nippers we found in his suit? You can't tell me he didn't have 'em at the time we searched his room. But where'd he ditch them?"

"I think," Westborough said slowly, "that I am able to answer that question."

"You're good if you can!"

"Hotel service is founded upon the taking of infinite pains over apparently trivial details," Westborough began. "To give an example, I learned the other day from Mr. Swann that on each guest's pincushion must be placed one black button, three white buttons of various sizes, two needles, twenty-four straight pins, one large safety pin, two small safety pins, twenty-four inches of white thread, and twenty-four inches of black thread."

"So what?"

224

"The chambermaid is supposed to take inventory of these items and to replenish any which are missing. The morning after Swink's death she found one of the objects I have named missing from Devon's pincushion. Can you guess what it was?"

"How old is Ann?" Mack grinned. "You tell me."

"The black thread."

"Probably sewed a button on his pants," Mack hazarded. Westborough said nothing, and Mack went on, "I'll bite, then. What did he do with it?"

"I should like to verify my conclusion by experiment," Westborough answered. "I suggest that we adjourn to his room."

Mack found the chambermaid on the point of going into a room at the end of the corridor and made her open the door, which she did under protest, vociferously maintaining that it was against the rules. Westborough went straight to the bathroom and pointed to an opening in the wall leading to a ventilating shaft and covered by a metal grille.

"Now if we remove that plate."

Mack yanked out a substantial-looking pocket knife and attacked the screws. "Damn!" he exclaimed as the blade broke at the first attempt.

"I'll get a screwdriver," Westborough volunteered. "There was one among the cleaner tools."

"That junk's all down at the station. Anyhow, this blade's working now."

He removed the grille, and Westborough triumphantly pointed to a fragment of black thread attached to one of the bottom screws.

"Neat idea," Mack commented. "All he had to do was to tie his toys to the thread, wrap the thread around the screw, and put back the plate. The jigger gun and nippers would be out of sight down the shaft, and the face of the plate hides the thread. No wonder Phelan and McCarter didn't tumble to it. I wouldn't myself."

"A houseman vacuums these shafts every so often," Westborough remarked, "so it's hardly satisfactory as a permanent hiding place. But for a day or two it serves quite well."

"O.K., let's get going," Mack urged, closing the door behind him.

"Were there any fingerprints on the pipe?" Westborough asked.

"Pipe? Oh, you mean the thing that slugged Jerry. No—not even Devon's. If you're such a smart detective, deduce something from that."

"It was wiped clean?" Westborough hazarded.

"Yeh, go to the head of the class. This mug probably wore gloves—there weren't any prints on Devon's throat either—but even so he was taking no chances. Our best bet now is the locks—Devon had to leave his calling card—and I'm going to get Clark on 'em right away."

Westborough walked with him to the elevator shaft, then returned to his temporary office in the sample room. He could hear the busy clicking of a typewriter from the corridor.

Miss Gant looked up from her work as he entered the room. "Well, my dear, and how it everything going?" Westborough questioned.

"Pretty well. Of course, I have to go rather slowly. Your typewriter isn't what it once was."

"Like its owner," Westborough smiled. "As a matter of fact, there is no hurry, my dear. No hurry at all. I find that urgent business calls me away from the hotel."

He bowed himself out of the room while Yvonne Gant continued at her typing. There was a great deal about Apollodorus of Damascus, and Yvonne began to conceive an admiration for this Leonardo da Vinci of the first century. A mental image began to form

226

in her mind. He was tall, of course, tall and blond—with a start she realized that she had been picturing Chris Larson. She pounded furiously at the keys until she heard a knock at the door. She opened it to admit Jerry Spanger.

"Where'd Westborough go?" the hotel detective demanded.

Yvonne Gant struck a few more keys on the machine. She had no particular love for Jerry Spanger. "He didn't tell me."

"Did he say when he was coming back?"

"No."

"O.K." Spanger started to close the door, then flung it wide open again. "If you ask me, Westborough's screwy."

Yvonne Gant rose from her machine and delivered what was intended to be a withering look. "I don't believe I remember asking you."

"Oh, climb down off your high horse," Spanger said cheerfully. "I was on the second floor when I heard someone making a racket on the fire escape. I peeped out of the window, and who should I see but your boss, Westborough, skipping down the steel stairs like a kid of ten."

XXIII

CHRIS LARSON knocked on the connecting door which led to Yvonne Gant's bedroom. "Yvonne," he called softly.

"Yes?" she answered from the other side of the door.

"Are you dressed?"

Her laugh sounded low and pleasant. "At seven-thirty in the evening? I should hope so."

"Then I'm coming in. Wait until I open this door."

He fitted a key to the lock and the door swung open. "Passkey," Chris explained. "I borrowed it from the desk downstairs."

Yvonne moved a chair toward him. "It's all right with me, but aren't you breaking a rule or something?"

"Several of them," Chris laughed. "In fact, I'll probably shatter the whole decalogue of house rules this evening."

"What on earth—"

"Yvonne, I'm in a jam."

"Sit down, smoke a cigarette, and tell me about it," she invited. "I've been in a few jams myself."

"You're a trump!" Chris exclaimed. "I knew you would be. What would you say if I told you I expected to be arrested for murder?"

"I'd say someone was crazy!"

"Not so crazy," Chris replied. "As a matter of fact, they've got an excellent case against me. You know how Swink was killed?"

She nodded.

"Things point definitely at someone who knows something of chemistry and had access to potassium cyanide. And that hits me on both counts. Besides, I was experimenting with some cyanide in the lab only about two weeks ago."

"Do the police know that?"

"Yes. I think Lieutenant Mack was on the verge of making an arrest last night when he was shunted off the track by what happened to Devon."

"You poor dear!" she exclaimed compassionately. "But they know you couldn't have anything to do with what happened last night. Why, you were with me!"

"Only until a quarter of eight. After that I was alone in my room. And I don't know what time Devon was killed. I had to leave just as the doctor got there."

"But why should they suspect you of killing Devon?"

"Why should they suspect me of killing Swink?" he countered. "The answer's easy. Somebody did it. They know it had to be someone in this hotel. And they want to make a showing."

"But there has to be a motive for a murder, doesn't there?"

Chris answered slowly, "As far as Swink is concerned, the police have found a motive, or think they have, which amounts to the same thing. I was alone in my room that entire evening without a ghost of an alibi. And then, on top of that, the cyanide."

"But the police can't prove that you took any of it from the laboratory, can they?"

"Of course they can't. But I can't prove I didn't, either."

"I don't know a great deal about law," she asserted, "but I have always had an idea that a person was supposed to be innocent until he was proved guilty."

"That's the theory of it," Chris answered, "but to make an arrest all they need are reasonable grounds of suspicion. They can charge me with the murder. I honestly believe I'd be acquitted, but, guilty or innocent, I'd be washed up here. This whole business is a black eye for Swann. He'd never keep a night clerk who, as far as the public knows, might be a murderer, even though he wasn't convicted." Larson's hand gripped the arm of his chair tensely. "And that would probably go for every other prospective employer too."

"I see," Yvonne sympathized. "It is bad, isn't it?"

"Well, it hasn't happened yet," Chris rejoined. "But the only way I can make sure that it doesn't is to find the real murderer."

"That's rather a large order, isn't it? The police don't seem to have been so successful at it."

"I have a plan. It may be a hundred-to-one shot, but anyway, I'm going to try it. Will you help me?"

She allowed her hand to rest on top of his. "You know I will."

"Thanks, Yvonne. I knew I could count on you. You're a thoroughbred all the way through, and I—"

"Tell me about your plan," she interrupted hastily.

"Twice since Swink was killed somebody has been in his room. It doesn't take much brainwork to guess that it was the murderer and that he was looking for something Swink had hid. Well, whatever it was, it must be well hidden, since the murderer has had three chances to look for it: once when he put the test tube over Swink's door and twice since then."

"Do you think he found it?"

"I don't know. If he did, I'm out of luck. But if he didn't, he's almost sure to come back. And he'll have to come back tonight or not at all."

"I don't understand that."

"Tomorrow Swann is putting new locks on every door in this corridor. If the murderer has a passkey it won't do him a nickel's worth of good after tomorrow morning."

"I heard Lieutenant Mack talking to Mr. Westborough. He seems to think that the lock was picked."

"Well, my argument still holds good. Swann is all worked up over this business, and, if there is such a thing as a pick-proof lock, he's going to get them for these doors."

"I see," Yvonne said again. "But what's your plan?"

"It's very simple," Chris answered grimly. "All I have to do is wait in Swink's room until the murderer shows up, then grab him."

"And you say that's all! But if he has a gun—"

Chris shook his head. "He hasn't. Hammond was the only suspect with a gun, the police found the other night, and he checked out of the hotel this morning."

230

"Even so, it's still too risky. Why don't you tell the police what you've just told me and let them keep watch?"

"Yes, and if nobody showed up I'd be worse off than ever! No, I'm not passing the buck on this thing. It's my idea, and I'm going to carry it through."

"But what will Mr. Swann say when you don't show up for work?" she objected. "You'll be fired for sure then."

"I told Larry Collins about it, and he was a prince. He gave me the passkey, and he's going to stay at the desk tonight. I've already told Swann I'm sick."

"Chris Larson, it's one of the craziest ideas I ever heard, but I'm with you. I always did like crazy fools, particularly when they've got nerve."

Chriss grinned. "Nerve and no brains. That's me."

She said, "I'm going to wait in there with you, of course."

"You are not."

"I am."

"Whose idea is it?"

"If you think that I'm going to let you—"

"You can't help me a bit in there." Chris's thumb jerked in the direction of the other room. "But if you stay here, you can do a lot."

"What do you want me to do?"

"Swann may call up to see if I want anything. If the phone rings, knock on the door and I'll go answer it."

"Is that all I can do?"

"All? That's a whole lot. It may save my job."

"But Swann will know if you catch the murderer?"

231

"In that event, I'll probably be the white-haired boy around this place," Chris laughed. He rose to lock the connecting door which led to his own room. "I don't want you involved in this if anyone gets suspicious. Won't you tell me now why you didn't what to change your room yesterday, dear?"

"When you are not able to pay your bill," she replied, tapping the point of her slipper against the carpet, "you don't like to ask favors. At least, I don't."

"Why didn't you say something to me?"

"Because at heart I'm a conventional little stick, I suppose. Anyway, I just couldn't."

"You would be that sort. But from now on—"

"Oh, I'm all right now. Mr. Westborough gave me an advance."

"How do you like working for the walking encyclopedia?"

"He's an old dear. And don't make the mistake of thinking because he's all wrapped up in his Roman history that he hasn't a brain. I must tell you what happened today."

"To Westborough?" Chris inquired.

"Yes, he was nearly arrested."

Chris whistled. "The deuce he was! Tell me about it."

"I had better begin at the beginning." She lit a cigarette and took a meditative puff. "He was out most of the afternoon and didn't come back until four-thirty. Then he began to glance over the manuscript I had typed. 'Dear me!' " Her mimicry of Westborough's nervous hesitancy was perfect, and Larson chuckled. " 'An excellent job, Miss Gant, and from very poor material. My dear, you have succeeded in a feat which the children of Israel found impossible— the making of bricks without straw.' I had taken the liberty of rearranging some of his sentences and changing a word here and there, and I was glad he liked it. Some men blow up if you alter a single comma, and the stuff they dictate! Well, just then in walked

Lieutenant Mack, very angry. Not openly, of course, but I could see it in his eyes—the pupils were contracted to pin points. He stood there for some seconds, too mad to talk or do anything but glare. Finally he said:

"'Westborough, I don't like being played for a sucker.'

"Mr. Westborough—he's so mild and apologetic— didn't turn a hair. He looked up from his manuscript and said in a tired, patient voice, 'Whatever have I done now?'

"That was too much for Lieutenant Mack, and he exploded. It was almost comical, though I confess I didn't see the funny side of it then. 'Done! You know what you've done! Devon got into *your* room, you dirty little double-crosser!'

"That didn't bother Mr. Westborough in the slightest. He said, in the same calm, patient voice, 'Then it was my lock that the scratches were on?'

"Lieutenant Mack smashed his fist so hard against the writing desk that I thought he'd broken it. 'You know damn well it was! Don't try playing innocent with me.'

"Mr. Westborough didn't even hear him. He just sat there looking way off somewhere into space. 'Dear me! But in that event, why did the—'

"I never did learn just what he was going to say because at that point Lieutenant Mack interrupted. He was just as mad as ever, but it was a different kind of anger. 'You're as smooth an article as I've ever met, but I can see a whole lot of things now. Those notes of yours, for instance, that you pestered me with until I read them. You tried to throw suspicion on everyone in the corridor. It was a very clever trick, but that section on poisons would have been a dead giveaway—if I hadn't known Jim Westborough. You know a lot more about that subject than an ordinary man has any business knowing. And when I told you we were going to examine the locks— God, you were slick about that! Cutest trick I ever saw the way you tried to sell me on the idea that Devon was killed in Swink's room.

233

But he wasn't. It was your room, and you're going to headquarters. Tell me now why you choked him.'

"Mr. Westborough held out his hands—you know what tiny, frail hands he has for a man—and said, 'With these?' Lieutenant Mack was flabbergasted. He looked at Mr. Westborough's hands as if he couldn't believe his eyes, and then looked at his face. He opened his mouth twice but couldn't manage to get out more than a sort of grunt. Then Mr. Westborough asked him, 'Have you talked to my sister-in-law?' Lieutenant Mack said, 'Yeh, we sent a man up there!' Mr. Westborough didn't even wait to hear what the man had found out. 'You know my sister-in-law personally?' Mack said, 'Yeh,' and Mr. Westborough told him, 'Then you know that Mrs. James Westborough is scarcely the woman to serve as accomplice to a murderer. Especially if he should be a brother-in-law for whom she doesn't particularly care.'

"Lieutenant Mack didn't take his eyes off Mr. Westborough's face, and Mr. Westborough didn't take his eyes off Lieutenant Mack's face. Neither one would stop staring at the other. Only Mr. Westborough wasn't really staring. His eyes were actually twinkling behind those big glasses of his, and finally the other gave up. 'Was that scratch a plant?' It was plain to me that he thought a lot of Mr. Westborough's opinion.

" 'Either a surprisingly stupid one,' Mr. Westborough said, 'or—
'

"He stopped, and Lieutenant Mack asked, 'Or what?'

"Mr. Westborough slumped back into his chair, and somehow I got the idea that he was exhausted. He's so little and frail, I wondered if he might have heart trouble. Anyway, I left my chair and came over to him. 'Anything I can do for you, Mr. Westborough?' I asked. 'No, thank you, my dear, I am quite all right.' Then Lieutenant Mack said again, 'Or what?' and Mr. Westborough smiled a wan little smile.

"'Dear me! I really don't know.'"

Chris Larson rose to his feet as the girl concluded her narrative. "I can't visualize Mr. Westborough as a murderer."

"He's the last person in the world"

"But then," Chris went on, "I can't see anyone else here as that either. They're all nice, ordinary everyday people."

"Is a murderer essentially different from other people?" Yvonne wanted to know.

"Here, I'll light it for you!" Chris exclaimed, crossing the room to hold a match to her cigarette. "Yvonne, when I heat manganese dioxide with potassium chlorate I know I'll get oxygen every time. But you can't put human beings into a test tube and be sure of always getting the same reaction."

Her eyes, blue as larkspur, smiled at him through her cigarette smoke.

"Meaning?"

"Meaning that I can't take people to pieces and see what makes 'em tick. Maybe a murderer has got a sort of warp in his psychological make-up. Maybe he can stay a kind old gentleman like Mr. Westborough. I don't know. But I do know that if this particular one comes into the next room tonight, he's going to be nabbed." Two quick strides brought him to the connecting door, and he inserted his passkey in the lock. Suddenly Yvonne's tall, graceful form was beside him.

"Chris?"

"Yes, dear."

She laid her hand on his forearm. "You—you'll take care of yourself?"

Larson turned away from the door. "Does it mean anything to you?"

"Yes," her lips said simply, but her eyes admitted more.

235

"Yvonne, when this is all over will you mar—"

"Not for years and years," she laughed, evading his outstretched arms. "You have to finish college."

"I could chuck chemistry"

"You do, Chris Larson, and I'll shoot you."

"Bloodthirsty little wench." This time she failed to elude his arms. For perhaps half a minute they clung together, her eyes pleading. Larson answered, as though she had spoken aloud: "*En avant, toujours, en avant.* You didn't know I knew French too, did you?"

"It's pronounced 'ahn', not to rhyme with 'hen', and the 's' is silent," said the little carping demon which lies hidden in every feminine soul to Yvonne Gant. But to the demon she paid little heed. Aloud she answered, "*En avant,*" as Chris turned the knob. The door opened noiselessly on its well-oiled hinges. Then Chris's head bent down to her face before the door closed between them. She could hear the click the bolt made as it slid into place. Chris had locked the door from his side—for her protection, she knew.

She sank into a chair and toyed with a nail file. Just to wait. Was there, could there be anything worse than waiting? Waiting while a man—the man you love, she told herself—was in that room? The room which had taken at least one man's life! That ghastly, sardonic mocking room!

"Please don't let anything happen to him," she breathed, and then she smiled at the absurdity of that. You stood alone in this world. You were alone outside of the help which friends could give. Chris had only his own strength to depend upon. Beyond that—nothing.

She lit another cigarette, took a few puffs, and then crumpled it out in a quick, nervous fashion. She looked out of the window. She went to the dressing table and looked into the mirror. She put a dab of powder on her nose and a touch of rouge on her cheeks. But she did this mechanically, scarcely noting the effect produced. Then she placed her ear against the connecting door. Was it imagination, or could she actually hear Chris breathing in the next room?

"It must be imagination," she told herself, and went back to her chair. There were no more cigarettes in the cylindrical receptacle beside the ash tray. "There's a fresh pack in my purse," she remembered. She was about to tear the pack open when she heard a noise from the next room. Chris's room. Not Swink's. Chris's phone was ringing. Loudly and insistently. Clamorously, in the imperative manner in which phones order you to drop everything and come to them at once.

"Chris ought to know that," she thought and went to the door. Her knuckles rapped softly, and she waited for his answering call. But there was only silence. Yvonne knocked louder. "Chris, oh Chris."

Still no answer. This ominous, predatory silence! "Chris, Chris, Chris darling!" She hugged the door and clung to it, her ear strained to catch every sound emanating from the next room. But there were no sounds. No, that wasn't true, either. She could hear something now. The din of the telephone in the next room ceased, and she realized that she could hear very distinctly indeed. It was the click of another bolt being drawn in a lock. It was the creak of a door swinging open.

Yvonne Gant ran screaming into the corridor.

XXIV

CHRIS LARSON had locked the door which led to Yvonne's room and restored the key to his pocket. No matter what happened in here tonight, he told himself, she, at least, was out of it.

Outside darkness had settled upon the city, and the room was illuminated only by a faint glimmer from the transom. He drew up a large wing chair to face the door and settled to his vigil. But waiting there in the semidarkness for something, he didn't know what, turned out to be not the easiest task in the world. The trouble was not with his nerves. His nerves were excellent. But Chris Larson was becoming sleepy.

In his dual role of student and hotel man Larson averaged, as Edison had done, not over five hours sleep a day. But, unlike Edison, he had never been able to accustom himself to it. He was always fighting sleep—in the classroom listening to a lecture or at the desk trying to discover if Mr. William Smith had really managed to leave the hotel without paying his bill or if that impression was due to a cashier's mistake. With plenty to do—immersed, swamped, submerged in work as he usually was—Larson could fight sleep at any time and win. But tonight, despite the two cups of black coffee he had downed only an hour or so ago, he was losing the battle. His eyelids were overpoweringly heavy. He blinked and jerked his head up—tactics which earned only a few minutes' respite and then left him more drowsy than ever. Perhaps if he walked about the room? No, that wouldn't do at all. The slightest noise might frighten away the intruder he expected. This thing had to be fought—and whipped—mentally. Give his mind something to feed upon; that would stop it from sinking into lethargy.

He began with a problem in calculus; then gave it up as a bad job and turned to chemistry. He tried to recall the atomic weights and numbers of the ninety-three elements, but, as a method of keeping awake, that proved about as efficient as the old-fashioned counting of sheep.

Mental effort was all very well, but it must be something simpler. Without moving his lips he began to recite a jingle which he had committed to memory years ago because the dash and swing of it had impressed themselves upon his adolescent mind. "Laska used to ride on a mouse-gray mustang close to my side," recalled Chris

238

Larson. "With a blue something or other and a bright-belled spur, and then something else again. Little she knew of book nor creed." It was beginning to come back to him now. "And Ave Maria sufficed her need. And little she cared . . ." His eyelids were lead weights pressing against his eyeballs. "Little she cared . . . cared . . . cared . . ."

Chris Larson fell asleep, his head lolling against the wing of the chair and his right arm dangling helplessly at his side.

How long he slept, he didn't know. Afterwards he realized that it could not have been for so very long. He was roused to consciousness by an insistent rapping. "Yvonne," he thought sleepily and was about to call to her when a second sound struck his senses with the shock of a cold shower. He sprang to his feet, his body tense and tingling, as slowly, very slowly, the door to the corridor commenced to open.

Mack affixed a mirror to Westborough's transom and stepped down to survey his handiwork.

"Slick job if I do say it," he commented. "We can see everything going on in the hall, and nobody will tumble that we're watching them."

"Did anybody see you enter?" Westborough questioned.

"Sure. Old Four-Eyes down by the employees' entrance. That's all. I sneaked up the back stairs and waited till the corridors were clear. If anybody knows I'm here, he's got second sight, that's all." He tilted a chair backward until its front legs were off the floor and puffed comfortably on a cigar. "The minute Swann said the locks on this corridor were to be changed I got my big idea. I thought, 'Whoever bumped off Swink wants something in that room, and tonight will be his last chance.' Funny that Larson should get the same hunch, isn't it?"

"Larson?" Westborough repeated.

"Yeh, didn't I tell you? Collins didn't like to run to Swann about it because Larson had already told Swann he was feeling rather seedy, but he figured somebody ought to know. So he gave me a ring."

"Larson did?"

"No, Collins. Larson told Collins he was going to wait all night in Swink's room."

"I see," Westborough answered. "That action requires considerable courage."

"Well, I guess Larson isn't yellow," Mack admitted. "I've more or less changed my mind about that fellow. He couldn't have done for Devon, anyhow. The Gant girl said she was with Larson most of the day yesterday, and they didn't get back to the hotel until a quarter of eight. I don't believe that girl was lying."

"A woman," Westborough deliberated, "is supposed, theoretically at least, to be willing to swear to practically anything for a man if she loves him. I speak without practical experience."

"Maybe." Mack nicked the ashes of his cigar to the carpet. "But I'd take oath any time that the Gant girl's straight."

"Perhaps," Westborough suggested, "a glass of brandy would lessen the tedium?"

"Now that's what I call a swell idea," Mack grunted. Westborough produced a bottle and brought out the glass from his bathroom. He poured a good stiff drink, and Mack smacked his lips. "That the same stuff you gave Jerry Spanger?"

"The identical ichor. I believe there is a saying relative to the impossibility of a man standing upon one leg?"

Mack waved away temptation. "I could drink that all night, but I know my limits. I won't be much good if I start seeing two mirrors."

"Whom are you expecting to come tonight?" Westborough inquired.

"I could act wise about it, but what's the use? Hell, I don't know, and that's flat!" Mack tilted up the glass and consumed the last few precious drops of the brandy. "Hammond's alibi checked," he said.

"You found the garage, then?"

"Yeh," Mack declared, the liquor loosening his tongue into unusual garrulity. "And the guy remembers changing his tire and says it was about seven-thirty or so."

"My impression was that you were going to be suspicious of alibis," Westborough reminded.

"I am, but if they check, there's not much you can do about it. Yours, Hammond's, and Larson's seem to be O.K. Jasper's is lousy and so is Colmar's."

"Do you suspect either of those gentlemen?" Westborough wanted to know.

"I'm not sure," Mack said slowly. "If you want the truth, I haven't a case yet against anybody, and unless something happens tonight I probably won't have." He looked quizzically at his host. "Westborough, you're a damn queer duck, but I can't help getting the idea that you know a lot more about this than you're letting on. What's your slant on this?"

"That's a frank question and calls for a frank answer," Westborough replied. "I only wish I could give it to you, but, since confessions are in order, I have to admit that I am as completely at sea as you are. Up to this afternoon—"

"This afternoon?" Mack repeated quickly.

Westborough's thin hands played with a pen, pressing the point against the blue desk blotter. "Let me elucidate by means of an analogy. The situation is not unlike the mechanism of a pin-tumbler lock."

"I'll be taking locks to pieces in my sleep," Mack declared with emphasis. "There's five pin tumblers, and the wedges on the key have to raise 'em all in line before the plug can turn. That what you mean?"

"Exactly. To carry the parable a step farther, I might add that four of my tumblers have reached the proper height, but an obstinate fifth prevents the lock from opening. Could I surmount that obstacle—"

"What's your fifth?" Mack demanded.

"Devon's cigarette lighter," Westborough returned promptly.

"But I thought we'd settled this morning that it'd been planted in the south corridor?"

Westborough's head moved in a negative gesture. "That explanation was perfectly valid—this morning. Since then conflicting evidence—"

"I get it," Mack broke in excitedly. "You mean that this guy we're looking for—the killer—wouldn't plant the lighter to point to the south corridor and then put the scratches on your lock to point right back at the west corridor again?"

"The leaving of two directly contradictory false clues is not a logical procedure," Westborough confirmed. "The next question is, 'Has our murderer a logical mind?' Judging from the skill with which he plotted the death of Swink, I cannot help but answer that question affirmatively. Therefore, one of the contradictory clues must be genuine. But the marks upon my lock are a false clue. There is no doubt about that. 'No probable, possible shadow of doubt,' as the Grand Inquisitor said in *The Gondoliers*. Hence, the cigarette lighter must be the genuine clue. But it follows inevitably that Devon was not strangled in the west corridor." He shook his white head in bewilderment. "As I have heard you observe so many times, 'It doesn't make sense.' "

"Nothing makes sense in this case," Mack declared gloomily. He stepped toward the telephone. "Keep your eye on that mirror, will you? I'm going to call Larson off before he goes in there and gets hurt."

"Are you sure he's still in his room?"

"We'd have seen him if he'd come out, wouldn't we?" Mack rejoined, taking down the receiver and asking for Larson. A prolonged buzzing indicated that the operator was trying vainly to complete the connection. "Funny it takes so long," Mack began. He was interrupted by Westborough tugging anxiously at his sleeve.

"Quick! He's just gone in."

"Larson?" Mack asked, replacing the receiver.

"No. The man we're waiting for."

"Did you see him?" Westborough nodded.

"My God! Who?"

Westborough told him. Mack dashed across the room and flung open the door in one quick motion. "If Larson is in there, we've got to act quick. He packs a gat, and if he starts shooting, Larson won't have a chance."

Hurrying after the detective, Westborough said, to no one in particular, "This is the most unexpected event which could happen. Dear me, it utterly frustrates all of my calculations!"

XXV

MACK SWERVED in time to avoid a head-on collision with Yvonne Gant in the corridor.

"Thank God!" she gasped, clutching at his arm. "Chris! In there! With—with the murderer!"

Mack grasped the doorknob and grunted, "Locked!" From behind the closed door came a noise like a chair being knocked over. "Sounds like the roughhouse had started," Mack pronounced grimly.

"I'll procure a passkey," Westborough volunteered, darting down the corridor with surprising agility. The scuffle within the room redoubled in violence as a second chair crashed to the floor.

243

"Can't you do something?" begged Yvonne in a tone that was almost a prayer.

People poured from near-by rooms—Graham, Jasper, Mrs. Blakely. Their exclamations sounded grotesquely in the girl's ears.

"What's going on here!"

"What's all the racket?"

"I'll complain to Mr. Swann if this noise isn't stopped at once."

"Go right ahead and complain!" Mack advised Mrs. Blakely. He yelled in stentorian tones at the locked door, "Come out of there!" There was no answer. "Looks like I'll have to shoot the lock," he declared, but Yvonne caught the arm holding the revolver.

"No, no! You'll hit Chris! Break the door down!"

Mack restored the gun to its holster while Graham dealt a tremendous kick at the door. "One more ought to do it," he shouted. Mack grasped his shoulder roughly as he was raising his foot for the second effort. "Stay out of this!" the detective growled.

"Run at it from across the corridor," Jasper suggested.

"When I want advice I'll ask for it," Mack snarled. He drew back and lunged against the door with his entire weight. Though it bent a trifle under the onset, it continued to hold firm. A third, and louder, crash from inside the room was followed by an ominous silence.

"Somebody took the count that time," Jasper chuckled. He was leaning lazily against the wall in obvious relish of the situation. Mack made a second, and equally unsuccessful lunge at the door.

"Cut it out," a muffled voice drawled from within. "I'm all ready to open it."

The bolt clicked back and the door opened to reveal Larson clutching another man firmly by the shoulder. The night clerk's blond hair was tumbling down over his face, his necktie was twisted

244

askew, and his forehead was bleeding from a gash over one eye. But Yvonne flung her arms about his neck and kissed him unashamedly.

"Chris Larson!" she gasped. "You *have* been in a fight!"

"Take a look at the other guy!" Larson grinned. For the first time Yvonne noticed the pudgy individual whom Lieutenant Mack had taken in custody.

"Mr. Spanger!"

"Yeh, Jerry Spanger," Mack confirmed, surveying the house detective critically and impersonally. "Swell sight, aren't you? Larson gave you a beauty on the beak!"

Spanger rubbed his nose, from which a crimson trickle descended to his chin. "He got me by surprise. I'll take the bastard on again any time."

"You've got other fish to fry," Mack told him. He adjusted handcuffs about the house detective's wrists. "Spanger, I arrest you for the murder of Elmo Swink and—"

Spanger, glancing with hurt bewilderment at the handcuffs, protested, "See here, a joke's a joke, but you're going too far. It's Larson you want!"

"Oh yeah?" Mack retorted.

"The big gorilla was laying for me the same as he did in Devon's room the other night," Spanger went on vindictively. "This time, though, he didn't have such a pushover. I didn't have a gun on me, or I'd have brought him in for you."

"It's a lie!" Yvonne began indignantly. Mack motioned her to silence.

"This bird's not fooling me one bit. Just why did you go into that room?" he demanded sternly of Spanger.

"It—it's a long story," the house detective gulped.

245

"Yeah, I'll bet! Well, you're going to have plenty of time to tell it—here or at headquarters."

Spanger fumbled uneasily with his grizzled mustache. "All right," he yielded, "I'll tell you just what happened in there. First I step into the room and close the door—"

"Who locked it?" Mack demanded.

"I—I did, I guess. It locked when I closed it."

"All right, go on."

"I heard a scream from the next room, and then this gorilla socks me. Wham! I felt it coming and jerked my head back; then I pasted him one in the puss. A chair or two gets knocked over; we're fumbling around in the dark and neither of us can see very well. I paste him another and then go right for his belly. Somehow I don't connect, and he gives me this clout on the beak. The next thing—"

"Can the blow-by-blow description," Mack advised wearily. "He licked you, and that's enough. What the hell were you doing in that room?"

"That's my business," Spanger answered sullenly.

"Gonna be tough, eh? What made you turn the room topsy-turvy the two other times?"

Spanger continued to fumble at his mustache but said nothing.

"You laid yourself wide open the other morning," Mack went on. "You got peeved when I said it was a lousy idea to rip the mattress open and told me the same mattress would stay in a room for years. I checked up with the housekeeper, and you were right, but I can see now how you laid yourself wide open. Only I couldn't realize that a guy who had once been on the force could turn into a low-down crook!" he concluded angrily.

"Who're you calling a crook?"

"You!"

"The hell I am!"

Popping mysteriously out of nowhere, Theocritus Lucius Westborough ejaculated, "Dear, dear! So Mr. Spanger is the key to our riddle?"

"Yeh," Mack answered, "he was in a deal with Swink and bumped him off because he wanted to cop all the profits himself."

"Swink didn't know a thing about—" Spanger checked himself too late. Mack seized the opening and beat down the other's guard with sentences like sledge-hammer blows.

"You searched his rooms. Don't lie. Do you talk now or—"

"Oh, hell, yes. I'll talk," Spanger said reluctantly. "I'll come clean. To go back to the beginning—"

Westborough interrupted. "I would suggest that Mr. Spanger relate his story in the comparative privacy of my room."

"All right," Mack concurred. "Come on, Jerry." They followed Westborough down the corridor.

"I've got more or less of a personal interest in this case," Jasper declared. "It got me a night in the hoosegow and kept me here, cooling my heels, since Saturday. I'm going to listen in at the finish."

"Larson," Westborough suggested, "is certainly entitled to be present, and Miss Gant is an extremely competent stenographer. Perhaps she would take down Mr. Spanger's confession in shorthand."

"Swell idea," Mack grunted, "Get her some paper and pencils, will you?"

Graham had followed the others inside. "If you want another witness to this, I'm your man. It was my room he broke into."

"And I am certainly entitled to know—" Mrs. Blakely began.

"Yeah?" Mack demanded. "I'm not ready to give this to the newspapers yet. If you're in on it, it'll be all over the hotel in half an hour. Outside."

"Well, I never heard such insolence!" Sarah Blakely sniffed. She stalked down the corridor, and her door slammed indignantly.

Westborough closed the door to his room. "There doesn't seem to be nearly enough chairs," he fretted, watching the efforts of his guests to make themselves comfortable.

"Never mind the chairs," Mack declared. "Miss Gant, will you please take down the confession? And, Spanger, you know as well as I do that anything you say—"

"Nuts!" Spanger interrupted. "I'm going to cut this short. You remember that shooting fracas I got into nearly a year ago? When Jake the Gent got killed?"

"What about it?"

"Jake would never have pulled a damn fool stunt like that one if he hadn't been drunk. His play was to come quietly along to headquarters. If his brains had been working, he'd have known we didn't have anything that'd stick in court. Why, we went over the whole house from top to bottom, and there wasn't a smell of the big green rock—"

"What on earth—" Westborough began.

"Emerald," Spanger elucidated. "Five-carat emerald worth fifty grand. Jake hooked it from an old duck called Lynn Van Elman. I know something about jewelry, and I'm telling you that emerald was as slick a piece as you'll ever find. It came from Colombia, where most of the good ones come from, and it didn't have a flaw. If you know anything about emeralds, you know that almost never happens."

Mack broke in grimly, "What's the Van Elman emerald got to do with Swink's room?"

"Plenty. Old Van Elman had it step cut and set in a brooch, which he gave his wife for their twenty-fifth wedding anniversary. Then Jake got it. One of the slickest jobs he ever pulled."

"The Van Elman robbery was on the eleventh of June," Spanger recollected. "And on the twelfth we were combing the city looking for Jake but couldn't stir up a trace of him. But on the thirteenth I get a tip from a stool that Jake's just rented a room on North Clark Street. You know what happened there."

"Yeh, you got yourself a hundred bucks for 'heroism,' " Mack remarked with a sarcastic emphasis thrown upon the last word.

"But not the emerald," Spanger grinned. "It wasn't on Jake, and he hadn't ditched it in the house. You knew Jake. He played a lone hand and never ran around with a mob. Smart guy! I doped it out that Jake must've got rid of the emerald sometime during the twelfth. But I didn't think he'd passed it on. Jake didn't trust anyone. No, he'd gone out and hid it some place, but I couldn't figure out where."

"Safety deposit box," Mack said shortly.

"Maybe. But that doesn't sound like Jake either. He was cagey. Deposit boxes have a way of being found and opened up, and besides, we checked that angle pretty thoroughly. I wanted to find that emerald badly because Van Elman had posted a reward of five percent—two and a half grand—and I could sure use that dough. But it didn't turn up at any of the fences. I didn't think it would, either. The way I'd doped it out Jake was planning on handling the sale himself after the fuss had died down a bit. He had a lot of good connections—"

"Oh, lay off Jake! He's got about as much to do with what you're going to take the rap for as my aunt Harriet up at Niles, Michigan."

"You and your aunt Harriet!" Spanger chuckled. "Well, I finally had to give it up as a bad job. Then I quit the force—I'm not so young as I was, and my feet bother me something fierce—"

"For God's sake, Jerry! You don't need to go into that either!"

"About ten days ago," Spanger continued, "Swann told me to cooperate with a firm of lawyers that were handling a divorce case. They were trying to dig up evidence to prove a dame's husband had spent a night with another dame at the Equable. So I take the ambulance chaser into the office, and we start to go over last year's register. He doesn't find a thing, but I do. I'm no expert, but I'd seen Jake's writing before, and the name, Cecil M. Deering, staring at me from the register, was just the sort of fancy moniker that Jake went in for. The date was right too—June twelfth. Well, if you've got a hunch, there's nothing like making sure, so I went down to headquarters and borrowed a specimen of Jake's writing from the files. Then I studied the two side by side: you can tell a lot from the alignment, spacing, how the stems are crossed, the flourishes are made, and so on. I'm no expert, as I said before, but if Jake wasn't Cecil M. Deering I was ready to eat a new spring hat right then and there."

"Had this Mr. Deering taken the room which Swink had?" Westborough wanted to know.

Spanger nodded. "Right the first time! 'It all fits,' I told myself. 'Jake hid out here for the day. He didn't dare stay any longer than that because we'd have been sure to find him, but that one day gave him the chance he wanted to get rid of the emerald. He ditched the thing somewhere in 315, and it's probably there yet. Two and a half grand in your pocket, and all you have to do is to go and pick it up!' But having got that far, I didn't know how to go on. Room 315 was occupied, and it would be risky to give it a combing. Besides, I'm the house officer, and Swann'd be real tough if there was any monkey business going on in one of the rooms."

"If you'd done the square thing, you'd have gone to Swann with the whole story," Mack observed.

"Yeah, that would've been a bright idea! Swann would've collared the whole twenty-five hundred—as an employee of the hotel I was merely doing my duty and so on. I know that bird! No, sir, this was my baby, and I intended to do the collecting. But the best thing I could think of was to wait until the room happened to be vacant, and—"

"But that took so long you decided to empty it yourself," Mack suggested.

Spanger glared angrily. "By God, I didn't! But when it happened, I didn't see any reason why I shouldn't take advantage of the break. If the room was found all torn up it'd be credited to the account of the guy that did for Swink. After you fellows had left the other night, I sneaked back in and took the place apart. I got as far as the mattress and the chair upholstery, but I wasn't able to turn up a thing, and it was getting too late to be safe, so I gave it up for the time. Nearly everyone was away from the corridor on Sunday—even nosy Old Lady Blakely—so I had another try. I thought that Jake might've dug out a little hole in back of the dresser and puttied it up, or he might've done the same thing to the back of the shelf in the closet. But he hadn't done either. Well, I was right in the middle of the job when I heard somebody walking down the corridor. Nothing to get excited over about that, but it didn't sound right to me. It was a slow, heavy tread, and I heard a guy breathing hard like he was doing real work. I figured I ought to investigate and stepped outside. There wasn't a soul in sight, and I wondered if my nerves had gone jittery. Then I saw Devon's lighter—"

"Just a minute," Westborough broke in, his eyes glittering strangely. "You saw the lighter. In which corridor?"

"This one—west."

"Not in the south corridor?" Westborough exclaimed. Spanger shuffled his feet embarrassedly. "I stretched the truth on that, I'll have to admit. I didn't want to let anyone know that I'd been in the west corridor. Not with Swink's room still messed up."

"That's it!" Westborough almost shrieked. "That's my fifth tumbler—the one I hadn't been able to get into line. I didn't see any reason why Spanger should lie about the place where he found the cigarette lighter, and I didn't dream that he had done so. Lieutenant Mack, you may now remove Mr. Spanger's handcuffs."

"Why the hell should I?" Mack demanded belligerently.

Westborough's voice soared triumphantly. "Because I am now able to tell you the name of the true murderer!"

XXVI

"FOR THE LOVE of God, who?" Mack clamored.

Westborough smiled his patient smile. "If you don't mind, Lieutenant Mack, will you permit an elderly historian to proceed in his own blundering manner? You see, there are so many different and seemingly contradictory elements involved—"

"O.K. If you've really solved this case, you're entitled to put on a show, I guess." He turned to Yvonne, seated at the writing desk. "Are you getting all this, Miss Gant?"

"Every word," she declared with enthusiasm.

Westborough slouched against the door, directly facing his audience. "To begin with, there is the time question. Mr. Hammond reported that he had heard someone—suppose for the time being that we call him Mr. Z—in Swink's room at nine-thirty. Mr. Spanger, if his story is true, could not be Mr. Z because, by his own admission, he did not begin his search of the room until early morning. Unquestionably, then, the Mr. Z whom Hammond heard must be the true assassin."

"Always supposing that both Hammond and Spanger weren't lying," Mack qualified.

"If Hammond had not been lying," Westborough continued, "there were, besides himself, only six people who apparently possessed the opportunity of committing the crime—myself, Mr. Larson, Mrs. Blakely, Miss Colmar, Mr. Colmar, and Miss Kriskrowski, the night housekeeper. But the time element proved to me puzzling. Four other people, able to produce witnesses to testify

252

to their whereabouts at nine-thirty, had uncertain alibis for ten. Mr. Jasper was gone from the bar for about fifteen minutes around that time. Mr. Swann returned to the hotel at ten, ascended to his quarters on the top floor, and then left again. Mr. Devon entered the lobby at the same hour. Miss Gant retired to her room between nine-thirty and ten. If Hammond was mistaken in the time at which he heard Z, these four could be included with other suspects. I determined, therefore, that the logical starting point in my analysis was to test Mr. Hammond's sense of the passage of time. On Friday evening I conducted some simple experiments, for which, however, he was not prepared and so would have had no opportunity to delude me. The results convinced me that Hammond was gifted with an acute perception of time. Therefore, if he said that he heard our Mr. Z at nine-thirty, Mr. Z must have actually been there very close to that hour. Certainly not as late as ten."

"You're using up a lot of words to tell us what we already know," Mack objected.

"The laboratory method," Westborough retorted, "is to construct a hypothesis only upon a base of verified and indisputable facts. Am I not right, Mr. Larson?"

"It works that way in chemistry," Larson confirmed.

"Now let us review the case of Devon," Westborough resumed with the air of a university professor lecturing his class. "His immolation appears pointless unless we assume that he was killed because he knew the identity of Swink's murderer, our Mr. Z. But how did he learn that identity?"

"You tell me," Mack grinned.

"The theory that Z, Swink, and Devon were involved in the same transaction cannot be substantiated. True, Swink and Devon were both criminals, but they were criminals of a different social strata. Nothing in the past life of either points to a possible connection. Therefore, the reasonable assumption is that Devon did not learn the identity of Z until after Swink's death."

"Wait a minute," Mack broke in. "Devon could've seen your Z friend searching Swink's room."

"Only if the culprit were Spanger," Westborough corrected. "If we assume that Z is other than Spanger, there is no evidence at all to show that he did enter Swink's room at any other time than on nine-thirty Thursday evening. But Devon was physically unable to have surprised Mr. Z in the commission of the crime. Because Devon could not have been in the hotel at nine-thirty.

"Let us trace his movements of the evening. According to his statement, since substantially verified, he was calling at a home in Rogers Park at a quarter-past nine. He took the 'L' from Rogers Park to the Randolph and Wells station, walked east to Michigan Boulevard, and caught a northbound bus to the hotel. If we assume that the 'L' journey occupied twenty-five minutes, the walk across the Loop another ten minutes, and the bus trip another ten, this brings Devon back to the hotel at ten o'clock—the hour at which he was actually seen to enter.

"During those forty-five minutes—on the 'L,' walking on Randolph Street, or in the bus—Devon learned something which enabled him to penetrate to Mr. Z's identity. There is no other possible foundation for our belief that he did know."

"You're doing a lot of assuming," Mack protested.

"No," Westborough denied, "I am making but one assumption: that Devon was strangled because he discovered Swink's slayer. Without that assumption, no reasonable motive exists for Devon's death."

"Not much motive for Swink's either," Mack grumbled.

"True. But Swink's death is an accomplished fact. That we do not know the cause does not alter its essential reality. Given a primary condition, we are justified, always, of course, within the rigid boundaries imposed by logical inference, in the correlation of a second event to the first."

"It sounds great, but I haven't the least idea what you're talking about."

"Truth," Westborough continued, without heeding the interruption, "is a jewel of many facets. Let us consider another of them. Devon's violent death was known to have occurred between seven and seven-thirty on Sunday evening. Six people were questioned by Lieutenant Mack and Captain O'Ryan: three of these produced alibis which allowed of checking and appeared, superficially at least, to be valid. Two had alibis which were worthless. One had no alibi at all. The situation was exactly what might be expected of six people chosen at random and asked to state their whereabouts at a definite hour.

"Let us examine the five alibis—both the good and the worthless. Of my own, I shall say nothing. Mr. Larson is vouched for until a quarter of eight by Miss Gant. But that *per se* does not entirely eliminate him, although the good faith of Miss Gant need not be questioned. There is the inevitable human factor. If the doctor's estimate should prove wrong or if Miss Gant erred by so brief a period as fifteen minutes, it would be necessary to include Larson once more among the list of active suspects.

"In Mr. Hammond's alibi, established by a garage mechanic on the Elgin road, a flaw also appears. Mr. Hammond states that he left Elgin at five-thirty and did not arrive at the hotel until eight-fifteen. Why two and three quarter hours for a fast driver to traverse a distance of about forty miles? Mr. Hammond explains the length of the interval by saying that he picked up a nail in his tire, stopped to put on his spare, and then stopped again at the garage where he had the tube vulcanized. But might not Mr. Hammond have punctured his spare tire by driving the nail into it with his hand? Might not he, after strangling Devon at seven o'clock, have been able to drive to the garage on the Elgin road by seven-thirty, have his tire vulcanized, and return once more to this hotel by eight-fifteen? Lieutenant Mack, you were going to conduct some experiments with regard to the driving time. Is the procedure I have outlined physically possible?"

"It's drawing it pretty fine," Mack replied, "but I think it's just barely possible—given all the breaks on lights, of course."

"Therefore," Westborough resumed, "we must restore Hammond to the list of active suspects. Now for the two men whose alibis were admittedly worthless: Mr. Jasper and Mr. Colmar. These two men have denied acquaintance with each other. Yet both were attending the same motion picture at the designated time, and—a coincidence even more curious—both are employed by the same individual, Mr. Ezra Whittington of New York. Coincidences by the hundred occur in daily life, and yet the mind instinctively revolts at them, seeks to establish a relation of cause and effect between apparently separate events occurring simultaneously. Does such a relation exist between Mr. Jasper and Mr. Colmar? Yes, to a certain extent, since Mr. Colmar would not have been in Chicago yesterday were it not for Mr. Jasper's incarceration on Saturday night. The question of a further relationship between the two men is, to say the least, an interesting one, and I regret that the stern dictates of logic brand it as altogether irrelevant. The truth is that none of the gentlemen I have named executed Devon."

"How do you make that out?" Mack wanted to know.

"Because the death of Devon was not a premeditated crime. We know this from two facts, the validity of which may not be questioned. Devon was not killed in his own room. And an instrument was found—I believe it is termed a 'jigger gun'—which had been concealed the night of Devon's death. The inference is extremely simple. The instrument had belonged to Devon, who had used it to effect an entrance into the room of another guest. But, obviously, the other guest could not have known in advance that Devon would effect such an entrance. Therefore, Devon's death, at least in the manner in which it occurred, could not have been premeditated."

"That's A-B-C stuff in fancy language," Mack cut in. "What you mean by saying that none of the guys could've killed Devon?"

"Dear me," Westborough murmured, "it appears to me to be so extremely simple. A large hotel—particularly the first floor—is a veritable beehive of activity. There are guests surging in and out of the lobby. There are sharp-eyed and observing bellmen and elevator pilots. To say nothing of the room clerk, who is trained by the nature of his profession to keep a watchful glance on everything going on about him. Now, to kill Devon and yet escape detection, any of the people I have mentioned must have entered and have left the hotel unobserved. Isn't that right?"

"Yes," Mack agreed, "And so far as I know none of them were seen. We've checked pretty carefully with the help too. But what of it?"

"Neither entering nor leaving the hotel unobserved is an impossibility," Westborough continued, "as I presently hope to demonstrate. But it is not possible to do either without taking certain precautions, which Devon's murderer did not take. Why? Because, *up to the minute he reached his own room, he did not know that he was going to hill Devon. Therefore, he could make no attempt to establish an alibi.*"

"What the hell!" Mack exclaimed, glancing in genuine bewilderment from the handcuffed Jerry Spanger to each of Westborough's other four listeners. "But you're contradicting yourself, Westborough. A little while ago you said the same guy killed both fellows."

"The second crime," Westborough confirmed gravely, "is unquestionably the direct, logical outgrowth of the first."

"But the guy you're driving at couldn't have done for Swink. He might Devon but not Swink."

"Your second error, Lieutenant Mack, and I trust that you will forgive me for pointing it out, was to be unnecessarily suspicious of alibis. But your first mistake was not to be suspicious enough. The murder of Swink was as obviously premeditated as that of Devon was not."

"I still don't see," Mack floundered.

"Let us return to Devon's journey on Thursday evening," Westborough suggested. "During the forty-five minutes between nine-fifteen and ten o'clock Devon uncovered a secret which led to his death. Where did he learn that secret? Hardly while riding on the 'L,' nor does the bus offer more attractive possibilities. There remains only the walk eastward on Randolph Street at a time known to have been between nine-forty and nine-fifty. What would he pass on Randolph Street that has any bearing on this case?"

Mack scratched at his temple, his face blank. "Damned if I can see anything. There's a beer joint—"

"The United Artists Theater," Westborough returned promptly. "What Devon saw was a guest of this hotel buying a ticket from the cashier. A guest who, if he had told the truth to the police, should have been inside the theater for nearly an hour."

"It's a lie!" Graham shouted and leaped to his feet, his face purple.

XXVII

MACK'S REVOLVER flashed from its holster. "Sit down, you!"

"Prove it!" Graham shrieked. "Prove it! You've called me a murderer before five witnesses. That lays you wide open for slander, and I'm going—"

"Sit down!" Mack bawled again.

"I'm going to put the matter in the hands of my attorney," Graham concluded defiantly.

"You're going to sit down and shut up!" Mack informed him. The eyes of the two men clashed for perhaps five seconds before Graham, making a visible effort to regain control, subsided into his chair. Mack restored the revolver to its holster, but his hand remained conspicuously within his coat.

"How could Graham get the cyanide without leaving a back trail?" he demanded.

"Graham had had it for months—perhaps years— prior to the crime. In fact, I will hazard a guess that the possession of the poison suggested the modus operandi."

"Easy to say," Graham sneered. "I'm going to call my attorney—"

Mack blocked his way to the telephone.

"Back, or I'll paste you one!"

"I mentioned that possibility in my first notes," Westborough reminded as Graham sullenly returned to his chair. "You will recall that I even went so far as to tabulate the occupations of potential suspects."

"Yeh, but I never heard of an artist that made drawings with cyanide."

"It was largely by chance that I stumbled upon the necessary connection," Westborough expounded. "I found Graham making a pen-and-ink sketch upon a photostat. He explained that the photostat would later be bleached to leave only his ink lines. Does that suggest anything to you?" Larson put in quickly, "The light sensitive salt would be silver—"

"Silver bromide, I believe," Westborough interrupted, "and a bleaching agent would have to be a substance capable of dissolving this chemical. But, as Mr. Larson pointed out on the night of Swink's death, potassium cyanide is an excellent solvent of all silver halides."

"Rather farfetched," Mack said doubtfully.

"I do not believe so. Mr. Graham admitted to me that he had done a great deal of work upon photostats at one time. What more natural than that the means of bleaching them should remain in his office?"

"Think we didn't look there?" Mack demanded irately.

"Naturally he would not leave the poison for you to find."

"Humph!" Mack ejaculated, obviously far from being convinced. "Two women testified that Graham was in the show. His wife might've lied to shield him, but you can't tell me that Mrs. Hammond was in on it too."

"No, I do not believe so."

"Then why would she lie?"

"I don't believe that she did."

"She said she was with Mr. and Mrs. Graham all evening."

"No, she merely implied that. At eight-thirty there are comparatively few vacant seats in Loop cinemas, and a party of four would be liable to experience difficulty in securing adjacent chairs. Wouldn't it be natural for Graham and Cedric each to take— 'singles' is I believe the term used by the ushers—in order that Mrs. Graham and Mrs. Hammond might sit together?"

"The Hammond woman never said that happened."

"Naturally not. Since she had been to a certain extent involved with the murdered man herself, she would scarcely weaken an excellent alibi by a voluntary admission of this nature. Particularly since she did not know that Graham and Swink were acquaintances and had no reason to suspect that Graham had left the theater. Graham, of course, had seen the picture before and was able to discuss every detail of it."

Spanger grinned broadly. "Go to it, kid! You're talking these bracelets off me with every breath you draw. Here's a thought to help the good work along: Mrs. Graham told us her hubby talked of nothing but the picture all the way home. He did that just for the Hammond woman's benefit."

"Yes," Westborough confirmed. "Under the circumstances it would not be a difficult matter to delude Mrs. Hammond into the belief that he had actually remained in the theater the entire period.

In fact, it would be odd if she had thought otherwise. It is strange," he reflected, "that the most obvious clues—the test tube, the acid, the hairpin—should be the true ones and yet I should persist so long in my failure to perceive this simple fact."

"You weren't the only one," Spanger chimed in. "Graham was pretty foxy in having the nerve to use the tube from his kid's set and not trying to get another. It might've been traced, and a tall guy like Graham's fairly easy to identify."

"I am afraid that I wasted a great deal of thought in speculating upon the whereabouts of a nonexistent second bottle of acid," Westborough admitted with chagrin. "My error was, of course, to accept at face value Cedric's assertion that no acid had been removed from the bottle. I forgot that he had not been allowed to see the chemical set for several days, and consequently his estimate of the volume of acid which the bottle had contained could scarcely have been reliable."

Mack growled, "Now that you two fellows have finished saying what might've happened, I'll give you just four reasons why you're all wrong.—Graham! If you get up from that chair again, so help me God, I'll smash your face!—One: No one can sneak into the hotel and out again without being spotted by somebody. You said that yourself, Westborough, and then forgot all about it, I guess. Shut up, Graham! I'm doing all the talking that's being done right now.

"Two: Remember the Colmars in the south corridor with the door open? Remember the night housekeeper in the linen room in the north corridor? Even if Graham had managed to sneak through the lobby, he couldn't have got into the west corridor without being seen.

"Three: Graham didn't have the key to his room and would have to pick his own lock as well as Swink's. And Graham's lock was picked. You read a lot of tripe in fiction about how easy it is to pick locks, but I'm telling you it's a darned hard job—especially cylinder locks. The fellow who put the tube over the door was there at nine-thirty, and that gives Graham less than an hour to get back to the hotel, pick two locks, and mix up his chemicals. I'll bet fifty bucks against a plugged nickel that Graham can't pick one lock in two hours—let alone two locks in half an hour.

"And here's my fourth reason, and it's right up your own side street, Westborough. Logic. Cold, hard logic that you're always spouting about. Why was Graham's alibi good? Because Hammond heard your Mr. Z in the next room at nine-thirty. But Graham wouldn't have been able to count on Hammond's being there, or on hearing him even if he was. That's logic, isn't it?"

"It is indeed," Westborough concurred, "but the answer is fairly simple. True, Graham could not have foreseen that Hammond would hear him at nine-thirty, and so establish his alibi. Nevertheless, for that purpose he could count upon another event, occurring daily with the regularity of clockwork. I refer, of course, to the chambermaid who visits each room in this corridor near the hour of nine."

"I forgot about the chambermaid," Mack admitted.

"Passing to your third objection," Westborough continued, "I find it easier to believe that Graham was able to procure a passkey than that he possessed the necessary technical skill to pick the locks."

"What about the scratches?" Mack cross-examined.

"As we already know, Swink's lock was picked the evening before by Jasper. Perhaps Graham had conducted preliminary experiments in lock picking on his own in order to ascertain the feasibility of that mode of ingress."

"Smart fellow!" Mack grunted. "But you still haven't answered my toughest ones."

Westborough said slowly, "You refer, of course, to Graham's unobserved progress to the west corridor?"

"You know damn well I do!"

"That feat, Lieutenant Mack, was easily accomplished. He used the fire escape."

"The fire escape?" Mack echoed. "It's raised to the second floor on purpose so nobody can sneak in by it!"

Spanger broke in with, "It hangs too low. I told Swann we ought to have it yanked up a couple of feet, but he thought I was screwy. A tall guy with a cane could jump high enough to be able to hook it down."

"I never carried a cane in my life," Graham snapped.

"Besides," Mack objected, "you're forgetting that all the fire-escape doors were bolted."

"On the contrary, I—"

"Bolted from the inside," Mack declared emphatically. "Graham might have been able to get in that way—he could unfasten the bolt before he left—but he couldn't go out again and leave the door bolted from the inside."

"Examine the bolt on the fire-escape door," Westborough told him.

"I did. Why?"

"In the open position the handle of the bolt is horizontal; when locked the handle is turned vertically upward. Moreover, the handle is below the doorknob."

"Well, what of it?"

"This afternoon," Westborough explained with thoughtful deliberation, "I looped a piece of string about the handle of the bolt, stretched the string over the doorknob to secure the necessary leverage, closed the door, and jerked the string sharply, holding it, of course, by both ends. The bolt immediately moved upward—into the locked position—and I was on the outside. By holding only one end of the string it was a simple matter to pull it through the crack between the door and the jamb."

"The oldest trick known to detective-story writers," Mack groaned.

Graham sprang to his feet. "It's all a lie—a damned lie!"

Mack acted with amazing quickness. His fist smashed into Graham's face as the artist was in the act of springing at Westborough's throat.

"I told you I'd have to poke you if you didn't stay still!" the detective growled.

Clapping a hand to his bleeding mouth, Graham staggered back to his chair. His eyes glowered vindictively at Westborough, who, seemingly undisturbed by the contretemps, had not moved from his position against the door.

"Your behavior is both foolish and futile, Mr. Graham," the historian admonished gently. "Please note that my deductions up to this point have been entirely theoretical. I believe it was Einstein who observed that in a complete theory there should be an element corresponding to each element of reality."

Mack angrily demanded, "You mean you've been wasting my time spouting a lot of hot air?"

"Please have patience," Westborough smiled. "I have secured the physical confirmation of my hypothetical conclusions. The tangible evidence which gives my theory its one-to-one correspondence with reality. But I am afraid," he added hesitantly, "that to obtain it I have been guilty of a statutory offense."

"The hell you have!" Mack exploded.

Westborough continued. "You will recall that at the beginning of the encounter between Mr. Spanger and Mr. Larson I was delegated to procure a passkey from the room clerk. I secured this article, but upon my return the need for its use had passed. Seeing, however, that Mr. Graham was in the corridor and his attention fully occupied, I seized the opportunity to slip unobserved into his apartment. Reason had told me that a certain object should be there. And," he concluded elatedly, "I found it."

"Found what?" Mack demanded, his eyes regarding Graham watchfully.

"Can you not guess?" Westborough smilingly challenged.

"Spill it," Mack ordered peremptorily. "I don't like riddles."

"Does anyone care to solve this simple problem in logical inference?" Westborough invited. There was an expressive silence. "I am surprised," he averred, "that no one has as yet brought up one vital matter: the reason for Devon's presence in Graham's apartment."

"That's not hard to answer," Jasper broke in. "If you knew what to look for there, he probably did too."

"You are exactly right. Is anyone able to deduce the nature of this object?" The question was followed by a second period of silence. "Dear, dear!" Westborough remarked, "I fear that we have sadly underrated Mr. Devon's intelligence."

"I've got it!" Spanger suddenly shouted. "Graham's cane! The iron rungs would've left scratches on its handle."

"My first thought," Westborough admitted, "but Mr. Graham, since living in this hotel at least, has not possessed a cane." He paused briefly, but there were no volunteers. "It was raining the night of Mr. Swink's death," he added quietly.

"An umbrella!" Mack yelled. "An umbrella with a crook handle! That's what he used to pull down the fire escape!"

"It is still within Mr. Graham's closet," Westborough informed. "If you will examine it, you will find a long and deep scratch across the under part of the crook. A scratch in such a position is unlikely to have been made by other means."

Mack relieved Spanger of his handcuffs and transferred them at once to Graham's wrists. "Will you talk now or at the station?" he demanded.

"Oh hell, what difference does it make? Now," Graham replied resignedly. "Yes, I killed Swink. My lawyer will tell me I'm a damn fool to admit it, but I'm sick of this mess. Westborough had the right slant on the photostat bleaching. I got the cyanide over three years ago. Hydrocyanic acid," he added bitterly, "is also used for exterminating vermin—and that includes Swink!"

"What'd you have against Swink?"

Graham pressed his lips together firmly. "I'm not saying."

"I wouldn't take that attitude," Mack threatened. However, as Graham continued obstinately silent, the detective was forced to shift his tactics. "Was your wife in on the job, too?" he asked.

"No!" Graham declared emphatically.

"Did she know about it?" Mack persisted.

"Perhaps. I can't say for sure, but it's difficult to conceal a thing like that from a person who knows you as well as your wife. I've seen the question trembling on her tongue a dozen times a day, but she was always afraid to ask it."

Yvonne's flying pencil halted momentarily. "Oh, the poor thing!"

"One minute she would look as if I were something untouchable," Graham said grimly, his mood plainly one of self-flagellation. "Then the next instant she'd throw herself into my arms and be sobbing her heart out. I tried to comfort her, but there wasn't much I could say. Something—I don't know just what to call it—had smashed between us. But Lu could know I was sixty murderers and she wouldn't give me away," he concluded proudly.

Mack's mind was obviously elsewhere. "What if Hammond had decided to go to the movie with you?" he conjectured.

"That was my original idea," said Graham. "Hammond had the best motive for killing Swink of anyone in the hotel, as far as anyone would be able to tell. He certainly wouldn't be likely to weaken an airtight alibi because I hadn't happened actually to sit with him. In fact, I nearly threw the whole idea up when Hammond refused to go. Then I realized that Norah would serve my purpose as well as her husband—or nearly."

"Did you pick the lock to Swink's room?"

"No. Westborough was right about the experiments on my own lock, but I couldn't get the hang of it. So I had to make a passkey. Oh, it was easier than it sounds. I'd noticed that the chambermaid on this floor was often careless about leaving her key in the outside of the lock while she was doing a room. I made a little wood box, hinged it in the middle and filled both top and bottom compartments with molding wax. It was a matter of only a few seconds to get an impression of the key—both sides at the same time. I went into a locksmith shop on the south side and talked with the proprietor until I'd got him to go into a back room to dig up some more padlocks. While he was out of the room, I stole a blank of the proper size and filed it to fit my mold. Of course, I threw the thing down the nearest sewer on my way back to the show."

"Did you kill Devon, too?"

Graham smiled malignantly. "He had the umbrella in his hand when I found him here last night. I hadn't thought about the fire-escape steps scratching the handle, or I'd have got rid of the thing today. I don't know whether Devon had deduced that or whether he merely wanted a weapon. Anyway, he tried to sock me. I ducked and twisted the umbrella out of his hand; then he told about seeing me outside the theater and demanded hush money. That's where he made his big mistake, for I throttled him then and there. It was easy, but the hard part was to get him back to his own room. Fortunately, the key was in his pocket."

"Why'd you lock Spanger in the closet?" Mack wanted to know.

"I had to get rid of Devon's pick, of course. I wanted to be sure Spanger'd stay out of the way till I had a chance to hide it. I figured it would be safe in the wastepaper bag until morning, but I slipped there. The houseman had emptied the bag before I could get to it. Even so I wasn't particularly worried, as I had a second string to my bow. I thought the marks I'd made on Westborough's lock would give the police plenty to think about if they found the pick. Westborough had been altogether too nosy—I wasn't sorry to do him a bad turn."

The scholarly face of the historian blushed to a vivid crimson, and Mack interposed quickly, "He was too much for you, anyway. I wish to heaven I'd had sense enough to take some pictures of the tumblers on your lock when we first had it apart. As it was, there was no way we could tell it had been picked again. Well, this case is about closed. Just one more thing, Graham. Why'd you do it?"

"I said I wasn't answering that question," Graham maintained obstinately, his lips setting in a thin line.

"Down at headquarters—" Mack threatened.

"You can beat me with your rubber hose from now till Christmas, but I'll keep my mouth closed," Graham defied. Mack, temporarily at least, accepted defeat.

"Miss Gant, if you'll write out a confession from the notes you've made, I think Graham'll sign it."

"Yes," Graham agreed. "I'm ready to take my medicine."

Miss Gant suggested using Westborough's typewriter, still down in the sample room, and Larson accompanied her. Jasper, mumbling something about "catching a train if you don't want me anymore," left also, and Spanger rose to his feet, saying, "I'm going to hunt Swann up and give him the low-down." Only Mack and Westborough remained with the prisoner.

"Now that we're alone maybe you'll tell what you had against Swink?" Mack suggested confidentially.

Graham shook his head emphatically. "I'm not talking about that, as I told you several times. Any objections to my smoking?"

"I don't see any."

Graham fumbled so awkwardly with his manacled hands that Mack finally had to assist him in securing a cigarette case from his breast pocket.

Westborough heard a knock on the door and went toward it. "Not back already, Miss Gant?" A woman's voice—not that of Yvonne—answered.

"Is Mr. Graham in there?"

Westborough glanced inquiringly at the detective. Graham, seemingly oblivious of the voice from the corridor, was tapping his cigarette against the case.

"I know he's there!" the woman went on insistently. "I heard him talking. You've got to let me in!" Her fists beat a tattoo against the door.

"What you want with him?" Mack demanded.

"It sounds like Mrs. Graham," Westborough began, turning toward the artist. He darted suddenly across the room with all the speed he could muster. Graham was drawing deeply on his cigarette.

Westborough dashed the cigarette to the floor—a tiny white dab against the dark carpet. Mack had opened the door to the corridor, and Luella Graham, her face strained and eyes haggard, brushed the detective aside and ran toward her husband.

Graham half raised his head. "Hello, Lu! They—"

He crumpled forward in his seat. Luella Graham dropped sobbing to her knees, both arms grasping the unconscious figure of her husband.

"Ronny! Ronny dear!"

"Your culprit will never be tried in court," Westborough pronounced gravely to the detective.

"Isn't there something—"

Westborough's head moved slowly sideward. "I'm afraid not. If there had been time—but I didn't suspect, I didn't dream!" He stooped to pick the cigarette from the floor. "He buried a capsule of potassium cyanide in this—the effect of the poison was practically instantaneous."

His frail hands patted the shoulder of the sobbing woman. "My dear Mrs. Graham, I am sincerely sorry."

The woman raised her head, and Westborough recalled vividly the time he had last seen her—a baby-doll blonde with wide blue eyes who didn't look a day over twenty-two. Now the mascara from her eyelashes was coursing in sooty rivulets down her cheeks while her voice was tight and choking.

"He was the best man who ever lived! Did he tell you why he killed that devil Swink?"

Mack, his usual brusque manner perceptibly altered, jerked out a large white handkerchief and blew his nose—hard. "That's the one thing he wouldn't talk about," he admitted.

"Then I will."

"My dear Mrs. Graham, there is hardly the necessity at the present moment," protested Westborough, offering his arm to escort her to a chair.

"But I want to tell," her voice shrilled. "I want you to know everything that Ronny's done for me!"

Westborough placed his arm about the shoulders of Luella Graham. "Yes, my dear," he said in his grave, kindly manner, "please, do."

270

PART SEVEN: *Tuesday Morning*

XXVIII

SARAH BLAKELEY, who had breakfasted upon grapefruit, cereal, wheat cakes, and sausages, peered about the lobby for a comfortably upholstered chair in which she could permit her digestive processes to take their due course. She bore down upon a tall and angular woman, exclaiming, "Good-morning, Esther!"

Esther Hatteras glanced up from her copy of *Murder at Eight Elms*, a typical representative of the type of fiction to which she was addicted. She had read as far as page 97 and did not seem inclined to stop for a chat with her friend and crony.

"How you can sit there calmly and read about a murder in England when all the time more exciting things have been happening in this hotel than were ever put between the pages of a book is more than I can see!" Sarah Blakely ejaculated all in one breath.

The narrow eyes of Mrs. Hatteras showed more than a flicker of interest. "You don't mean to tell me they've caught the murderer?"

"It's on the front page of all the newspapers!" Mrs. Blakely exclaimed aghast. "You don't mean you haven't heard?"

"You are well aware, Sarah, that I never read morning papers."

For the next three quarters of an hour Mrs. Blakely's tongue wagged like a bell clapper. "And so," she concluded, "I got every word of what was going on even though that Lieutenant Mack wouldn't let me stay in the room. All I had to do was to put my ear against the door, and, if I do say it as shouldn't, I've good hearing."

Mrs. Hatteras' mind, trained in the technique of mystery fiction, had already scented a serious flaw in the Blakely narrative. "But the motive, Sarah? You haven't told me his motive."

"Well, it's a whole story in itself," Mrs. Blakely replied. "Mrs. Graham told the police everything. She seemed to feel she ought to justify her husband, although how a double murder can ever be justified is more than I can ever see. The Lord says, 'Thou shalt not kill,' and not, 'Thou shalt not kill except under certain circumstances.' That was the law He gave Moses, and that's been His law ever since."

Mrs. Hatteras, refusing to be drawn into a theological discussion, inquired once more for the motive.

"It goes back nearly twelve years ago on a Fourth of July," Mrs. Blakely began, and Esther Hatteras settled back in her chair with a deep sigh of relief. "Mrs. Graham, who wasn't married then and had come to Chicago from a little town in southern Illinois to get a job, took the train out to one of the tracks to go to the horse races. She hasn't got much character, as I said the first time I ever looked at her, and her story certainly proves I was right. There are things that become a woman, and going alone to the horse races is certainly not one of them. On the train she struck up an acquaintance with another girl whose name was Mary Winters and who didn't have one whit more character than she did. Those two girls actually let themselves be picked up by two men, and if there's anything that's cheaper than that I don't know it!"

"Was Mr. Swink one of the men?" asked Mrs. Hatteras.

"Yes, Mr. Swink was. I don't know the other one's name, but it doesn't matter. But here's what you should remember: Both men had been drinking, and they got the girls' names mixed up. Mr. Swink paired off with Mrs. Graham and he kept calling her Mary Winters. The girls thought that was a good joke, and neither of them bothered to correct the men. The four of them drove back to the city in the other man's car and spent the night drinking at his apartment. In the morning, when Mrs. Graham woke up after they'd caroused all night long, she found Mr. Swink in bed with her—shameless hussy! She began to take on, although you can't tell me it was her first experience, and Mr. Swink woke up and promised to marry her.

"They left the others and went down and got a marriage license. But you've got to remember he thought she was Mary Winters, which fact she'd forgotten in the morning, and when he came back from the clerk with the license made out in that name she nearly fainted. However, she wanted to be married in the worst kind of way after what had happened, and she was afraid Mr. Swink would back out if she gave him half a chance, so what did she do but go and be married under her friend's name!"

"What did the real Mary Winters say to that?" Mrs. Hatteras questioned eagerly.

"Not a thing! She didn't have a chance to, because both she and Mr. Swink's friend were killed that very day—he'd been drinking again, I suppose, and he tried to drive through one of the tunnels under the Chicago River that only streetcars can use. However, the girl was identified as Mary Winters, and then out popped the fact in the papers that Mary Winters had been married on that day to Mr. Swink. You can imagine how mad *he* was at Mrs. Graham when he found out what she'd let him do."

"Well, they lived together for a year or so, and he finally left her about the time Cedric was born. She posed as a widow, and when she met Mr. Graham, five or six years ago, she ups and marries him without bothering to find out first if she was still married to Mr. Swink. In fact, she'd never told Mr. Graham a thing about her first marriage until about two weeks ago after she'd seen Mr. Swink again."

"He tried to blackmail her, of course," Mrs. Hatteras commented.

"Yes, she was certainly in bad with the law. To impersonate another person for the purpose of marrying means a one-to ten-year sentence in the penitentiary, and, on top of that, she might have got still another sentence for bigamy. Mrs. Graham said the matter was in such a terrible mess that only a first-rate lawyer could straighten it out, and she had always been scared to go to a lawyer.

"She made a clean breast of it to Mr. Graham, and she said he was marvelous. He didn't reproach her once, just went quietly and had a talk with Mr. Swink. He offered Mr. Swink every cent he had in the bank, but Mr. Swink just laughed in his face and said he couldn't bother with chicken feed. Right then and there, I guess, Mr. Graham made up his mind that the only way to save Mrs. Graham from going to jail was to kill Mr. Swink. He didn't take Mrs. Graham into his confidence either. That man was a cool one, and make no mistake about that! Well, 'the wages of sin is death,' as the Bible puts it, and it was death for Mr. Swink and Mr. Devon and Mr. Graham, but not for the woman who was the cause of all of it. And, Esther Hatteras, if that hussy isn't out of this hotel in twenty-four hours I'm going straight to Mr. Swann and give him the worst talking to he ever had in his life. Imagine me being forced to live on the same floor all this time with that trollop!"

"Since a metric carat weights a fifth of a gram," Westborough remarked, "a five-carat emerald would weigh just one gram."

"Sure," confirmed Jerry Spanger, who was trying to restore order to the room in which Elmo Swink had lived and died. "What of it?"

"Are you averse to a monetary proposition?" Westborough queried. "That is, if we are able to deduce the whereabouts of the said emerald."

"If you mean will I split fifty-fifty, I'm with you! I've about given up hope myself. Lord knows I could use the dough, too! The only reason Swann didn't fire me was so he could dock my pay for the damages to this room."

"Very well, then. Now that matter is settled, let us proceed with our deductions. The emerald, as I have already stated, weighs one gram, and the specific gravity of the stone, I ascertained this morning, is 2.74. From these figures it is a matter of simple arithmetic to calculate that our emerald will have a volume of 0.0225 cubic inches."

"Screwy!" Spanger ejaculated.

274

"What was the longest dimension of the emerald?" Westborough inquired.

Spanger rubbed his chin thoughtfully. "About a half inch. Why?"

"And were the other dimensions approximately equal?"

"I guess so. I only saw it once, remember!"

"Excellent! In that event—" he began to make calculations upon a piece of scratch paper. "Dear me, I can never remember just how one goes about to extract square root."

"Who the hell ever wants to?" Spanger demanded.

Westborough concluded his calculating. "Arithmetic shows again that the two smaller dimensions of the emerald will be approximately equal to 0.2 inches. Yes, it should fit very nicely into the place I have in mind, the diameter of which is equal to a full quarter of an inch."

"My God, where?" Spanger shouted.

"I shall need," Westborough observed, "a screwdriver. No, never mind, Mr. Spanger, I believe the blade of this knife will serve excellently."

He crossed the room and stooped down.

"The closet doorknob!" Spanger exclaimed.

"Yes, the chance was extremely small that it would be disturbed here before it could be reclaimed." He unscrewed the knob and shook it, but there was no sound. He probed with a pencil at the hollow interior of the doorknob and a small piece of tissue protruded. "Stuffed with paper, of course, to preclude rattling," Westborough commented. He probed again, and the emerald lay in his hand—a thing of velvety green beauty.

"Fifty thousand grand!" breathed Spanger in an awed whisper.

"And under the terms of our agreement, I am to receive fifty percent of the proffered reward for this stone. Right? Excellent!" The little man held the emerald up to the light. "A pretty bauble. I believe it was Pliny who said of these stones 'neither dim nor shade, nor yet the light of a candle, causes them to lose their luster.' "

"That may be what he said. But what I've got to say about that piece of green ice in your hand is more to the point." Spanger chuckled. "That hunk of colored glass is worth just twelve hundred and fifty bucks apiece to each of us. And boy, can I use it! Once I get my hands on that cash I don't give a damn if the stone turns white and makes a liar out of Pliny."

Westborough's eyes were far away, and he didn't seem to be paying any attention to the excited Spanger. "Wasn't it the Arab, Ahmed ben Abdalaziz, who mentioned the curious tradition that a serpent which fixes its eyes upon an emerald becomes blind? Oh, Mr. Spanger, before it slips my mind—I should like my share of the reward to be turned over to my amanuensis, Miss Gant, as my wedding present to her."

Spanger shook his head. "It's your dough, and you can do what you want with it, but if you ask me, you're screwy."